GLACIER FIRES

FIRES

— AND —

Ornaments of Value

INK START MEDIA
5710 W Gate City Blvd Ste K #284
Greensboro, NC 27407

GLACIER FIRES

CHAPTER 1

MOBILE TELESCOPE

"Hey Art, did you think we were going to attract this much attention?"

Laughing, Art replied, "Nope, but I figured we'd have some rubberneckers, just not so many. Seems like everyone passing us is wondering what we have concealed in the truck bed. Next time we should take the tube off the mounting and just have the pedestal stick up. Maybe that won't draw so much interest."

"Yeah, the kids looking at us are pretty funny. Some just point, but a few of them make faces, so I return the favor."

"That's all right, you're just a kid yourself … still a teenager until last month."

"Look who's talking. You're only a couple of months older than I am."

The two young men in the cab of the 1992 dark blue Ford pickup had an object made primarily of steel and glass attached to the bed of the vehicle. Tim and Art were driving east on Route 542 toward Mt. Baker, only 58 miles east of Bellingham, Washington. The object in the back of the truck was wrapped with an old threadbare blanket, torn and oil stained from putting it under the truck when the two college boys were attaching a telescope mount to the vehicle. The old blanket was now being used to protect the telescope during highway travel. Particulates from the highway and bug guts were not good for the telescope, especially the optics. The reflecting surface needed to be as pristine as possible, bug spots and chips in the mirror would prevent obtaining high quality photographic images of stellar objects.

The pickup was moving slightly below the speed limit with Tim driving and Art riding shotgun. Although the telescope was covered with a blanket and tied down with a rope, the drag from the air on the fabric caused it to flap. The sound reminded Art of playing cards attached to the fenders of his bicycle when he was a youngster. The spokes striking the cards simulated a noise like that of a motor, but the cards and the clothespins didn't stay on the bike for long.

The two young men had used most of their free time during their junior year at the University of Washington designing a telescope mount and planning the method of attaching the structure to the truck bed. Tim, a physics major and Art, an engineering student had been lab partners in sophomore physics and had formed a strong friendship, acting more like brothers than students competing for grades. They enjoyed teasing one another at the slightest provocation.

Tim had been an amateur astronomer for years but hadn't purchased a telescope of his own until this summer. He had previously used borrowed scopes and binoculars for stargazing. But now, with a quality digital camera and clear, cold mountain nights, Tim and Art had teamed up to carry out some astrophotography. Art had more than a passing interest in astronomy, having made a small reflecting telescope as a project for scouts. His father had taught him how to weld and use a mill, lathe and drill press.

Tim had used money from summer jobs at Boeing to purchase the much larger telescope, mount and the older model pickup. All were nearly paid for, but he bought a camera on credit and was making slightly more than minimum payments on it. Tim figured he would be able to pay off the camera in about two years; most of the balance owed, if any, after that period would be paid when he was out of school, working or in graduate school on a stipend.

Brian Michaels, Tim's father, was an aeronautical engineer at Boeing and Tim's mom, Sharon, was a substitute elementary school teacher. Fourth graders, avid readers and full of questions, were her favorite students. Questions she couldn't answer were written down and discussed with her son and husband. She always wished she had taken more university science courses. Sharon usually had the entire summer off but this summer she was attending a symposium in Iowa:

Teaching Science at the Elementary Level. Three weeks of summer instruction was sponsored by the National Science Foundation. Mr. Michaels normally had ten days off, including the July 4th holiday, during the summer. Tim's parents had rented a chateau-like cabin in Glacier, Washington, from June to August, but wouldn't be able to join their son until the first week of July.

Art was born and grew up in Walla Walla where his parents, Harvey and Helen Daniels, owned a vineyard and operated a winery. Normally, Art would work all summer at the winery, maintaining the Blue Mountain Nectar website. Helen always had a to-do list of website modifications for Art following the conclusion of spring semester. This year, Art's parents had agreed to let their son stay with Tim in Glacier until Independence Day. Art had talked about the telescope project for nearly a year. Knowing how much their son wanted to be involved in the project, Harvey and Helen decided the activity would be Art's reward for making good grades and managing their website. The boys were issued two provisos by their parents: no alcoholic beverages and no girls at the chateau without chaperones. Neither of the young men was very interested in drinking, having experimented with both beer and wine, supervised by their parents. Neither young man could make any sense out of getting drunk. However, their interest in girls was pretty normal, neither Tim nor Art suffered a lack of testosterone.

"Hey Tim, what do you think about the scenery?"

"Awesome, Art, but I'm sure you mean the surroundings, not the females. Photos of this area could be on postcards like the ones sold at national parks. I've been watching other vehicles and I haven't seen any good-looking females near our age; they're either too old or too young. I'm thinkin' women our age aren't much interested in camping out."

"I've been checking out every vehicle on the road, but I haven't seen any chicks close to our age, Tim. Maybe we'll luck out and meet somebody. We've still got several weeks until the fourth. Let's pull over at one of the observation areas or a campsite, set up the scope and take a close up look at Mt. Baker."

"Good idea. We don't have to go very far to test the mount. I've been looking at the river. I'll bet the water is ice cold from melting snow and ice."

The rapidly flowing water was reflecting sunlight from a myriad of spots, reminding Tim of flickering starlight on a warm moonless summer night. The two college boys hoped to get above the warm layers of air for some useful astrophotography. Tim wanted to take a logging road to a hill or butte that had been logged so they would have clear vision nearly to the horizon. They would have to do some studying of their maps to find a higher elevation devoid of trees. But this outing was just a short trip to test the functioning of the telescope and mount, gaining information for necessary alterations, if any, to their current design. A rigid mount was a necessity.

A couple of days after spring semester at the university ended, Tim and Art had loaded the pickup with essentials for building the telescope mount and set off to Glacier. Other requirements, such as food and necessary tools, could be purchased at their destination. They were pleasantly surprised to find that the chateau Tim's dad had rented was equipped with a well-stocked shop. After two weeks of work and very little relaxation, they were on their maiden voyage to test their meticulously designed scientific instrument.

"Hey, Tim, take the next right. There's a campground on the other side of the road."

"Yeah, I saw the sign too," Tim replied.

Tim slowed the pickup, exited the freeway and drove through a tunnel to a relatively large camping area beyond the opposite lanes of the road. It took Art and Tim about ten minutes to find a spot that afforded a good view of glacier covered Mt. Baker standing out against the clear blue sky. After backing through some trees, they found a fairly flat location to park the truck, a good distance away from most other campers.

There was a loud squeal when Tim forced down the brake pedal. Art hunched up his shoulders and made a face at Tim. "We might need a brake job before long."

"Either that or we have a rock stuck in the breaks. That didn't sound good." Tim replied.

"Get the cover off the scope. I'll extend the stabilizing legs from the bed to the ground."

"You got it," answered Art.

They had incorporated two carpenter's levels into the bed of the pickup so the telescope mount could be approximately level to the ground. Further leveling could be done on the pedestal of the telescope mount. The pedestal could be rotated and locked into place.

As they oriented the telescope, two boys about twelve years old, approached the pickup from a campsite about eighty feet away. The boys wore jeans and sweatshirts with large white numbers front and back.

"Whatcha doin?" asked one of the boys.

Tim looked at the two boys seriously and said, "Who's asking?" He realized the boys were twins after taking a closer look.

They answered in unison. "We're the Ashford boys."

The boy in the red shirt said, "I'm Jim." He had 9 on the front of his shirt and 99 on the back.

"And I'm Tom," added the boy in the blue shirt. "We're camping over there." He pointed to a large RV with a small SUV attached to the back on a trailer. Their campsite was south of the pickup in a grassy area away from the trees. Tom had 11 on the front of his shirt and 99 on the back.

"Well, Tom and Jim, I'm Tim and my buddy here is Art. Glad to meet you. We're setting up our telescope to take a look the Mt. Baker glaciers."

"Heavenly body approaching on the right, three o'clock," alerted Art.

Tim looked away from the boys to see a brunette striding through the foot-high grass. As she came closer, she kicked a large pinecone out of her way.

"Boys! Don't bother these gentlemen. Come back to camp."

"It's okay, they're not bothering us," commented Tim. "You can't be their mom so you must be their sister," Tim grinned.

"I'm Samantha," stated the shorthaired pretty brunette.

"Sam, we're just watching them set up their telescope," Jim commented to his sister.

"Hi Samantha. I'm Tim and my ugly buddy here is Art."

"Thanks a lot, Tim. Pleased to meet you, Sam," stated Art.

Tim said, "Okay, I've got the top of the mountain in the field of view."

"Let me take a look." Art grabbed the edge of the truck and jumped onto the tailgate. Tim jumped down from the truck and stood beside Sam. Tim was nearly a foot taller than the young lady. The top of her head was near the bottom of his chin. Tim was six-two and he estimated Sam was at most five-four.

Tim looked down at the girl and asked, "Want to take a look?"

"Sure." She stepped back from the truck, took two quick steps and effortlessly jumped onto the tailgate.

"Wow. And I was going to help you up," Tim commented.

"You must be a jock," joked Art.

"Yep. I'm on the varsity gymnastics team. I'm a Cougar. I just finished my sophomore year. I'm majoring in Veterinary Medicine."

"We're both Huskies, physics and engineering," stated Art.

"I thought there must be something wrong with you guys," smiled Sam. She was joking but the guys took it more seriously.

Tim felt like saying "smart ass," but decided to let it go, besides, she was awfully cute. He knew he wasn't the handsomest guy around and didn't want to squelch his chances.

Art stepped away from the telescope and motioned for Sam to take a look. She looked into the eyepiece then lifted her head to locate the focusing knob. Sam rotated the knob in and out until the image was clear. Obviously, she knew how to focus optical equipment, probably from using a microscope.

"What's that shiny object?"

"What shiny object?" Art inquired.

"It's at the lower left," Sam instructed.

Sam leaned out of the way and Art looked through the lens.

"Tim! She's right, there's something reflecting the sun. It looks like it's maybe 800 to 1000 feet below the summit…just guessing."

Tim jumped onto the tailgate and the pickup bed shifted.

"Oops. We lost the mountain," Art commented.

Art jumped down from the truck and held out his hand for Sam to grab so she could jump down. She took his hand and hopped off the truck bed. She didn't need his assistance but thanked him.

Tim re-acquired the previous view of the mountain but couldn't see anything shiny.

"Art. What time is it?"

"It's 2:21." Art responded after looking at his watch.

"Write it down so we don't forget," directed Tim.

Jim and Tom had run out of patience and climbed onto the truck bed.

Tom asked, "Can we take a look?"

Tim said, "Sure." He backed away from the telescope so the younger boys could look at the mountain through the scope.

Art explained to Sam, "We'll look again tomorrow when the sun is in the right position to reflect off the object. I hope it doesn't snow up there tonight."

Sam nodded, "That's what I was thinking. I'll ask my dad if snow is in the forecast."

"Is your dad a weatherman or something?" asked Art.

"Something. My dad's a park ranger. He instructs climbers that want to ascend Mt. Baker. He knows that mountain like the back of his hand. Would you like to meet him?"

Tim gave Art a thumbs-up. "Sure. That would be great. We've got some questions for him."

CHAPTER 2

DINNER WITH ASHFORDS

"How long will you guys be here?" Sam inquired.

"We plan on staying until about ten tonight but it might be later. We want to check out the telescope when we can look at stars, like doubles," Tim replied.

"Okay. See you later. Come on boys. Mom wants you back at camp."

Sam started ushering Jim and Tom toward their camp. After moving about ten yards, she looked back over her shoulder and said, "Nice meeting you guys."

Art yelled back, "Nice meeting all of you too. See you later."

Tim was changing eyepieces and added, "Yeah. See you later."

"Hmm…Very interesting. I can see something up there. It looks brown or black and I'm guessing it's about six feet long. I think it's a cylinder. Take a look, Art."

"I think you're right. Let's try a little more magnification, the upper end of the object looks bigger and has an irregular shape, kind of like a blob."

Tim handed Art another eyepiece with a shorter focal length. Art inserted it in the rack and pinion mount and focused on the object. "Would you hand me that clipboard and a pencil?"

Tim complied and watched Art sketch what he could see at the higher power.

"Damn. The image keeps going in and out of focus."

"Not surprised. We're looking horizontally across warm and cold layers of the atmosphere. Wait for a clear view and then quickly draw it, then wait for another clear view. You should be able to accumulate enough information to draw the entire object."

"Jeez, Tim, you should be doing this. You have more experience than I do."

"You have to get some experience sometime, Art. It might as well be now."

"Yeah, I guess you're right. It's a bit frustrating though," Art replied.

As the afternoon wore on, Tim and Art observed the entire western side of the mountain under low power but didn't see anything else out of the ordinary. They could see some dark patches randomly distributed but thought them to be cavities, rocks or shadows on the surface of the glaciers. They made a note to bring up the topic when they talked with Mr. Ashford. Art began to feel some hunger pangs around 5:30 and heard Tim's stomach growling.

"Hey buddy, let's stop and eat," suggested Art.

"Good idea. I'm getting tired of looking at the mountain anyway. I'll get the cooler out of the cab." Tim dropped down from the back of the pickup and opened the driver's door.

He reached into the cab and grabbed a small cooler. He shut the door and started to open the cooler but stopped when he heard someone nearing the truck. Tim glanced toward the noise and saw one of the twins approaching.

As number 11 approached the truck, the boy said, "Hey you guys, want to join us for dinner? We're going to eat in a few minutes."

Tim put the cooler back in the truck cab, shut the door and looked up at Art in the back of the truck. Art turned his palms up and said, "Why not?"

"Sounds good to us Tom. Thanks for the invitation."

Tim and Art joined Tom and they began walking toward the Ashford's RV.

"Did you guys see anything exciting on the mountain?" Tom asked.

Art answered, "I don't know if you'd call it exciting, but we saw something that looks a little strange on the surface of a glacier. We'll ask your dad about it."

As they converged on the Ashford's camp, Mr. Ashford, who was cooking at a barbecue, turned toward his guests and extended his hand. He was about six feet tall and looked like an outdoorsman. His shirtsleeves were rolled up exposing body-builder's forearms. He was tanned and hadn't shaved in a couple of days. Tim thought Mr. Ashford could probably rip him in half with his bare hands. Not many people would want to mess with him.

"I'm Glenn and this is my wife, Donna."

They all shook hands. Tim and Art introduced themselves.

As they were greeting, Art smiled and said, "I can see where your daughter gets her looks, Mrs. Ashford."

Donna Ashford smiled and pushed her long dark brown hair away from her face.

"Thank you, young man. I'll have to warn Sam to watch out for you."

Mrs. Ashford looked at the RV and raised her voice, "Sam, your new friends are here."

The RV door opened and Sam stepped to the ground. She had changed her clothes and put on makeup.

Art elbowed Tim in the ribs and winked. They had lost all interest in Donna and Glenn Ashford for the moment.

"Hi guys," Sam acknowledged Tim and Art with a little wave of her arm.

In unison, Tim and Art answered back with, "Hi, Sam."

Donna gave everyone a paper plate and a napkin and told them to get some meat from the barbecue.

The twins each grabbed a couple of grilled wieners and some buns and headed for the condiments on a card table next to the RV.

"Boys…don't forget the potato salad," reminded Mrs. Ashford. "And keep it covered. We don't need to be eating any flies."

Tim approached the grill but hadn't made up his mind whether he wanted chicken or a couple of wieners.

Sam noticed his hesitation and said, "The meat is grilled porcupine. Dad shot one this morning with his shotgun. Watch out for the lead pellets."

Tim grinned and replied with, "Yeah, and I bet it tastes like chicken."

Everyone laughed. After they had gotten some salad, potato chips and a fork they sat down on fold-up lawn chairs to enjoy their dinner. Sam had told her dad about seeing a shiny thing on the mountain. He asked Tim and Art what their thoughts were. That's when they told the ranger about the cylindrical shape they saw.

"Where was this object with relationship to the position of the shiny gizmo?" asked the ranger."

Art said, "It was at approximately the same position, maybe at a little lower elevation than the other object."

Mr. Ashford looked at Tim.

"I didn't see the shiny entity, sir," stated Tim. "Art has a drawing of the dark object. Show him your sketch, Art."

Art pulled a piece of folded paper from his back pocket and handed it to the ranger.Ashford looked at the sketch and said, "That's on the Hadley glacier. It almost looks like an equipment canister for firefighters that was dropped from a plane. The irregular part could be a parachute."

"Do you think we could climb up there and retrieve it?" asked Tim.

"Well, have either of you ever scaled a glacier?"

Tim an Art looked at each other hoping one of them would say "Yes," but there was just silence.

The ranger smiled and stated, "Before anyone is allowed to climb the mountain, they must complete a climbing course. The training takes a minimum of three months. Someone out of shape and not used to any high altitude exertion might take eight months to complete the course. But don't be discouraged, guys. I have a group of climbers from Austria coming in next week and we'll try to find what you saw through the telescope. If you look at the object tomorrow, draw the position with a scale. Use graph paper so I can have a better idea where to look. Put in as many reference points as you can. The glaciers on Mt. Baker cover a large area."

Tim requested, "Please let us know when you are on the glacier and we can watch you with the telescope. We can communicate using cell phones and advise you where the object is relative to your position. Perhaps we can observe from a site that is closer to the mountain than we are now. Is there a place at higher elevation where we can set up to observe you on the mountain? We were thinking maybe on a hill that has been logged?"

"Sure. I'll get you a map that shows all the old logging roads and mining areas. I've got one in the RV. It's a little out of date but will show you what you need. But, you may have to try several different sites to make sure you can still see the object. I don't think snow is expected on the mountain for the next week or so."

"It seems funny to be talking about snow in June," Art commented.

"Storms blow in from the coast and at two miles above sea level it doesn't take much to snow," commented the ranger. "Sometimes it seems like snow appears just by thinking of it," he smiled.

Tom and Jim asked if they could investigate the camping area. Donna told them it was okay but not to go too far. They shouldn't get out of sight of the RV. The Ashford's talked with Tim and Art for nearly and hour. As the sun began to drop below the trees, the shadows lengthened and it became noticeably cooler. Both Tim and Art were exhibiting goose bumps. Sam excused herself and went into the RV. In about ten seconds, she reappeared with a plaid blanket wrapped around her shoulders. Her father squirted some fire starter on some kindling in a small fire pit around which the chairs were placed. He lit a match and tossed it on the dried grass and pinecones and they burst into flame. A few small logs were combined with the kindling and in about five minutes they were enjoying the warmth from the fire. Conversation continued for another half hour. Art and Tim decided it was about time to get the telescope ready for night viewing so they thanked the Ashfords for dinner and the conversation. They returned to their pickup. It was 9:17 p.m.

After donning jackets, Tim and Art climbed onto the truck bed. They were just able to make out Polaris at 9:30 p.m.

"What do you think of Sam?" quizzed Art.

"Besides being cute, she's smart as hell. She finished high school when she was sixteen. That makes her eighteen now. She'll be finished with Vet school and making a living before I even get out of grad school. She's too much for me. I have to think things out before I make good decisions; she makes the right choices with very little effort. There ought to be a law against people like her," Tim stated shaking his head from side to side.

"Yeah, I guess you're right. But god, she is an awesome looking chick."

"Four ears on the right. We'd better change the subject," Tim warned.

The twin Ashford boys appeared from the dark carrying a flashlight.

"Hi boys! I'll bet you want to look through the telescope," greeted Art. "It will be a few minutes. We have to align the polar axis on Polaris first."

Jim looked up to the northern sky and pointed out Polaris. "There it is! Right, Tom?"

"Yep. That's it," answered Tom.

"You guys are correct. How'd you know that?" asked Tim.

"Dad told us a long time ago. He said if we ever got lost, we could find our directions if we could locate the North Star," Jim replied.

Time passed quickly for the twins and the college boys. They observed double stars, some star clusters, Saturn and a couple of galaxies. At 11:00 p.m. Sam joined them and they spent another half-hour observing. She delivered the map of the area her dad had talked about. The Ashford's phone numbers and address were written on the back of the map. Their home address was in Bellingham.

Art said, "Sam, there are two cell phone numbers here."

"The one with threes is the RV, the other one is my dad's," she replied. She looked at the twins, "Come on boys, we have to go back to camp. We're leaving early tomorrow. Thanks for the interesting viewing. Good night."

"Good night Sam. Thanks for the entertaining evening. Hope to see you again."

"Good night Sam," Art added.

Tim said, "Let's try a couple of pictures of Saturn and call it a night."

"Sounds good to me," replied Art.

CHAPTER 3

THE CHASE

Tim and Art arrived back home around one in the morning. They drove into the garage, took their uneaten lunches into the kitchen and put them in the refrigerator. They sat down, talked for a few minutes then went to bed.

Art was first to wake up in the morning. It was 9:15 when he rolled out of bed. He pulled on a pair of shorts, picked up the map Mr. Ashford had given them and spread it out on the dining room table. The sun was streaming through the kitchen windows and reflecting off the front of the stainless steel refrigerator. He started to change his position to avoid the reflections but decided to make some coffee. He dropped a piece of bread into the toaster and added water to the coffee maker to make twelve cups. Tim had put a filter and coffee in the brewer right before they had gone to bed. Art returned to the map, this time sitting on the opposite side of the table. He reached to rotate the map and farted.

Art heard the toast pop up from the toaster, smeared some jelly on it and wolfed it down.

"Jesus Christ, Art. Light a match!" yelled Tim. "I don't need an alarm clock if you're going to do that when you get up." Tim ambled barefoot into the kitchen dressed in jeans and a T-shirt. He looked at the coffee pot and got two mugs down from the cupboard. Tim was grinning and joined Art at the map. He went over to a desk and got a pencil and a ruler. He returned to the map and bent over to draw a line from where they had been the day before to the position of the cylinder on the mountain. He drew the line and farted. "I think that was from the potato salad. But don't worry, my farts don't stink," he laughed.

Art said as he chuckled, "Don't light a match, you'll burn down the cabin.""I'll get the coffee. See if there is any high point near that line I drew. Want your coffee black?"

"One level teaspoon of sugar please," answered Art.

"Okay." Tim rejoined Art at the map with the coffee mugs.

"Here's a place. The elevation is 3900 feet. There's a logging road that leads to the top," Art answered. "The high point is just slightly south of the line, maybe 5-600 feet."

"That should work," replied Tim. He looked at the map. "Jeez, it looks like we have to drive two to three miles to get there. There are a lot of switchbacks. It's only about a mile closer to the mountain than where we were yesterday. But we should be able to get a better view of the object from there."

"That's much more of a remote site than yesterday's. We'd better make sure we have some things in case we have an emergency. Let's take more food and water with us," suggested Art.

"Good thinking. I'll get some toilet paper and my twenty-two rifle. Let's take some heavier jackets too; we'll be much higher in elevation than yesterday. Except for the food, we can put the stuff in the toolbox behind the cab. Make sure we have some matches."

"Yeah. We may need to light human gas!" laughed Art. "When shall we get out of here?"

"If we check out the shiny object first, we need to go back to yesterday's site. After about two-thirty, we can go to the new spot. So…we need to start out at 1:00 p.m. What do you think?"

Art said, "Sounds like a winner."

After eating breakfast, they spent the rest of the morning checking the weather reports, getting gas for the truck and gathering supplies for the new, more complex excursion. It was ten after one in the afternoon when they locked the cabin, climbed into the pickup and pulled out of the driveway. Tim reached over to the dash and turned on the radio. He tuned in a Bellingham station and they listened to a weather report. The skies were to be clear for most of the next week with cloud cover expected the following week on Wednesday.

"There sure is a lot of traffic today," stated Art. "I'm driving a little under the speed limit and everyone is shooting by. We seem to be the slowest vehicle on the road."

"This is Friday and I guess everybody is headed to the mountains for the weekend to climb, hike and fish. There are hardly any cars moving west toward Glacier," Tim replied. "Look how many vehicles have camping gear. Nearly everyone passing us has a tent or canoe on top of their car or they're pulling a boat."

Tim and Art were lucky to pull into the same position they had the day before. The camping area was nearly completely filled by 2:00 p.m. As they set up the telescope a family in a station wagon stopped to ask if they could pull into the space between the pickup and the road. There was plenty of space but the station wagon would make it difficult for Tim and Art to get out of their observation site. There were too many trees in the way.

Art talked to the driver. "We're going to leave at 2:30 and you can have our space. If you can wait until then, we'll pull out and you can drive in. We just need to get a look at the mountain between 2:15 and 2:30." The driver said, "Thanks, we'll look around until 2:30."

Observations of the western glaciers started at 2:15 as they had planned. They could see the dark object as before. At about 2:18 Tim noticed a bright spot, apparently sunlight being reflected from something. He estimated the reflection was originating a couple of hundred feet above and to the south of the dark object.

"Got it! Art, get your graph paper and get your butt up here. Draw where that thing is relative to the dark object."

Art vaulted onto the truck bed and took over the eyepiece. He quickly sketched the positions of the objects versus the bottom of the glacier and the peak of Mt. Baker.

"Check this out, Tim."

Tim traded places with Art and verified what had been sketched. Just after he had looked a second time at the position of the shiny object on the mountain, it vanished.

"It's gone! Let's get out of here and move to the new site," Tim stated.

They locked the telescope axes, threw the blue blanket over the scope and wrapped it with rope. Tim climbed into the driver's seat and Art snapped the seatbelt catch on the passenger side and they pulled out from behind the trees. The station wagon was waiting and drove into the spot the young men had vacated.

"That went smoothly," commented Tim. "I think you got the positions right on the nose."

"Thanks. You were right having me gain some experience drawing what could be seen through the telescope. This time, sketching the positions was much easier than before."

They drove about a quarter of a mile before taking a right and traveling across a bridge made of massive logs and what looked like six- by sixteen-inch planks. The bridge, about twelve feet wide, could carry only one lane of traffic. It was probably built for large trucks to carry logs from the mountains to a sawmill somewhere on route 542. A sign pointing southeast in the direction of the road said Dawson's Butte, 2.1 miles.

The grade increased abruptly about 200 yards after leaving the bridge. They went over a small hill and crossed another much smaller bridge spanning a creek ten to fifteen yards wide. It was a modern bridge put in to support small vehicles. The logging trucks must have driven through the water. To the east, the creek widened, coming from the north, turning west and traveling under the bridge. After about a hundred yards, the grade increased and they made two zigzags. Tim shifted into second and they slowly made their way up the side of the butte. Two more zigzags and a long incline carried them to a wide, level area. Tim thought that was where truck drivers tested their breaks before descending the butte with a full load of logs. The thermometer on the dash was getting close to the red mark, so Tim stopped for about five minutes. He set the emergency break and they got out of the cab and looked around.

The valley below was beautiful. Several streams and creeks could be seen delivering water to the North Fork of the Nooksack River. But they couldn't see Mt. Baker from their location. They would have to drive to the top of the butte. Western views completed, they got back in the truck and headed toward the top. The road went more than halfway around the butte to the summit. A large horizontal area clear of trees allowed them a great look at Mt. Baker and the valley below. The glaciers on the mountain were beginning to take on massive proportions. The small stream they had crossed on their way to the top of the butte could be seen meandering below. Tim slowed to a stop and looked around. He then drove to a position closer to the Northwest edge of the butte and stopped.

"Let's see if we can see where we were yesterday, Art."

Art unfolded the map and laid it on the hood of the pickup. Tim reached down and picked up a couple of stones to act as paperweights. Art leaned forward and put his forearms on the map.

"Jeez!" He pulled back his arms from the map. "That hood is hot!"

"Let's put the map on the ground and lift the hood," suggested Tim.

Art didn't need any more prompting. He repositioned the map on the ground and added two more stones to hold down the corners of the rectangular paper. Tim tripped the hood latch and lifted the hood. He stepped back to avoid the hot air rising from the engine block. He smiled as he thought this would be a good time for bacon and eggs. He had a small skillet in the tool chest in the back of the truck, but no bacon or eggs. The original blast of hot air had subsided and the warm air felt good on his face.

Art's voice interrupted Tim's daydream.

"I think I can see where we were yesterday. It's hard to tell exactly, nothing but trees. Very few landmarks can be identified from here. What do you say we take the cover off the scope and take a look around the valley, then the glacier?" asked Art.

"Ah…okay." Tim blinked his eyes to get out of his daydream and climbed into the truck bed. He unwound the ropes from the blanket and tossed them in the toolbox. The blanket was folded to use as a cushion on the truck bed if they had to kneel to make some adjustments to the pedestal. Tim rotated the telescope and tipped it below the horizon. Focusing on the meandering stream they had recently crossed; he saw a woman standing in the water.

Tim stated, "I see a chick in the stream below standing in water up to her knees."

"Notice any obvious globular clusters?" inquired Art with a grin.

"No wet T-shirt if that's what you mean. She has on a gray jacket and shorts," answered Tim. "Wait! Something's wrong. She's got her hands up in the air and is looking toward the edge of the stream." He moved the telescope to see the cause of the woman's actions, but trees prevented the view. Scanning the trees, he could see part of a red pickup with a white canopy on the back. Looking back at the stream, he could see a man holding a rifle at his waist pointing it in the direction of the female.

"Art! Call 911. I don't have my cell with me. I forgot it."

Art replied, "Crap! I don't have my cell either. I thought you had one so I left mine on my dresser."

"Cover the scope. Let's get down there! I'll drive," yelled Tim.

It took Art about ten seconds to comply. He jumped in the pickup and latched his seat belt. Tim had already started the truck and spun the wheels when he hit the gas. Dirt and gravel created a cloud behind the truck as the pickup shot forward. They descended the butte as fast as possible without rolling the truck. The second zigzag Tim came to was avoided by driving over the edge of the road and dropping nearly thirty feet at a steep angle. He narrowly missed some stumps, bouncing over rocks and small tree limbs, remnants of logging. When he reached the road again, the front bumper dug into the soft earth. The truck bounced but continued moving down the dirt road.

"Hey! Take it easy! I'd like to live through the rest of the day. God, Tim, don't do that again," Art exclaimed, obviously worried about the crazy driving.

"Don't worry, that's the only switchback I thought we could avoid. I didn't think that one was quite that steep. I know the others are too steep," answered Tim grinning. "I saw a small red pickup with a white canopy parked near the stream. That's what we need to watch for."

Tim exited the last zigzag and put his foot to the floor. The truck quickly came to the gently sloping road above the little bridge. He slowed to about 45 mph as they looked around for the red truck. No red vehicle could be seen, only a small dark blue SUV.

"I can't see anyone here, just an SUV," stated Art. "Keep going!" Tim's pickup shot over the last hill before they reached the log bridge. They heard something bang in the back of their truck.

"Jesus! Was that the scope?" Tim asked.

Art looked through the back window and saw nothing out of the ordinary. "Nope. It must have been something in the toolbox. I set the locks on the scope."

They flashed across the massive log bridge and continued toward the highway.

"There! I think I see the red pickup! It's about 500 yards ahead of us," Art pointed.

"I sure as hell hope we're gaining on them; whoever they are," uttered Tim.

CHAPTER 4

MIKKA

"We need to get ahead of that pickup. I've got an idea, but you'll have to drive," informed Tim. "As soon as we hit the highway, you take the wheel. I'll put it in cruise during the changeover. Give me that rearview mirror."

Art reached up to the mirror. He expected it to lift out of a holder but it was cemented to the windshield. He grabbed it with his right hand and jerked. The small rectangular mirror came loose in his hand. He looked apprehensively at Tim.

"That's okay, we can put it back on at the cabin." Tim briefly told Art what his plan was. They approached a stop sign but no traffic was present so they blasted right through the intersection and about five seconds later were on route 542 going west.

The red pickup was now about 300 yards ahead of them. They were going to catch it within the next mile or so.

Little traffic was on the westward bound section of the divided highway. Everyone was coming to the mountains, not departing. Tim accelerated to 75 mph, 20 mph over the speed limit, and set the cruise control. As he opened the driver's door, Art took the wheel and began moving into the driver's seat. Tim was on the running board and closing the door when Art took over the driving. With his left arm grabbing the window frame, Tim grabbed the tool chest and swung his body awkwardly into the back of the truck. He moved to the telescope and pulled off the blue covering, released the locks on the axes and pointed the telescope out the back of the truck bed. They were rapidly approaching the red pickup.

Tim moved to the cab and yelled, "Hand me the mirror!"

Art had the mirror in his left hand and transferred it to Tim. They were even with the red truck now. Tim looked at the truck bed cover and could see a girl through the canopy window. She appeared to be mouthing the words "Help me."

Tim yelled back as loud as he could, "Hang on!"

Art passed the red pickup as Tim was yelling. Art had taken the truck out of cruise and was now going 85 mph. Tim noticed the driver of the red truck had a surprised look on his face as the college boys shot by.

Art was now doing 90 and widening the gap between them and the red pickup. The pickup was going about 55 so the gap was increasing rapidly. Art changed back to the "slow" lane and turned to the right following a fairly sharp curve in the road. He imagined taking the curve on two wheels. He leaned to the right, but all four wheels stayed on the asphalt. About 100 yards past the curve was a small stream. Art started slowing his truck and when he was even with the stream he hit the brakes hard, skidding the pickup to a shuddering, squealing stop.

Tim quickly released his white knuckled grip on the telescope pedestal and stood up. He aimed the telescope to a position where he thought the red pickup would be after coming around the curve. Tim pulled out the eyepiece and held the pickup mirror so the sunlight would be reflected into the telescope. He made a last second adjustment and the red truck appeared from around the curve. Tim made a slight adjustment of the telescope to aim the beam of sunlight right into the driver's eyes. He guided the scope so the driver couldn't avoid the extremely bright beam. The red pickup swerved, moved to the shoulder of the road and skidded off the pavement.

Tim watched as the truck went down the embankment, hit some boulders, tipped onto the driver's side, hit another large rock and flipped upside down in the stream. Tim jumped down from his truck and ran to the inverted vehicle in the stream. He ignored the driver, went to the canopy and looked in the window. The girl was lying in about six inches of water, which was rising rapidly. She looked to be unconscious. Tim moved to the back door of the canopy and tried to open it. The door was locked.

Tim yelled at Art, who was standing on the shoulder of the road, "Bring me the ax and the rifle."

Art returned with the ax and handed it to Tim. Then Art retreated to the graveled shoulder to pick up the .22 caliber rifle and move to the front of the truck. The driver was climbing out of the cab through the driver's window. Soaking wet, the man stood in the middle of the stream with a handgun in his left hand. He started lifting the gun to point it toward Art. Art yelled at the man, "Put it down or I'll shoot!" Art dropped to the ground as a bullet went sailing over him. Art pulled the trigger and the man doubled over, dropping the handgun into the cold water. Art had shot him in the stomach, the biggest part of his target. The man sat in the cold water with one hand raised, the other holding his stomach.

As the shots rang out, Tim had begun to chop a hole in the canopy. It took him about 30 seconds and ten whacks with the ax to make a hole big enough for him to get into the back of the truck. The water had risen another couple of inches but the girl's mouth and nose were still above water. He moved her body so he could grab her from outside the canopy. After exiting the canopy, he reached back into the truck, grabbed the girl under her arms and tugged. When he pulled, she suddenly opened her eyes and then her mouth. Tim sensed she was about to scream so he said, "You're going to be all right. We shot the driver." She relaxed and let Tim help her to her feet.

"My brother! He hit my brother with a gun!"

"Your brother?" Tim quizzed.

"Yes, where we were wading," she answered.

As they began to talk, a siren could be heard from some distance. Apparently drivers had seen the rollover from the other lanes of the road and called the police. A siren of a different tone could also be heard. Tim guessed it was an ambulance. He went down to the man sitting in the water.

"Just sit there. An ambulance is on its way."

Art went over to the girl, who was shaking, and put his arm around her waist to steady her.

"We have some dry clothes in our truck. Would you like to change?" Art asked.

"Th…That would be great. I'm freezing. That water must be coming off the glaciers. Have you got a blanket or something?"

"Sure. I'll get you a blanket." They moved toward the pickup. Art asked, "What's your name?"

"Mikka Morgan. What's yours?"

"I'm Art Daniels and the guy that pulled you out of the canopy is Tim Michael."

Just as they reached Tim's truck a police car pulled up. Two officers got out with guns drawn.

"Drop the rifle and raise your hands," barked one of the officers.

Mikka yelled at the cops, "Hey! He's one of the guys that saved my life!"

Art cooperated and laid the gun in the gravel beside the road and raised his hands. The other officer put his gun away, frisked Art and picked up the small bore rifle.

"He's clean Bob," he told the officer that had issued the orders.

Art volunteered, "I shot that guy over there in the water when he tried to shoot me. He dropped his handgun in the stream. I can show you where it is. Can I get some dry clothes for the girl?"

"Okay, then I want you to show me where the handgun is."

Art climbed into the back of Tim's truck and opened the toolbox with the officer watching. He handed a pair of pants and a long sleeved plaid shirt to Mikka. She started to pick up the blanket from the truck bed but Art suggested, "You can change in the cab of the truck. Nobody will peak." Then he grinned, "I'll keep the cops from looking."

The closest officer heard what Art said and replied, "You're a real comedian."

Tim approached the officers and said, "That guy sitting in the water is going to suffer hypothermia if we don't get him out of the cold water. He's already got a hole in his belly."

Art and the two officers were moving toward the man in the

stream. Art was telling the policemen the sequence of events that lead to the shooting. The larger of the two officers waded into the water and picked up the man and carried him to the highway shoulder. Art picked up the blanket from the back of Tim's truck and gave it to the officer to wrap around the kidnapper. Bob was inspecting the man's wound when the ambulance arrived. After the medical people took over, the officer with wet trousers asked Art to point to the handgun. Art pointed between two large rocks sticking out of the slowly moving water. The officer reached into the cold water and retrieved the gun.

Art and Mikka, now in dry clothes, were talking to Franco, the smaller officer.

"Hey Bob, the girl tells me her brother was hit in the head by the guy that kidnapped her, the one that got shot. She wants to see if her brother is all right. It's about ten minutes from here. I'll take her and you can stay here, okay?"

Bob answered, "All right. Radio me when you get there. If the brother is okay, have the girl drive him back here so the ambulance crew can check him out. I assume they have a car?"

"Yeah. She says they have a blue SUV parked on the other side of the Dawson's Butte log bridge. We should be back in about 30-40 minutes."

Franco, unsure of the girl's name, said, "Miss, let's check out your brother."

As Mikka and the officer got into the squad car, a State Patrol car rolled up and the officer set up cones to keep cars out of the lane where Tim's truck and the ambulance were parked. Most all the traffic was still in the eastbound lanes, only a handful of vehicles passed by where the red truck had left the highway and wrecked.

Tim and Art related their activities to the State Patrolman and Bob Waters, the big police officer. Tim showed them the telescope and Art pointed out the skid marks on the pavement when he stopped Tim's pickup. Tim accompanied the two officers to the wrecked pickup and showed them the ax and the opening he had chopped in the canopy. He told them he thought he had to get Mikka out of the truck before she drowned and that she was unconscious at the time. Tim picked up the ax, carried it back to his truck and returned it to the toolbox. The officer handed the rifle to Art and suggested they lock the toolbox when the gun was in it.

Bob's radio came alive with a message from his partner. Mikka was driving the SUV. She was bringing her brother, Brian, back to the ambulance so the EMT could check him out. He had been knocked unconscious when the kidnapper hit him with the gun. Franco would follow in the police car. They should be back in about fifteen minutes.

Bob complimented Art and Tim for their quick thinking and clever use of the telescope.

CHAPTER 5

MOTHERS ON THE PHONE

Mikka and Brian got out of the SUV and walked to the ambulance. Because the siblings had been knocked unconscious, they were administered some tests by the EMT. Both were deemed okay but should be checked in the next twenty-four hours by a doctor. The police officers and the State Patrol interviewed Mikka. She verified what had started with her being kidnapped and ended with the rollover. She didn't know anything about the shooting; she had just regained consciousness and was confused. But Mikka remembered hearing two gunshots having quite different sounds.

The ambulance left the scene with the wounded kidnapper. He was going to be taken to the Bellingham Surgery Center about 50 miles away, handcuffed to a gurney and strapped down for the ride. After removal of the bullet, he would recover in a Bellingham jail.

The police and trooper finished their interviews of Tim, Art, Mikka and Brian. After giving the authorities contact information, the four were free to go.

"Art, let's call it a day. We'll start over again tomorrow," suggested Tim.

"Mikka, would you and Brian like to stay with us in Glacier? We have a large cabin with four bedrooms. You guys can rest and tell us all your family secrets," Art said with a big smile.

"What do you think, Mikka? It's an hour drive back to Bellingham and I have a headache," quizzed Brian.

Mikka said, "Sound good to me. I could use a bath and maybe

we can wash our clothes. Say, Art, whose clothes am I wearing? They almost fit me."

"They're mine. I'm five ten and you must be about five eight. We're nearly the same size, except for the butt," Art replied grinning.

Mikka frowned and then smiled. "Are you saying I have a big ass?"

Art looked her in the eyes and said, "Turn around, let me see."

Mikka turned her back to Art, bent over and looked at him between her legs.

"Well, what do you think?" she asked.

"I'm sorry. I made a mistake . . . a big mistake," laughed Art.

Tim shook his head from side to side. Even he wouldn't have stuck his foot in his mouth like that, at least not that far.

Mikka and Brian followed the pickup back to the cabin in Glacier. After they all cleaned up, it was time for dinner. Brian's headache had vanished and he volunteered to cook some steaks on the barbecue. Mikka and Tim made a salad and Art set the table, made coffee and retrieved some soft drinks from the large stainless steel refrigerator.

Brian's effort at the barbecue was minimal; everyone wanted his or her steak well done. While the meat cooked, he found some ketchup and A-1 sauce and set the bottles on the table. Tim microwaved some potatoes and they sat down for dinner.

"Brian, where do you and Mikka live?" asked Art.

"We're from Bellingham."

"By any chance do you know Sam Ashford?" Tim inquired.

"You know Smash?" Mikka quizzed.

"Smash?" Tim inquired.

"Yeah, Samantha Ashford is "Smash." She's on the gymnastics team and I'm on the volleyball team."

"Oh no! You're a Cougar too?" exclaimed Tim. "Art and I are Huskies. He's in Engineering and I'm taking Physics. What about you, Brian?"

Brian replied, "I graduated from WSU two years ago and took Physical Therapy at UW. I've been looking for a position in PT for a couple of months. I haven't found anything permanent yet. In the meantime, I've been working for a company that instructs climbers on glacier ascent. Mikka is double majoring in Phys. Ed. and Elementary Ed."

"So, you've climbed Mt. Baker?" asked Tim.

"Oh yeah. I've been up there five times. I've ascended the mountain from each face. I started climbing when I was sixteen."

"Then you know Glenn Ashford?" Art asked.

"Uh-huh. Climbed with Glenn several times. He's an expert climber. Saved me from falling into a crevasse once. That guy is strong, really strong!"

"Did you ever date Sam?" asked Art.

"Nope. I'm almost 25 and I think she's 18, too young for me. Right, Mikka?"

Mikka answered, "Right. Besides, she's too busy with gymnastics and studying. Sam wants to be a Vet. Smash goes out on dates but she really doesn't have a boyfriend.

She's a year younger than I am, and a hell of a lot smarter."

After cleaning up the dishes, they sat down in the great room.

Tim turned on the TV and they watched a Hallmark Hall of Fame movie. Mikka fell asleep after the first half-hour.

Art whispered, "Brian, why don't you wake up Mikka so she can go to bed. She's had a tough day…so have you. Your bedrooms are on the upper level to the right. There are new toothbrushes in a drawer in the bathroom. Help yourselves."

"That's a good idea Art. I'm beat too. I'm gunna hit the sack. I'll lock up. We can clean up the truck in the morning. Good night."

Tim walked around the house making sure the doors were locked and went to bed.

Art continued to watch the movie but couldn't keep his mind on it. He kept thinking of shooting that dude in the stomach. He finally convinced himself that it had to be or he might have been killed, maybe even Tim and Mikka. He turned off the television and went to bed. It was 9:30 p.m.

Mikka woke up around midnight and looked around, a little confused. The day's activities flooded through her mind. Earlier, she had meant to call her mom to tell her parents that she and Brian were all right. Mikka flipped on the lights, found a bathrobe, went downstairs to the phone in the kitchen and called her mother. They talked for about ten minutes; Mikka insisted they were okay, in spite of the lumps on their heads. Mikka gave her mom the phone number of the chateau and returned to bed.

Art was the first to get up to greet the sun. He made coffee and turned on the TV. The news anchor commented about the flip over on the highway near Glacier. No names were mentioned. Dressed in Art's shirt and pants, Mikka joined Art in the kitchen and asked about laundering her clothes. Art showed her the washer and dryer. The detergent was in plain sight. Mikka went upstairs and opened Brian's bedroom door. He was still asleep. Brian slept in the nude so she gathered up his clothes, underwear and all, and tossed them in the washer with her dirty stuff.

Mikka went back to the kitchen where Tim had joined Art. They each had a mug of coffee and Tim was putting some bread in the toaster.

"Good morning Mikka," Tim greeted the young lady.

"Morning, Tim," she replied with a smile. "I don't remember whether I thanked you for pulling me out of that stupid truck yesterday. So, thank you."

"You're very welcome. I had never done that before. It's something I can add to my resume," Tim answered with a big grin.

"What is that smell?" Mikka questioned as she scrunched up her nose.

Tim leaned over the toaster and inhaled. "Yep. It's coming from the toaster."

He ejected the two pieces of half toasted bread and looked into the toaster. After unplugging the toaster, he tipped it upside down and removed the cleanout tray from the bottom of the appliance. The source of the smell was a partially toasted mouse.

"Ah…a Saturday morning Mt. Baker delicacy, a dead field mouse," Tim joked. He dropped the toasted mouse carcass and two pieces of partially toasted bread in the garbage.

Mikka decided to play along and said, "Mouse on a shingle? A new breakfast treat. Have any A-1 sauce?"

They all laughed.

Brian came thumping down the stairs. A large dark gray bath towel was wrapped around his waist. Before he had reached the bottom step he said, "Mikka! Where are my clothes?"

"Well, nature boy, they're just about to be put in the dryer. You'll have to wait about ten minutes. Okay? They'll be nice and warm."

"Okay. What is that smell?"

Art replied, "Toasted mouse. Want one for breakfast?"

Art noted that Brian looked serious but he suddenly grinned and said, "Nope. I'd rather have some ham and pancakes if you have some mix. If not, I'll make them from scratch. In fact, I'll make the pancakes if one of you guys wants to cook some ham or sausage. How about some eggs, too?"

Grinning, Mikka said, "Brian has to keep up his muscle tone. After the pancakes he'll jog a mile or two. He went to WSU on a football scholarship. Flab is not his friend."

After breakfast, Brian retrieved his clothes from the dryer. Ten minutes later he headed out the door to jog. Tim and Art went to the garage, started cleaning up the pickup and inspecting the telescope for damage. The front bumper was a little bent and had a few scratches in it. Art found a chunk of dirt, gravel and weeds clinging to the support behind the bumper. They cleaned the ax and rifle, repacked the toolbox dond secured it with a combination lock.

They both got into the truck bed and uncovered the telescope. Art opened the eyepiece box attached to the pedestal and noticed one eyepiece was missing.

"Tim. One eyepiece is gone."

"Oh yeah. It's in my bedroom on the dresser. I took it out of my pocket last night when I went to bed. I'll get it."

He jumped off the truck and went into the house. Just as he picked up the eyepiece, the phone rang.

"Hello."

"This is Mikka's mom. Are you Art or Tim?"

"Tim speaking. Do you want to talk to Mikka, Brian or both of them?"

"Mikka please."

"Okay. I'll get her."

Tim started up the stairs and could hear the shower so he returned to the phone in the kitchen. "I'm sorry, she's in the shower. Brian is out jogging."

Tim wondered how Mrs. Morgan got their number so asked, "How did you get this number?"

"Mikka called me last night and gave it to me. I just wanted to check with her to see if she and Brian were all right."

"Well, Mrs. Morgan, they seem to be fine today. Do you want me to have Mikka call you when she gets out of the shower?"

"Yes. Please have one of them call me."

"Okay. I'll tell them you called."

"Thank you, young man. Have you called your mother?"

"Not yet. I'm afraid when my mom finds out what happened she'll start worrying about us staying here in the cabin."

"I think you should talk to your mother and tell her what a brave thing you did for my daughter. Thank you for stopping the kidnapping and pulling Mikka from the wreckage."

"You're welcome. We just reacted to a bad situation."

Tim saw Mikka descending the stairway in her own clothes.

"Mrs. Morgan, Mikka's on her way to the phone. Here she is."

Tim handed the phone to Mikka and took the eyepiece out to

the garage.

"Hey, Art. Mikka is all cleaned up. She is a choice woman, really fine. Wait 'til you see her great legs. Here's the eyepiece."

Art put the eyepiece in its holder and closed the box. "I'll have to check her out."

Brian sauntered into the garage breathing heavily.

"I should have taken a jacket or sweatshirt with me. It's still cold here in the morning. Not bad in the sunlight though."

Art said, "What are you and Mikka going to do today? Got any plans?"

"I don't know. I'll have to talk to Mikka and see what she wants to do. Why?"

"Tim and I want to go back on top of the butte and see if we can see an object on the glacier that we saw a couple of days ago. I wonder if you would like to come with us. It's a few miles from where Mikka was wading yesterday."

"I don't need to see that place again, but I'd like to see what you guys noticed on the surface of the glacier. I think Mikka would like to look through the telescope. She enjoys using scientific equipment; thinks it will help her when she begins teaching."

"Amen to that," uttered Tim. "Let's ask her."

Brian did some stretching and went in the cabin. As Tim and Art finished cleaning and realigning the telescope, Brian and Mikka came into the garage.

"Brian and I want to go with you guys to take a look through the telescope. When are we going to leave?"

Tim answered, "Let's get out of here right after lunch. We can take a few munchies with us, but we should be back here for dinner."

Art said, "You take care of the food, Mikka. Brian and I will get the tools and warm clothes together and Tim has to get gas for the truck. How's the gas for your car?"

Mikka answered, "We've got half a tank."

Tim said, "That'll do. You'll have to follow us in your car. The pickup can't haul all four of us without someone riding in back. I don't want to do that; it's a rough ride on those old logging roads."

CHAPTER 6

NEAR CANADIAN WATERS

In international waters off the coast of British Columbia, the ISZATSO was moving at ten knots, nearly her normal cruising speed. Captain Ziya Pasha had been flown to the ship from Seattle by seaplane to take over the operation of the shallow draft research/transport vessel. The captain wasn't impressed with the one-hundred foot long vessel with a twenty-eight foot beam. It was a small ship, hardly worthy of his expertise but the compensation was more than adequate.

Captain Pasha, of Turkish descent, had been looking for a ship in the Mediterranean ports. He had only spent a couple of days in Gibraltar when he received a message from the Castle Hotel's assistant manager. A Saudi businessman had requested the captain meet him for lunch at the O'Keefe Warren Hotel a few blocks away in an upscale region of the port.

Ziya looked in the mirror and decided he'd better shave. It had been a couple of days and he looked as if he had been drinking for an entire weekend. Actually, he didn't drink, but he smoked heavily and the stale odor permeated his clothes. He probably should have paid to get a shave but he was too lazy to leave his room. Besides, he would have to give a barber a tip. He was running a little short on cash, not having had a lucrative job in two months. After wiping the spots of shaving cream from his face with a warm wet towel, he looking in the mirror again. Much better, he thought, except his beard was so dark he looked as if he still needed a shave. He had always had that problem, since his teenage years.

His black pants fit a little tight around his belly. He was nearly six feet tall and weighed about 250 pounds. Eating was something he really enjoyed. A captain, he found it was easy to delegate the hard work to his crew so many of the delicious calories he consumed were unnecessary. His girth had been changing in regular fashion; he just let his belt out to the next notch. Smoking too much and consuming too much high calorie food were his only sins. Well, he did occasionally visit a harlot. Ziya had a favorite in almost every port. He had been a drifter for some time, occasionally taking jobs that were a little unsavory. At least, he didn't owe anyone any money.

He slipped into a white shirt, leaving the top two buttons undone and donned a black ill-fitting suit coat. After checking to ensure cigarettes were in his pocket, he left his room, locked the door and set off down Main Street. Walking the four and a half blocks to Elliots Way in the hot midday sun became uncomfortable after three blocks. He stopped, withdrew a handkerchief from his right rear pants pocket and wiped his brow. The shade at the entrance to a shop beckoned so he stopped and lit a cigarette. After a couple of puffs, Captain Pasha continued on toward the O'Keefe.

As Ziya was crossing the last street before getting to the cobblestone walk leading to the hotel lobby, a car sped by, the driver yelling at him in Spanish. He stared at the little red car and gave the driver the finger. He muttered, "Up you."

The captain entered the hotel lobby and surveyed the interior of the stylish establishment. The entrance to the dining room could be seen to the right. He walked across the burnt-orange carpet and spoke to a trim young lady at the arched opening to the restaurant.

"Mr. Benjamin Saud, please," Pasha requested.

"Name please?'

"Captain Ziya Pasha."

"Thank you sir. Please follow me," she replied with a British accent.

She moved quickly, dodging several occupied chairs and stopped at a small table, big enough for maybe four diners.

"Mr. Saud, may I introduce Captain Pasha? Captain Pasha, please meet Mr. Saud."

Saud stood and shook hands with Pasha. The young lady turned and moved quickly away from the men. A large man, well over six feet tall, dressed in a nicely tailored light-tan suit stood at Mr. Saud's left.

"Please have a seat Captain," he motioned to the chair opposite him.

Mr. Saud appeared to be about fifty years old. He sported a well-trimmed gray goatee, wore wire rimmed glasses and was dressed in a nicely tailored gray suit. He wore a black rope tie and gold cufflinks. He obviously took pride in his appearance.

Saud snapped his fingers in the air and a waiter came to the table. They ordered sandwiches and drank ice water as they silently evaluated each other. Saud waved his hand at the big man and the light-tan suit retired to an adjacent table and took a seat. Pasha noticed the large man had gigantic hands and feet.

Saud spoke, "Captain, I want to make you an offer. Please listen closely. I am not in the habit of repeating myself."

Pasha focused on Saud's dark blue steel colored eyes. The businessman was very serious. The captain was to be flown to Seattle, Washington. From there he would travel by helicopter to the ship ISZATSO, and steer toward Bellingham. He was to avoid taking on a pilot. If a government agency insisted on a pilot, he was to reverse course and retrace his original route. If boarded, his story was that the ship was going to Bellingham to pick up a diesel power supply for a research team in the Aleutian Islands. The reason he had reversed course was to meet with another vessel to pick up a refrigeration unit to be taken to Bellingham for servicing. Coordinates of his destination in the Aleutians would be given him when the power supply was loaded. If the ship made it to Bellingham, it should be abandoned.

"Do you understand?" Saud asked.

"Yes. What about a crew?"

"I'll get to that shortly."

Saud continued with his explanation of the project. Pasha was to assist three men to fly from the ISZATSO in small single seat helicopters. They will be part of an air show during an American

Independence Day celebration, July 4. They must fly from the ship on June 28 to prepare for the show. There will be three crewmembers: an engineer, a cook and an experienced helicopter assembler/troubleshooter. After the men have flown from the ship, Pasha was to reverse course. He would be picked up by helicopter and flown to Seattle.

"Where would you like to go from Seattle?" Saud queried.

"Malta."

"Malta it is. You will be provided with a plane ticket to Malta. Are your papers in order?"

Pasha answered, "Yes sir. When do I leave?"

Saud, slightly irritated, said, "Would you like to know what you will be paid?" Before the captain could answer, Benjamin Saud said, "Twenty five thousand American dollars; half now and half when you reach Malta."

Saud looked at the big man and motioned for him to come to the table. The giant held a stack of 125 one-hundred dollar bills in his enormous right hand. Ziya thought the money looked too small to be real. The captain picked up the top bill and looked at it. He could see the security lines in the paper and Benjamin Franklin's prominent face.

"I guarantee the money is real, Captain. I'll tell you something amusing. My real first name is not Benjamin. I adopted Benjamin as a business name. I borrowed it from the one hundred dollar bill." Saud seemed very proud of his inventive skill. "Well…have we a deal, captain?"

Pasha eyed the stack of money and said, "It's a deal."

"You leave in about…" Saud looked at his watch. "…two hours. My man will assist you to the plane. You'd better get started right after we have our sandwiches."

Following the quick lunch and very little conversation, the giant and Captain Pasha took a taxi to Pasha's hotel. They took the stairway to the second floor and stopped in front of the door. The big man pointed at the lock and held out his hand. Pasha gave him his key and the door was unlocked. A large suitcase was rapidly filled with clothes, some dirty, some new, still having store labels attached. Ziya retrieved his shaving kit from the bathroom and placed it in his luggage. After looking around the room, he picked up his passport, inserted it in his coat pocket and closed the suitcase. The big man pushed Ziya aside and reopened the case. He pointed to Pasha's pocket containing the money. The captain nodded, pulled out the money and added it to the contents of the suitcase. The expressionless giant closed the case, snapped the locks shut, and pointed a large index finger at his watch and then the door. Pasha moved to the open door, tossed his room key on the table and the two men were off to the airport. As was apparent with the money, the large grip looked small hanging from the huge left hand of the giant. In less than an hour, Captain Ziya Pasha was on his way to the United States.

Pasha's plane landed in Seattle at 10:05 p.m. the next day. It was Sunday, June 26. Pasha deplaned and was greeted by a young man of slight build about four inches shorter than the captain and perhaps ninety pounds lighter. The man had identified Pasha from a small wallet-size picture. All the man said was "Come with me Captain." The captain followed the younger man through a metal door and down a flight of stairs. They walked about thirty yards across the concrete to a seaplane that was being fueled.

"I thought I was to be flown to the ship by helicopter," Pasha commented.

The young man said, "Change of plans."

As they neared the plane the hatch in the fuselage swung down. The young associate transferred Pasha's suitcase to waiting arms in the plane. Pasha climbed the stairs into the fuselage and the hatch was closed behind him. The interior of the plane was dimly lit in red light. Pasha was ushered to a seat next to a window and a seat belt was tightened around his waist. Captain Pasha could distinguish three other men sitting against the body of the plane as he was. One man sat beside him and two more were facing them on the other side of the fuselage. The plane began to taxi and the usher disappeared into the front of the plane. There was a three-minute wait before the props began to accelerate. The pitch of the engines increased rapidly. The plane slowly began to move and within twenty seconds, the seaplane was airborne.

Pasha's eyes slowly adjusted to the dim red glow in the plane. In the center of the fuselage were three wooden crates and three black duffel bags. It looked as if the plane had been converted to carry cargo only; all the passenger seats had been removed.

He was pretty sure these men were the helicopter pilots and the crates and bags were their equipment. In just under an hour, Pasha felt the plane descending. He estimated they were over the ocean about 200 miles northwest of Seattle. The three men had not uttered a word during the trip; neither had Pasha.

CHAPTER 7

PASHA COMPLETES HIS JOB

The plane settled on the water, quickly slowed and turned right about ninety degrees. The engines revved and the plane slid through the calm water toward the ship. The pilot cut the engines and they drifted slowly, the plane riding the small swells, slowly oscillating up and down. Ziya could see the light from a small lifeboat moving away from the ship approaching the seaplane. The ship's navigation lights reflected off the deck of the vessel and the surface of the ocean. The outline of the ship was prominent against the dark night sky. If it weren't for the money, Ziya would never captain such a piece of junk. This scow was at least 50 years old, maybe older.

The other three passengers released the clasps on their seat belts and began to remove the tie-downs on the crates. The men spoke to each other quietly. Pasha was able to identify some of the French words. The man he had seen before returned from the front of the plane and handed Pasha a piece of paper containing a handwritten message. He was to steer the ship no closer than 60 miles from Bellingham. After the helicopters took off, he was to return to the present position. Another seaplane would return him to Seattle. When the hatch was opened, Pasha climbed into the skiff and was taken to the ship.

Ziya climbed the twelve feet to the deck on a rope ladder. His examination of the ship was unremarkable. A wheelhouse rose roughly eighteen feet above the aft deck. The deck was flat from the wheelhouse to the bow. It was obvious why this ship was chosen for assembling and launching the helicopters. He trudged up the steps to the pilothouse and looked over the antiquated controls.

Fortunately, the GPS system was operational. He checked the ship's location and jotted down the position. After looking at the charts, a quick calculation indicated he didn't need to rush; he had twelve hours to reach the liftoff site.

While he waited for the three men and their equipment to be transferred from the plane, he went below deck and met briefly with the crew. He was surprised; they all spoke English but he couldn't quite place the accents. They showed him the galley and his quarters. His suitcase was on the bed. From his room, he could hear some noises on deck. When he heard yelling in French, Pasha went up to investigate.

"What's the problem?" he asked the ship's engineer.

"Oh, not a damn thing. We dropped one of the crates about a foot to the deck. You'd think it was full of their mother's best china. Dumb arses! It was just an accident. The damn box was wet and it slipped from our hands."

Ziya said, "We'll let them move the crates next time. Don't worry about it."

"Aye, Captain." The blond engineer turned and went below deck.

The three pilots hoisted the duffel bags to their shoulders and descended from the deck to their bunks. Ziya noticed the bags were color coded, red, blue and green. Now he realized the significance of what he had overheard in the plane. He had heard rouge, vert and bleu, the French words for red, green and blue.

Pasha had not seen the previous captain transfer from the ship to the plane. He thought it was a bit strange, but not his concern. It was his job to make sure the ship went from point A to point B on time. Pasha watched as the engines on the plane started, idled for a minute or two and then revved up. The seaplane took off and quickly disappeared into the night sky flying east. He moved to the wheelhouse, started the ship's engines and pointed the ISZATSO toward the southern end of Vancouver Island and the Strait of Juan de Fuca.

Radar showed nothing within 50 miles but he could sense change was in the air.

The weather report on the radio indicated there would be cloud cover for most of the trip. There was a mild cold front approaching the Washington coast and it would be over the ISZATSO shortly. Pasha was wide-awake, having slept during most of the trip from Gibraltar to Seattle. He set the ship's autopilot and went to the galley.

All three ship's crewmen were sitting drinking coffee. Pasha filled a Styrofoam cup to the top with steaming hot coffee, added a spoonful of sugar and joined them. Out of respect for his position, they all stood as he pulled back a chair. He nodded to them and said, "Have a seat gentlemen. We can dispense with the formalities. This will be a short voyage. Tell me your names and where you're from."

Reg was Reginald, the cook, from Nigeria. The engineer was Joseph from Liberia and the mechanic was Jimmy from Australia. They had been hired in Hawaii and flown to the ship in a seaplane, as was Pasha. The ship had traveled about six hours before Pasha and the three helicopter pilots had arrived. Joseph had piloted the boat until the captain arrived. They were each paid 2,500 dollars and were to return to Hawaii after the short trip. They didn't have any qualms about accepting the money; they just thought they were lucky.

"Well, you gentlemen seem to be a good crew. I suggest you keep your distance from our three guests. They will be gone before long. They will fly their little helicopters from the deck sometime this afternoon."

Reg said, "Helicopters, Sir?"

Jimmy responded with, "That's what's in them crates, mate. I'm here to help put those little mosquitoes together."

Reg and Joseph looked at the captain.

Pasha looked them in the eyes and concurred, "That's correct."

Jimmy looked at his wristwatch and said, "I'm to sleep for three or four hours, mates. Then, I've got to help birth them choppers. G'night."

"And I've got to get back to the engines. Got to keep'em purr'n'," added Joseph.

"If you'll excuse me, Cap'n, the galley needs cleanin'." Reg stood up, nodded at Pasha, picked up a rag and started wiping down the counter tops.

Pasha refilled his cup, added the usual sugar and made his way back to the pilothouse. He checked the ship's position and leaned back in the captain's chair. A smile appeared on his face as he mused about the use of this shallow draft slow moving whale. Since he had climbed on board, the little aircraft carrier had traveled just over ten nautical miles. Increasing the speed to 12 knots would shorten the voyage by an hour. He could feel the vibrations of the engines change as he increased the speed from 10 to 12 knots, the normal cruising speed of the little ship.

Pasha had almost forgotten buying a western novel at the Seattle airport. He went to his room and picked up the book. He sat down to read "Cascade Killings" while watching the radar and visually checking the ocean in the proximity of the ship. After four hours and having read half the novel, he put the paperback down and walked around the deck. The sky was getting lighter and he noticed the ship was not black, as he had originally thought, but dark green. However, ISZATSO did need a paint job.

The captain had a bit of trouble lighting his cigarette, the wind had picked up significantly and would assist the ship moving toward its destination. Pasha returned to the wheelhouse and resumed reading. He looked up from his book when he heard, "Morning Cap'n." It was Jimmy sipping a cup of steaming hot coffee.

"Morning Jimmy," Pasha replied. "Are you about ready to work on those mosquitoes?"

"All set. Those blokes 'ad better get up soon…sun'll be up before long."

The Captain said, "Speak of the devils."

The three men appeared on deck and started wrestling their crates into separate areas with room to spare between them.

"I'd better get down there Cap'n."

Jimmy walked across the deck, pried open each crate with a small crowbar and dumped out the contents. Tubing, fasteners of various types, a small motor and rotor blades were easily recognized. Normally three wheels would have been in the kits, but they were omitted so more gas could be carried, extending the range of the mini choppers. Within an hour, all three small helicopters were assembled. Each of the three men opened their duffel bag, withdrew a heavy coat and a coil of rope. The coats were placed on the seats and the partially filled duffel bags were lashed to the undercarriages of the mosquitoes. The oversize gas tanks were filled and the engines were started. When Pasha heard the engine noise it reminded him of a lawn mower. The rotors were engaged briefly to check the controls and the motors were shut down. Each pilot topped off his tank with gas.

Jimmy came up to the pilothouse after his work was completed.

"Cap'n, what d'yah think is in them bags?"

"I don't know, you tell me," Pasha answered.

"Climbin' gear…for mountain climbin'. Seen that stuff before in New Zealand."

Pasha thought to himself. These guys are not taking part in a 4th of July celebration that he ever heard of. They must be going to Mt. Baker. That's east of Bellingham. Why are they flying in there using these little helicopters? They can't go high enough to reach the timberline. What could they be after? Well, after they leave the ship, I don't give a rat's ass.

The ship was entering the Strait of Juan de Fuca. Other ships were present, mostly big cargo carriers three to four times the size of ISZATSO. Pasha just had to stay away from them and make his way down the Strait toward Bellingham. Three hours had elapsed since the mosquitoes had been assembled and tested. The pilots were on deck making last minute checks of their equipment. A slight breeze came from the west; the overcast sky was a light gray and occasional drops of rain splattered against the deck. They slipped into their heavy coats and synchronized watches. Each man had an armband, one red, one blue and one green. They huddled together briefly for a last minute discussion of some sort and climbed into their tiny helicopters. Each man pulled a pair of goggles from his coat pocket, put the eyewear in place and started his engine. Thirty seconds elapsed and all three men took off from the deck of the ISZATSO. There was no hesitation of motion, the mosquitoes moved just above the water and disappeared into the distance.

Pasha turned from watching the little choppers leave the ship and moved to the ship's controls. He swung the ISZATSO around and headed back through the Strait toward open sea. Still, there was nothing on the radio from the shoreline stations about having a pilot take the ship into port. It was time for more coffee. Pasha went to the galley, filled his cup with steaming hot brew and picked up a glazed doughnut. He thought the combination of a doughnut and coffee must be an American invention. Pasha climbed the stairs, checked the autopilot and resumed reading chapter 13 of his book.

"Captain!"

Pasha heard rapid steps on the stairs to the wheelhouse and then he heard the voice again, louder this time.

"Captain!" Joseph almost yelled.

"What is it Joseph?" Pasha queried.

Joseph entered the wheelhouse holding a piece of two by four.

"Look what I found in the engine room," Joseph uttered and held up the piece of wood.

Pasha focused on the object and realized it wasn't a piece of wood. It was an explosive charge wrapped in brown paper with a detonator poking through the paper. Pasha took the object from Joseph and slowly pulled the detonator from the brick-like package. The captain stepped to the open window at the side of the wheelhouse and flipped the detonator into the ocean as if it were a cigarette butt.

"Where was it in the engine room?" Pasha asked.

"Under engine number two covered with an oily rag. It was in a shadow and hard to see. I dropped a wrench and when I picked it up, I saw the oily rag. I thought that was a bad place for an oily rag… could start a fire," Joseph replied.

"Let's get down there and check for more of these," Pasha commented.

Pasha set the autopilot and the two men descended to the engine room. An intensive search was rewarded with two more explosive charges. They removed the detonators and threw them overboard, followed by all three explosive bricks.

Joseph said, "Do you think that's all, Captain?"

"Let's all do a complete search of the ship. Look in all the access plates next to the hull. Let's go!"

The four men combed the ship and didn't find anything. They assembled in the galley for a discussion.

"Gentlemen, I have a plan," Pasha said. "We will beach this whale and get off the ship to safety of land. If the ship blows, we won't have to worry. What do you think?"

Jimmy responded, "Sure 'nuff someone's try'n to kill us, Cap'n."

Reg said, "I'm all for it!"

"Me to," added Joseph.

"Okay then. Get your things together on deck. I'll point the ship toward the shore. We've got about fifteen minutes before we hit the Washington shore. Make sure you've got a good hold so you don't get hurt when we ram the coastline."

Pasha turned off all the automatic equipment in the wheelhouse and set the ship on a collision course for the shore. Not more than five minutes passed when rotor noise could be heard. The sound got louder and all of a sudden a large helicopter appeared off the bow. At a hundred yards, the helicopter circled the ship. It hovered for about ten seconds then moved closer. When it was about 40 yards away, Pasha could just see something being extended from the open side door of the chopper. It was a rifle barrel.

"Get down, he's got a gun!" Pasha yelled.

It was too late for Jimmy. Bullets strafed the deck and Jimmy was killed immediately. He wasn't able to get to cover. Joseph got wounded in the stomach and fell on the open deck. A second volley of bullets struck the ship and Joseph was shot again, this time fatally.

"Reg! You okay?" yelled Pasha.

"Yes Sir!" I'm in the galley.

"Stay there, I'll join you."

Pasha darted under the superstructure and descended to the galley. A porthole view indicated the ship would hit the shore in a few seconds.

"Hang on, Reg! We're going to hit!"

There was a grinding sound as the ship shuddered when it struck the shore and stopped. The screws were still turning and the ship started to swing starboard. The two men couldn't hear the helicopter's engine so thought it was safe to go on deck. Pasha went to the wheelhouse and opened the captain's compartment. He reached in, pulled out a snub-nosed .38 revolver and went back down to the deck. Pasha could see the helicopter sitting on land about fifty yards away.

Reg was watching the helicopter when a head poked up from the edge of the ship.

Someone had climbed the rope ladder and was coming aboard.

Reg yelled at the man, "Who da hell are you?" Reg had a large knife in his right hand and was ready to stab the intruder. Pasha recognized the man instantaneously. It was the giant man that was with Mr. Saud in Gibraltar. The big man calmly got on deck, turned and looked at Reg. He pulled a gun from his belt and shot Reg twice in the head.

Reg dropped to the deck, dead.

Pasha stepped out from behind the wheelhouse superstructure and shot the big man twice, in the stomach and the leg. The big man just kept walking toward Pasha. He raised his gun and shot Pasha in the chest. Pasha fell to the deck still holding his gun. He rolled to his left, lifted his pistol and shot the giant two more times. This time, the bullets hit the big man in the neck and right eyeball. The big man looked at Pasha, shot Pasha a second time and fell forward. Pasha new he was dying but he was still curious about the big man. Pasha crawled to the big man and looked in his open mouth.

Pasha said, "I knew it. He has no tongue." Pasha wasn't dead yet, he felt as if he had just awakened but couldn't open his eyes. He heard movement on the deck. He could feel the ship moving, backing into the Strait. Helicopter rotors were making a rhythmic thumping, decreasing in intensity and then nothing.

As the helicopter rose into the air, moved away and hovered a few hundred yards from the ISZATSO, the chopper pilot pressed a red button and the ship in the Strait exploded. In less than thirty seconds it sank below the surface.

CHAPTER 8

BETTER VIEW

When Tim was getting gas for the pickup, he called his mother on his cell phone. He told her of the previous day's incidents and assured her that everyone was okay. She thanked him for calling and told him they would be at the chateau on July 3 instead of after the fourth as originally planned. As soon as he returned to the chateau, Tim used some superglue to reattach the rearview mirror to the windshield.

All their tasks completed, Mikka, Art and Brian were shooting baskets as Tim checked the toolbox and put his fully charged cell phone in the truck cab. This time they would be better prepared for an emergency. Tim joined the others for a game of horse, which Mikka won. Volleyball was not the only game she was good at, but maybe it was her competitive spirit and lack of rivalry. After she had given the guys a good natured and generous amount of ribbing, they had lunch. They sat in the great room and talked about glacier climbing, posing many questions to Brian, who was a fountain of information. Everyone listened attentively and asked more questions. After fifteen minutes of discussion, Art got to his feet.

"Does everybody have jackets?" Art asked. They all answered in the affirmative.

"Well, let's hit the road. I'll lock up," Tim commented as he rose from the sofa and shook his keys.

Tim and Art led the way and in about thirty minutes majestic Mt. Baker was clearly in view from the top of the butte. In spite of the bright sun and clear sky, they all donned jackets. There was a cool breeze coming from the mountain.

"Oh my gosh!" Mikka exclaimed when she looked into the valley opposite the mountain. "That is really beautiful. I wish I had a camera."

Brian agreed with Mikka and inquired, "Where did you see Mikka in the water yesterday?"

Art stepped over to the edge of the butte and pointed down to the stream about a mile away.

"You can see the metal bridge and the big log bridge from here too."

Tim swung into the back of the pickup from the running board, removed the blanket from the telescope and rotated the instrument toward the mountain. Mikka was excited about looking through the telescope and climbed into the truck bed. Tim thought it was a good time to teach Mikka about the scope so he asked her to hand him an eyepiece from the box attached to the side of the pedestal.

Mikka opened the box and was a little bewildered. Eight eyepieces were neatly arranged in two rows.

Tim expected to see her hesitate and said, "They're arranged according to focal length. The one on the upper left has the longest focal length. It's used when we want to survey a large area at low power. The one on the lower right has the shortest focal length and will give the highest power. We don't use that one very often. It's only good for the best observing conditions; those rarely occur."

Mikka asked, "So how do you know which one belongs in each position? They all look the same to me."

"Take one out and look at the metal part on the side of the eyepiece. There is a number; that's the focal length in millimeters. The smaller the number, the higher the magnification or power."

"This one says 20 mm," stated Mikka.

"Okay. Hand me the one with the biggest number, please."

Mikka put the eyepiece back and took out the one at the upper left and gave it to Tim.

"Very good, Mikka. You catch on fast. You're going to make a good amateur astronomer."

Tim inserted the eyepiece and focused on the mountain. The dark object stood out clearly against the ice and snow of the glacier. Tim turned the focus knob so the telescope was out of focus.

"Okay, Mikka, take a look." Tim stepped aside and Mikka moved to look through the eyepiece.

"It's all blurry."

"It's not focused. Turn the knob on the eyepiece holder and clear up the image," Tim coached.

Mikka found the knob and rotated it. "I got it! That is so easy! What's that dark thing?"

"That's the sixty-four thousand dollar question," Tim answered.

Brian had been listening and said, "Hey Mikka, don't be a hog. Let me take a look."

"Okay, brother dear. Get your big butt up here." She glanced at Tim and grinned.

Mikka got down from the truck bed and started talking to Art about her new accomplishments.

As soon as Brian looked through the scope he commented, "How about some more power, Tim."

"I was just going to up the power. This one should more than double the power."

Tim exchanged eyepieces with Brian. Brian looked at the object intently for a couple of minutes and asked for even more power. They exchanged eyepieces again.

After another minute or so, Tim asked, "What do you think that thing is, Brian?"

"I don't think it belongs to the forest service. It's too big and the ratio of the width to the length is not correct for firefighting tools. It's got to be something else. Why don't you take a look?"

Tim studied the object in the field of view. The object was not a cylinder with a smooth outside curve as they had thought. It was hexagonal shaped and looked as if it would come apart in six long triangular sections. The irregular shape at the top end was clearly a large parachute with a camouflage design.

"Brian, please hand me the 25 mm eyepiece. I want to look for that shiny object we noticed."

Brian swapped eyepieces with Tim again. Tim released the axes and tipped the scope at a slightly higher angle to the ground. After several minutes he said, "Eureka!

I think I found it." He locked the telescope axes in place and asked Brian to take a look.

Brian observed the new object and said, "I have no idea what that thing is."

Art said, "Hey, let me take a look."

Brian jumped down from the truck and Art climbed up to the telescope. Art went directly to the eyepiece. Five seconds later he said, "Let's push the power up some more, Tim."

Tim thought it might be too much for the seeing conditions but handed Art an eight mm eyepiece. Art refocused the telescope and said, "Wow! Take a look at this!"

Art leaned away from the eyepiece and Tim looked at the object.

"Does that remind you of anything?" he asked Tim.

"I don't believe it! That damn thing looks like the inside of my PC! Look at those circuit boards!"

Brian, eager to look at what Tim and Art had seen, jumped onto the back of the pickup. Art and Tim both got down from the truck and let Brian scrutinize the unusual sight.

"Well, I'll be damned! You guys are right. That looks like the guts of a computer.

What the hell could that be for?" Brian spent another minute studying what he was seeing and said, "Tim, how do I get the other object back in sight?"

Tim told him how to release the locks on the axes and scan the telescope across and down the glacier to the other object.

"Okay, I've got it!"

Brian peered into the telescope for another minute, then stepped away and looked at Art and Tim standing on the ground. Mikka had returned from observing the valley below and looked up at her brother. She anticipated that Brian was about to offer his conclusion about the objects.

"What's your conclusion Brian?" Mikka asked her brother.

"You guys might think I'm nuts, but I believe that small object is a guidance system for rockets that are secured in the large black canister. I'll bet the target was Seattle, maybe Boeing."

Tim and Art looked at each other raising their eyebrows.

Tim spoke first. "You know, Brian might have hit it right on the nose."

"Yeah! It was an automated system that broke apart on landing. But who the hell would have dropped such an assembly on top of Mt. Baker?"

"I guess the logical conclusion is terrorists, probably from the Middle East," suggested Art.

"I've got another idea," offered Brian. "What if rockets in the canister carry incendiary devices to start forest fires? Maybe it was dropped in the wrong place, courtesy of bad weather?"

"I don't know. Where would terrorists get that type of technology?" Tim questioned.

Mikka suggested, "North Korea, China or Pakistan might create something like that for the right money…funding from Middle East terrorists."

"Before we go off half-cocked, let's think about this scenario. Can we imagine any alternative explanations?" asked Tim.

Brian said, "Mikka, what have we got to eat? I can't think but superficially on an empty stomach."

Mikka answered, "Brian! What a time to want to stuff your mouth!"

"I could eat something, too," Tim stated.

Art said, "Me too."

"God! You guys are all the same, food, mountains, and guns, or in your case, telescopes! That's just about all you think of," Mikka said feigning disgust and trying not to grin and laugh.

Art said, "Come on, Mikka, that's not true. We think about other things."

"What, for example?" she challenged.

"Sex!" Art answered almost immediately. They all laughed.

"I'm sure of that," Mikka replied, still laughing. "That was something I forgot to mention."

"Come on, sis. We talk about other things. We were just talking about terrorists setting the forests on fire."

Mikka didn't pay any attention to her brother but she went to the car and returned with a large picnic basket full of snack food and sandwiches she had made before they left the cabin for the butte. She opened the basket and grabbed a sandwich, looked at the three men, smiled and said, "I was just joking. I'm hungry too. Here, have a sandwich and a can of pop."

As they ate, Tim conjured up another idea.

"What do you think of this idea?" he said. "The computer section isn't automated. It has to be assembled to fire the rockets. The rockets have to be removed from their shipping container and set up for firing. So, it's not really an automated system. If so, it wouldn't require as much technology as a high-tech system. However, it would require some manpower to set everything up."

"Yeah! That wouldn't have required NASA or the military establishment to develop it," added Art.

"Well, who do we contact with our ideas? Someone that wouldn't think we are a bunch of nut balls?" quizzed Brian.

"I know… Smash!" answered Mikka. "Her dad's a ranger and he knows all of us."

"That's right. And ranger Ashford's supposed to be going up there on Monday with an Austrian climbing team," added Art.

CHAPTER 9

A CALL FROM SMASH

About thirty minutes later, the foursome was back at the cabin. Both vehicles, dirty from the back roads, were placed in the garage. They would be cleaned up the next day, Sunday, June 26. Everyone had suffered from sunburn and wanted to bathe and put on ointment to sooth their pink skin. In their excitement to look at the objects with the telescope, putting on sunscreen hadn't even crossed their minds. Dust from the unpaved roads leading to the top of the butte had been deposited in a thin layer on their sunburned faces, necks and backs of their hands.

Mikka brought in the picnic basket and put the leftovers away while the young men headed for showers. Brian and Art were first to occupy the bathrooms. Tim sat down in the great room and clicked the on button for the TV. To his surprise, the officer Franco was talking to a reporter about the turnover on the highway the day before. He was explaining how two young men had rescued a young woman from a kidnapper. He divulged the names of the young men but not the girl or her brother, stating that the college boys had performed a heroic stunt to save the young woman. Within five minutes of the broadcast about the thwarted kidnapping, the phone rang.

Tim requested, "Mikka, will you please answer the phone? My face and neck are so burned I don't want to move."

After the third ring, Mikka picked up the phone, "Hello."

There was a pause and then the voice on the phone said, "Mikka! Is that you?"

"Hi Smash! Yes, it's me! Why are you calling Tim and Art?"

"Wait a minute. Why are you at Tim and Art's place?"

Mikka had not seen nor heard the newscast about the flip over.

"Tim and Art were just mentioned on the TV news. But neither the policeman nor the reporter mentioned the girl's name. Were you the one kidnapped?"

"Yes, I was the victim. Some idiot hit Brian…knocked him out. Then he locked me in the canopy of his truck. God, he smelled bad, probably booze and sweat. Tim and Art saw it happen through their telescope and rescued me. Did you hear what they did?"

"Yes! What they did was awesome. They were really clever!"

"Yeah. That's what I thought, too."

"Is Brian all right? They said he got knocked out."

"He's okay. I got knocked out too. When the truck flipped over in the stream, Tim cut a hole in the back of the truck with an ax and pulled me out of the water that was seeping into the canopy. Do you know how cold that water is?"

"I can imagine. It's probably coming from one of the glaciers on Mt. Baker."

Tim overheard the conversation and walked into the kitchen. He looked at Mikka's dusty pink face and said, "Is that Sam…ah…Smash?"

Mikka replied, "Yes, want to talk to her?"

"Yes, please."

Mikka handed the phone to Tim.

"Hi Sam. How are you?"

"I'm doing great. You know, you guys are heroes! What you did was awesome. Was that your idea?"

"Pretty much, but it wouldn't have worked without Art being there. It was a team accomplishment. Art shot the bad guy and I rescued the damsel in distress," he smiled at Mikka.

"I'm so happy you saved my roomy!"

"Your roommate? She didn't tell us that! I wonder what else she's hiding from us?"

"I don't think she was hiding that we are roommates, it probably just didn't come up."

"Yeah, I guess you're right about that. Say, where are you now?"

"We're in Glacier getting some gas for the RV."

"Can you come over to the cabin? We have some important information for your dad. It could be vital to him when he ascends the mountain Monday. I'll give you the directions."

Tim explained to Sam how easy it was to get to the cabin from the main road through Glacier.

"Okay, I'm sure Mom and Dad would like to see Brian and Mikka… ah…and you and Art, too. The boys like both you guys."

He grinned, "What about you, Sam?"

"Couldn't you tell? I like both of you."

Tim couldn't resist and said, "You like Art better than me?"

There was silence at first then Sam broke out laughing. "You are so funny! I didn't think a physicist could have such a good sense of humor! When we first met, I thought all you wanted to talk about were galaxies and red shifts."

Tim joined in the laughter and then became serious. "Make sure your dad knows we have something important to tell him."

"Okay. We'll see you in a bit. Bye."

"Bye Sam."

Within fifteen minutes, Ashford's RV pulled into the driveway.

Mikka ran out to the door of the RV and waited for it to open. When the door opened, the Ashford twins jumped to the ground. Mikka had to step out of the way or get run over. Sam was next. She hugged Mikka and said, "It's good to see you and I'm so happy you are all right."

Glenn and Donna exited the vehicle and surveyed the chateau. They were impressed with the large windows, walls of rough-hewn logs and river rock chimneys of the home. Brian, Tim and Art came from the main entrance of the cabin to greet them. The twins had found the basketball and were dribbling the ball around the half court, passing the ball and shooting. Everyone, except the twins, shook hands. Mikka had her arm on Sam's shoulders and Sam held Mikka around the waist. They appeared to be sisters who hadn't seen each other in years. Actually, it had been only a few weeks.

Mikka and Tim had not yet cleaned up from their dusty round trip to the butte so everyone was invited in to relax and have a cold drink. Mikka ran upstairs to shower and Sam joined her so they could talk. Mikka and Tim each took a few minutes to shower, change clothes and lather on some sunburn ointment to sooth their reddening skin.

Art had been relating the previous day's activities to the Ashfords when Tim and Mikka returned to the great room. Brian explained how the kidnapper had approached him and without warning, hit him in the head with a handgun. That was the last thing he remembered until Mikka came back and found him leaning over the hood of their Honda.

Donna and Glenn offered to take everyone to dinner but Tim and Brian thought it would be better to stay at the cabin and tell Glenn what they had seen from Dawson's Butte with the telescope. They didn't want any civilians to hear what they imagined was contained in the cylindrical package and the smaller object resembling some sort of computer. Rumors about terrorists trying to set fire to the national forests might not sit too well with the locals or people vacationing in the area.

The women volunteered to make dinner. After they went into the kitchen, the men gathered in the great room near the fireplace to talk to Glenn. Tim lit a fire with six-inch stick matches and with the burning logs sounding like someone making popcorn, the young men told the ranger what they thought they had seen.

"Well, that is quite a story," commented Glenn. "You know, I respect you guys for stopping the kidnapping and probably saving Mikka from a fate worse than death, but don't you think it's a bit of a stretch to conclude there are a bunch of rockets on Mt. Baker that will be launched to set fire to the forests?"

"What do you think is in that long hexagonal package, Mr. Ashford?" Tim queried.

"I think it's probably some kind of weather package that went awry. It was probably dropped from a cargo plane by university researchers either in Canada or the US. The hexagonal package may have crashed before it could unfold. Perhaps it was supposed to deploy at a lower altitude and the automatic routine wasn't able to activate at high altitude."

"You make that scenario sound more plausible than ours, Mr. Ashford. You sure know how to deflate our bubble of intrigue," Art responded with a trace of chagrin.

The ranger smiled and said, "I'll tell you what I'll do. I'll contact the Forest Service, the Air Force, the Coast and Geodetic Survey, the National Weather Bureau, the University of British Columbia, and the University of Washington and ask them if they know of any activity utilizing the objects you've described. Where is your computer?"

Tim's attitude suddenly changed from disappointment to hope for their ideas. "It's in there." He pointed to a room adjacent to the great room. They all stood and went into the study in the back of the large cabin.

"Dinner's ready. Come and get it!" ordered Donna from the kitchen.

"Okay, Donna, we have to do something immediately so we can enjoy dinner," answered Glenn.

Tim logged on the brouser and Glenn sat down at the keyboard and accessed his ranger account. In less than a minute he had composed a letter that he could send to all the pertinent agencies. He added the addresses of all the organizations he had previously named and clicked on the send icon. Glenn leaned back in his chair in front of the computer, looked up at Tim, Art and Brian, smiled and said, "Let's eat!"

Tim suddenly thought Boeing might be involved and said, "I'll have my dad check with the Boeing Research Division. Maybe they'll know something. I'll send him an email after dinner."

Dinner was very enjoyable. The ladies had come up with an

idea to change the subject of the conversation. They didn't feel like talking about the objects on the mountain. Everyone had to tell a funny story. Tom and Jim were first. They told how they had tricked their mom by exchanging clothes so she would get confused. Donna interrupted and said, "They really had me going for a while but Tom has a little mole on his right shoulder so I pulled on their shirts and could tell which boy I was talking to. Now that they're bigger, it's easier to tell them apart."

Art was next. He apologized for returning to the subject of the objects on the mountain but without cracking a smile, he said he thought what he had to say was extremely important.

"I think the large object is a vending machine for wine. Mt. Baker Lodge had it dropped from a plane but it never reached the lodge. The lodge manager decided to leave the wine on the glacier since the ice would keep it cold."

Art received some smiles and several boos for his, at best, amusing story.

"Jeez, I thought it was a funny story," Art commented with a grin.

After all the stories had been related, Donna and Glenn announced they were going to have to return to Bellingham. In the morning, Glenn had to report to the mountain to meet with the Austrian climbing team. The ranger had to pick up some climbing equipment from home before going onto the glaciers. He would check his email for replies to his questionnaire about the objects on the mountain. He left his email address with Tim in case Tim's father found out anything from Boeing. Brian and Mikka also had to return home but would return to the area for more camping later in the week. Tim and Art were left to clean up the dirty dishes. Tim left Art to load the dishwasher while he sent an email to his father in Seattle.

CHAPTER 8

FORECAST: SNOW AND WIND

"What do you think about the women?" Art asked Tim excitedly.

"Well, Mrs. Ashford is a nice woman. Mikka and Sam are nice if you know what I mean," Tim replied.

"I know, you mean really hot."

"Yeah…awesomely hot. And they're not idiots like some great looking chicks are."

"I noticed a faint tan line on Sam's temples. I think she has contacts and occasionally wears glasses," added Art.

"That doesn't bother me," Tim countered.

"Oh! Don't get me wrong. That was just an observation. I just mean…well…she's not perfect," Art said, feeling a little foolish.

"Well, she's damn near perfect. I'd say just short of 10." rebutted Tim.

"How would you rate Mikka?" quizzed Art.

"God, she has great long legs, and a nice bod. I would rank her about 9.7 or 9.8, just a little less than Sam," Tim stated.

Art came back to reality. "I wonder what they think of us?"

Tim answered, "I already know that. They both think we're a couple of nerds."

Tim had always felt a little unsure of himself around members of the opposite sex. He had never dated much but enjoyed being around girls near his age, even if they were more accomplished socially.

They had finished scrubbing the kitchen countertops and started the dishwasher.

Art announced he was going to watch the news and turn in.

"Let me know if the weather is expected to change, especially on the mountain. I'd like to get one more look at the computer package, or whatever that smaller object is. Maybe we can determine whether batteries or photocells are attached to the circuit boards. Want to hit the butte with me tomorrow morning?"

"Sure. Nothing else to do except wait till the sun goes down so we can try out the camera. Right?"

"Right," confirmed Tim. "I would like to get a time exposure of that computer module…see if the camera can pick up some LEDs. That would verify there is an active power system present. After that, we can take some shots of double stars or maybe a planetary nebula. Saturn might be a good target too."

A few clouds were drifting across the northwestern sky when Tim and Art rolled out of bed in the morning. Art stepped outside to look up at the irregular puffs of cotton drifting to the east. His outdoor visit was short lived; it was noticeably cooler than the previous morning. The top of the butte should be even more frigid, but better for higher power with the scope. Maybe more details would be evident observing from the butte with increased power. He went back to the cabin and found Tim at the computer.

"Hey Art, look what I just received from my dad."

Art looked at the 23-inch computer screen and read the bold letters. "**The Boeing Aircraft Company has not developed or used a scientific package of that description.**"

"Well, that's one organization we can cross off the list," stated Art.

After breakfast, the young men made a quick trip to the butte and scrutinized the computer module with the highest power yet. They couldn't see anything significantly different than they had observed the day before. The remainder of the morning passed quickly.

Tim and Art returned to the cabin and checked their email. Glenn Ashford had sent them a copy of a letter from the National Forest Service. No equipment of the type described had been dispatched to any area of the United States. They speculated the large object was probably of foreign origin. Ranger Ashford would contact the FBI after investigating the objects, provided, in his estimation, they were potentially destructive.

Tim sent ranger Ashford a copy of the statement from Boeing.

Tuna fish sandwiches didn't do an adequate job of filling them up so peanut butter and jelly and red delicious apples supplied more calories for the active young men. One of the perks of living in Washington State was the year around access to delicious fruit.

After eating, they slept for a couple of hours so the late night-early morning hours wouldn't exact too much of a toll. They didn't eat again until about 8:00 p.m. Cheeseburgers, cokes and some fresh vegetables dunked in Thousand Island dressing were their dinner fare. Tim went to the closet and grabbed his heavy coat and filled the pockets with Twinkies; Art filled two Thermos bottles with steaming coffee, one decaf and the other high-test. They climbed in the truck and headed for the top of the butte.

The jaunt to Dawson's Butte had been uneventful. Tim drove more slowly than usual even though they had made the trip a number of times in the last week. The long shadows of late evening made the gravel road look a little different than in broad daylight. Tim glanced to the Northwest as he planted his feet on the ground. Some distant dark clouds signaled the weather might be about to change. Art was in the back of the truck removing the cover from the telescope. Art manipulated the telescope to its usual position and focused on the smaller of the two objects. He noticed the orientation of the circuit boards had changed. The integrated circuits were more difficult to discern than earlier in the day. Initially, he thought it might be the low light level of dusk, but something else had happened.

"Hey Tim! The object containing the integrated circuits looks different tonight. Take a look."

"You're right. It looks like the module has sunk into the snow and rotated slightly. Let's get the camera on it and take a long exposure. Maybe we'll be able to detect some photons emitted from LEDs."

Art took off his jacket and donned a heavy coat he had stored in the toolbox. He had suspected the temperature was going to drop significantly tonight. It looked as if a cold front was approaching from the west or northwest. Dark clouds, in fact nearly black, seemed to have gathered in the western sky since the sun went down. A sliver of yellow orange sunlight could be seen along the western horizon. Art reached into the right hand pocket of his coat and pulled out something covered with cellophane…a Twinkie! Tim must have sneaked it into his coat pocket when they were setting up the telescope.

Tim had the camera attached to the telescope and was waiting for the last vestiges of sunlight to disappear. They both watched the western sky as a pinpoint of light disappeared. Tim turned to the scope and started a time exposure.

"What do you think, Art, five minutes?"

"Hell, I don't know but why not? It's just an experiment. We've got plenty of time…and thanks to you, Twinkies!"

"Oh, you found my sweet gift."

"Yeah. Thanks. You are such a sweet person, Tim!" Art said affectedly.

"Jeez, Art. Are you sure you like women?"

Art had taken a bite of the Twinkie and laughed, nearly spitting out the soft filling and sponge-like crumbs. "Sometimes you really crack me up, Tim."

The alarm on Tim's wristwatch sounded and he turned off the camera. "Let's take a look at this with the monitor in the truck."

They plugged the power plug for the monitor into the cigarette lighter socket and attached the camera to the monitor with a small cable. Tim downloaded the time exposure frame to the monitor and they could see four bright-red LEDs and four very faint ones.

"Look at that, Art, the damn thing has power. It must be battery powered. It may have photovoltaic cells keeping the batteries charged."

"I see eight LEDs," stated Art.

"I believe the faint ones are just reflections from the bright ones."

"Yeah. I think you're right."

"You know Art, I'm still having trouble with the idea of that thing being an undeployed weather package. What if our suspicions were correct and terrorists are going to start fires, or worse, on July 4th?"

"Hmm. July 4th is only a week away. I hope Glenn Ashford can discover what that thing is before long. I wonder how long it will take him to get there. He was supposed to meet with the Austrian team today, so they'll probably start the ascent tomorrow."

Tim said, "Let's get some photos of Saturn and Mizar, the double star in the handle of Ursa Major. It's starting to get pretty cold, so zip up your coat."

Before going into the cold air outside the truck, they each had a cup of coffee and a slightly squashed Twinkie. Decaf was their choice; they didn't want to stay up all night. After realigning the telescope and spending another hour taking photos, The duo called it a night. They arrived back home in the early morning of June 28th.

During the trip home, a weather report on the truck radio predicted four to six inches of snow above 8,000 feet. The glaciers on Mt. Baker would be more hazardous than usual. The new snow would create weak bridges over the crevasses. Winds gusting to 25 mph were expected in the afternoon. The skies were expected to be clear tomorrow morning.

As soon as they got in the cabin, Art headed to the bathroom saying, "Be right back, too much coffee today." Tim brought the computer out of standby and logged onto his email account. There were several new messages, all from Sam. Except for one, all were copies of statements sent to Ranger Ashford. None of the organizations he had contacted had any knowledge of a scientific package of his description.

Sam's message asked if it would be all right if Brian, Mikka and she could stay with them at the cabin while her dad was on the mountain. Could they go to the butte and use the telescope to watch the climbers?

Art returned from his trip to the john and asked, "Anything new about the object?"

"Yeah. Sam sent copies of emails that had been sent to her dad. No one knows anything."

"I knew it!" Art emphatically snapped his fingers.

"Oh, Sam wants to know if they can stay with us while her dad is climbing."

"Are you kidding me? Tell them to get out here. Here, let me send the message."

Tim grinned and said, "Wait a minute, have you washed your hands?"

Art grabbed Tim's arm and yanked him from the chair, sat down and wrote a message to Sam. *"Sam, you and Mikka can come, but leave Brian at home. Just kidding. We'll be expecting all three of you later today. A & T."*

Art clicked on the send message and turned off the computer. Leaning back in the chair he said, "I'll have good dreams tonight!"

"Unfortunately for you, fortunately for the girls, you'll only have dreams," Tim replied with a smirk. "Remember, Art. We're a couple of nerds."

CHAPTER 9

ALIEN ENCROACHMENT

It was about ten in the morning when the front door alarm sounded. Westminster chimes announced Tim and Art had visitors. Tim rolled over in bed and said, "What the hell was that?"

Art had gotten up about a half hour earlier, was dressed and in the kitchen. He had poured himself a cup of high-test coffee and was reading a book about climbing glaciers.

"I'll get it. You'd better get up though, I think visitors from Bellingham just arrived."

Art practically ran to the door and jerked it open. A girl, about nine to ten years old, was surprised at the sudden entrance opening. She stood there in a jacket and blue jeans and an older woman was standing about twenty feet away next to a small green SUV.

"Wo — Would you like to buy some Girl Scout cookies?" the youngster asked.

"Sure," Art said with little interest. "How much are they?"

"Four and a half dollars a box. Here are the different kinds we have."

The scout held out a brochure and Art said, "Here's ten dollars. Give me two boxes of whatever you have the most of. Keep the change."

Art took out his wallet, handed the girl a ten-dollar bill and accepted two boxes of cookies from the scout.

"Thank you, sir!"

"Sure. Happy scouting."

Art closed the door and put the cookies on the kitchen countertop.

Tim was in the kitchen pouring a cup of coffee and said, "Who was that?"

"Oh, a Girl Scout," he said disappointedly. "I bought two boxes of cookies. Can you believe it; she called me sir. When the doorbell rang, I thought it was Sam and Mikka…and Brian."

"Hey, what's with the doorbell? I thought I heard chimes."

Art said, "I changed the setting from ding-dong to chimes. Don't you like it?"

"Nope. Change it back please. Those chimes sound stupid."

Art smiled and said, "Aw, you're no fun. But I agree, the chimes sound kind of stupid. I just wanted to give it a try. I'll change it back."

With a barstool in his hand, Art went to the front door. Standing on the barstool, he removed the plastic cover from the doorbell. Just as he was about to change the setting, the chimes sounded. He was startled and nearly lost his balance. He leaned against the wall to keep from falling and could see outside through the window above the door.

"Hey Tim! Our dreams just arrived!"

He yelled to Sam outside, "Don't come in yet. Wait one minute."

Art quickly reset the doorbell, jumped down from the barstool, and opened the door.

"Hi guys! What took you so long to open the door? Were you in the bathroom?" Sam quizzed.

"I was fixing the doorbell. If you had opened the door I would have been knocked off the barstool."

Mikka added, "And you aren't even drunk?"

Tim laughed and said, "That was a good one, Mikka. Come on in. Where's Brian?"

"He's getting some things out of the car. We brought a bunch of climbing equipment. Can he put it in the garage?" asked Sam.

"Who's going climbing?" asked Art.

"All of us, unless you're scared," Sam replied.

"Let's help him transfer the equipment to the garage," suggested Mikka.

There were five coils of rope, a box of pitons and carabiners, five ice axes, several probing rods and a burlap bag of crampons. Brian had also brought some compasses and a GPS locator system. Sam brought extra clothing for use while climbing. It was her dad's but she thought it would fit Tim. Brian's extra gear would fit Art. After the equipment was placed in the garage, they went in the cabin. Brian explained to Tim and Art that it was Mikka's idea to go climbing. Since Sam and Brian were both experienced climbers, they would be the instructors. Art remarked that he had been reading a book on climbing glaciers when the phone rang. Tim answered and held out the phone to Sam. "It's your mom, Sam."

Sam listened attentively and smiled. "I remember Mrs. Goldsby. She called dad about goats eating her flowers. They weren't goats; they were deer. Okay, Mom, we'll go talk to her. Bye."

Sam hung up the phone and announced to the group, "We need to see Mrs. Goldsby. She wants Dad to check on something for her. She thinks it's important. Someone has to protect the forest."

Tim said, "Is she a kook?"

Sam replied, "She doesn't see very well and she misinterprets things. Can we go talk to her? Dad's not available; he's on the mountain."

"Sure. Let's see what she has to say!" answered Tim. "Where does she live?"

"I'll show you. Mikka and I will take my car and you guys follow in the truck. Okay?"

"Sounds good to me," Art commented.

They drove about a mile south of Glacier to a small meadow containing an A-frame. There was an aluminum boat, twelve feet long, and an old motorcycle in the driveway. They went to the front door and Sam knocked. They waited for nearly a minute before an elderly lady came to the door.

"May I help you young people? Are you lost?" she inquired.

Sam said, "Mrs. Goldsby, I'm Ranger Ashford's daughter. My father is on the mountain today and can't come see you. My mother asked my friends and me to talk to you about the forests. What did you want to talk to my dad about?"

Mrs. Goldsby smiled, "Come in, come in, all of you! Let me tell you what I saw this morning. You can call me Gladys; that's my first name."

Gladys was eighty-six years old, pleasingly plump and about five feet four inches tall. She wore bifocal glasses and her gray hair was in a bun. Gladys reminded Art of a German lady he met one time when he was a kid. The German woman owned a bakery.

"Can I get you something?" she asked.

Sam seemed to be speaking for the group and replied, "No thank you Gladys. Tell us what you saw this morning."

"Please be seated everyone," requested the old lady. "Well, I went outside to wave goodbye to my husband. He was going fishing. Did you see him? He was in an old green Ford pickup."

"No, we didn't see him," replied Sam as she shook her head.

"Well, just as Fred pulled away from the house, I heard the sound of lawnmowers. But there's no one around here that has a lawn; there's just rocks, weeds, and wildflowers…and, of course, lots of pinecones. The sounds got louder and I looked up and saw the strangest thing. A man in a dark jacket sitting on a bag with a propeller over his head came flying by, then another and another. There were three of them. I wondered what they might be doing. Could they be trimming trees and collecting pinecones in those bags? I just didn't know, so I called the number for Ranger Ashford. I thought he should know about this strange happening. Oh, I just thought of something. Could it be they're making a movie like Mary Poppins?"

Art said, "I don't think anyone is making a movie, Gladys. I think those men were traveling in mini helicopters to Mt Baker to do some climbing." He looked questioningly at the others.

Brian added, "The bags probably contain their climbing gear. I don't know why they would be using helicopters for travel though. Maybe they are just a group of thrill seekers? I'd be afraid to fly around in one of those little helicopters."

Gladys commented, "I guess my imagination just ran away with me. What you said is very logical. They are probably going to climb the mountain. I'm so glad you all came to see me. Fred doesn't say much; he just fishes and I don't get out very often. So, I guess my pea sized brain comes up with some crazy ideas."

Mikka commented, "Gladys, you had good reason to wonder about those men. Your ideas aren't crazy."

"What do you do, dear?" Gladys asked Mikka.

"I'm studying to be a teacher."

"Well, I think you'll be a good teacher."

"Thank you, Gladys."

"Can I get you something?" Gladys asked. "I have chocolate chip cookies and coffee."

Tim was a little sympathetic, smiled and said, "I'd like that very much."

"We'll help you. C'mon Mikka," Sam offered.

Subsequently to cookies and coffee, the young people said good-bye to Gladys and returned to the cabin in Glacier. They gathered in the great room and discussed Gladys's observations.

Brian spoke first. "I think those three guys are ex-servicemen that used to fly helicopters and now get their thrills from climbing mountain glaciers. What do you think, Tim?"

"Your explanation is as good as anything I can come up with," he smiled. "Do you think they're spraying Agent Orange on the trees? I don't think so. Let's figure out where we're going to learn to climb glaciers. Art, pull out that map of Mt. Baker."

Art unfolded the large map and they crowded around the dining room table. Brian had just started to talk when Mikka's cell phone rang.

"Hello? Oh, hi Mom."

Mikka listened for nearly a minute raising her eyebrows, frowning several times and said good-bye to her mother.

"Guess what guys? The kidnapper confessed. He was procuring women for someone at $2,500 each. He was supposed to get four girls and take them to a cabin outside of Maple Falls and hold them there until July 7th. He didn't meet with anybody; he just got a phone call and half the money from general delivery at the post office in Bellingham."

Art said, "I wouldn't have done it for less than $5,000 each. Mikka is worth at least that much, don't you think?"

Mikka grabbed a magazine, rolled it up and slugged Art on the head.

"Ow! Take it easy!"

"You're lucky that wasn't a piece of pipe," Mikka exclaimed.

"Jeez, guys, I'd have done it for nothing," interjected Brian with a big grin.

"Okay, brother dear. I'll get you for that. Just wait."

CHAPTER 10

ON THE GLACIERS

Glenn Ashford welcomed Tuesday's weather. The wind out of the northwest had calmed and only a few snowflakes were still floating to the ground. There was about six inches of new powder on the slopes but it would begin to harden with the bright sun shining on it. As the team of climbers crossed over the glaciers, they would have to be careful of already weak snow bridges concealed by the new snow. The ranger predicted the group of relatively experienced climbers wouldn't have any difficulty. Their leader, Franz Anich, was an experienced climber and had a reputation for keeping his climbers out of trouble. Franz had climbed nearly every major peak in Europe and New Zealand. He had never been to the United States so had not had the opportunity to climb in the Cascades. He was eager to add new skills to his resume and Mt. Baker would offer a challenge, although not too great, for him to instruct his younger climbers as they traversed several glaciers.

When the snowstorm hit the mountain, Ranger Ashford discussed the weather with Franz and they decided to wait until the storm subsided before attacking the glaciers. Franz gathered his team and in the comfort of the large chalet, the ranger reviewed the potential problems they might encounter while traveling over the glaciers blanketed with new snow. One enthusiastic young French-speaking climber wanted to attack the mountain while snow was still falling. Glenn squelched the climber's idea by saying he didn't want to risk encountering any whiteout conditions and end up dead. There were no emergencies requiring the climb to begin under poor conditions.

During one of the coffee breaks, Franz approached the ranger. The Austrian stood about five nine and probably weighed about 180 pounds. He had a barrel chest and massive biceps. He reminded Glenn of an Olympic weightlifter, short blonde hair and no neck.

"You know, Ranger, our group normally has just five members. Those three guys joined us at the last minute." Franz nodded in the direction of three men sitting together separated from the others. "I do not know much about them; our financial officer told me to take them along. I had no choice. They seem to speak French mostly, but occasionally I hear some spots of English and I think Arabic. I am worried about their climbing skills. They might be Internet climbers and have no actual experience. We will have to watch them."

"Thanks, Franz. I'm glad you gave me that information. I'll keep an eye on them. I hope they don't cause trouble by dragging any of us into a crevasse. I originally thought we would have three groups of three but now I believe a group of four and a group of five would be better. I'll take your second best climber and two of those guys. You take the third guy and the rest of your original team. After you, who is your best man?"

"That would be Otto Mohr. I'll have him join us." He turned toward the massive stone fireplace and said, "Otto. Please come here."

Otto stood, excused himself from his friends and walked toward his leader and the ranger. In his late twenties, Otto was about two inches taller than Franz. He smiled as he joined the pair of experienced climbers.

"Yes sir," he said as he stuffed the last bite of a cookie in his mouth. He chewed for a moment and said, "Umm, very tasty."

"Let's sit down over there," Glenn said as he pointed to a small table next to a large window extending from floor to ceiling. The three men sat down and Glenn picked up a napkin, took out a pen and began to draw a diagram of the object Tim and Art had described. Franz and Otto looked intently as the ink flowed from the tip of the pen. As the ranger finished the sketch and rotated it for the other two men to see, Otto said, "What is that?"

Franz asked, "Where is that object located?"

Glenn replied, "Two of my daughter's friends saw this object near the top of Hadley Glacier. I'm guessing, but I think it is on Mazama Glacier at about 9,000 ft. They saw it telescopically from Dawson's Butte, about three miles west of here. The telescope is a 12-inch reflector, so the object was easily detected. They also saw something that looked like it had circuit boards in it, perhaps some sort of computer. The young men think there are rockets in the big object and the smaller object is a guidance system. I told them there was a greater chance it was some sort of weather instrument that had not deployed properly. We contacted all the institutions that might have the capacity to produce such a package but they all denied any involvement."

"It looks like the hexagonal tube of a fairly large telescope. Can we check it out?" quizzed Otto enthusiastically.

"That's what I wanted to ask you gentlemen. Would you want to do that?"

"What do you think, Franz, should we try to recover the object, or at least find out what it is?"

"Why not? It will give us a chance to pull some sleds. We haven't done much of that. It will provide some good experience."

"Well, it's settled then. Let's get our gear together and take a truck to the north slope of the mountain. Much of the first part of the climb will be over rock. We'll have to adjust the loads for three people to carry sleds. We'll redistribute the loads when we get to the glacier. Make sure each man has an extra day's rations. We'll meet in the parking lot in a half hour."

Back at the cabin in Glacier, Sam and Brian were directing the three novices how to pack for the climb. It appeared they wouldn't have enough equipment to venture very far onto a glacier. Tim remembered having never looked in a large closet in the garage, so he checked it out.

"Hey Sam, come here," Tim called excitedly. "Can we use any of this stuff?"

Sam swung the door open wide and looked in the large closet. "Wow! There's enough gear here for six climbers, maybe more. This is perfect! All we need now is some food."

"Make me a list and I'll get the food at the grocery store," instructed Tim.

Sam gave the list to Tim and he drove to Brannigan's Market. Rose Brannigan knew just about everyone in the small community. She made it a point to keep things in stock that climbers might want for mountain climbs.

As Tim entered the store, Rose said, "Hi Tim, what can I help you with today?"

"Hi Rose. Sam Ashford sent me to buy some things for our climb today. She and Brian Morgan are going show three of us how to climb a glacier. Here's her list."

Rose looked at the list, picked up a small box from behind the counter and began gathering the items. Tim watched the middle-aged lady pick articles from the shelves and pack them neatly in the box. Rose was humming something but Tim couldn't place the tune.

"What's that you're humming?" he asked.

"I don't know. I just can't get it out of my head. Some young man came in this morning. He said his name was Mr. Green. He was singing in French and I've got it stuck in my little peanut brain," Rose replied with a grin. "Is this all you want today?"

Tim thought for a moment and said, "Toss in five energy bars and that will do it, Rose. Thank you. I'll put it on my debit card."

As Tim went out the door, Rose called to him, "Make sure you drink plenty of water with those bars you bought or you'll get sick."

"Gotcha! Thank you!"

Tim drove back to the cabin to find his friends packing Sam's SUV. He gave Sam the food and helped her distribute it throughout the five packs.

"Mrs. Brannigan told me to make sure we drink plenty of water with the dried food."

"Oh, my gosh, I nearly forgot! We have to take water with us. If we were going for a longer climb, we could always boil some snow or ice for water but we aren't going to take any equipment for making a fire today."

After inserting insulated water bottles in all the packs, Sam made sure the novices were dressed appropriately for glacial travel on the sunny day.

Brian checked all the packs and Sam joined him to double-check the equipment. In a few minutes they were ready to go. They climbed into their vehicles and started toward the northern part of Mt. Baker. It would take them nearly forty-five minutes to reach a point to start their climb.

Sam and the Morgans took the SUV; Art and Tim followed in the pickup. They drove on Route 542 to Wells Creek Road past Nooksack Falls and took a sharp right turn at a junction. The drainage from Hadley glacier, Dobbs Creek, was crossed about six miles from the junction and they turned left at the next junction and followed the road to a fairly large, nearly empty, parking lot. Few people seemed to be in the area today to climb Hadley Peak or the glacier.

They all wore light jackets and carried their heavier coats tied to their backpacks.

Art and Brian each carried a coil of rope to be used on the surface of the glacier. Each climber carried a probing rod, also used as a walking stick. Brian led the group and Sam followed the three novices. They hiked for almost two hours before taking a break to eat a sandwich, an apple and drink some water.

"Hey Sam! Where's the glacier?" asked Tim, a little weary of climbing goat trails and rocky areas after being in the trees and meadows for the first hour.

"We'll cross over between these buttresses in about thirty minutes and we'll be on the glacier. We'll be on the ice for about an hour and then turn back. We don't want to overexert on our first climb. Okay?"

"Sounds like a good plan! Thanks!"

"Good question, Tim," acknowledged Art. "I was wondering

the same thing."

Well short of Hadley Peak on Chowder Ridge, they crossed to the north between two small rock buttresses and were immediately on Hadley glacier sloping down and to the northwest. All five climbers put on crampons and they roped up with Brian leading, followed by Tim, Mikka, Art and Sam respectively. The climbers spent the first half hour learning how to use an ax to make an ice anchor called a bollard. In addition, Sam and Brian showed the novices how to use the ax for stability and to self-arrest a fall.

Sam looked at her watch and said, "Let's get off the ice and head home."

Art was intensely interested in glacier climbing and said, "Teach us one more important thing and then we can go, okay?"

Sam looked at Brian and he said, "Okay, one more thing. Mikka, we'll put you in a crevasse and rescue you."

"What? Why me? Why not Tim or Art?"

Brian said, "So, you're afraid?"

"Well, how deep is the crevasse you're talking about?"

"We'll find a shallow one around here; maybe 20-30 feet deep. Don't worry; we'll pull you out in less than thirty minutes. Put on your gloves, cap and heavy coat. It will be colder in the crevasse than it is up here. We don't want you to suffer hypothermia."

Sam and Brian found a suitable crevasse and they lowered Mikka down until her stomach and butt were lodged between the two ice walls. They had her release the rope on her harness and they pulled it up. Brian showed Art and Tim how to seat two anchors correctly and lower a rope for Mikka to tie to her harness. Sam used two ice axes to pad the lip of the crevasse for the pulling rope. Brian showed them how to use the single pulley system to raise their "victim", Mikka. Brian was correct with his estimation of the time to retrieve Mikka; she was extracted from the crevasse and they were on their way off the glacier in a little over half an hour.

"What was it like in the crevasse, Mikka?" questioned Art.

"It's a little claustrophobic and my movement was hindered by the ice. I'd hate to be in that position without someone to help. It would be impossible to climb out if I were hurt or without an ax and crampons. I think the best bet is to avoid falling in."

As the party of five continued down the south side of Chowder Ridge, Sam's cell phone rang. As Sam talked, the others took energy bars from their packs and sat down in the meadow to rest. Sam found a big flat rock to sit on and continued the conversation.

"We just came off Hadley glacier and are in a meadow taking a break. Where are you?"

The ranger replied, "We're on Mazama Glacier about 2000 ft above and to the east of you. We should reach the big object tomorrow around noon. I'll call you when we get there. Love and kisses. Bye!"

"Love you, Dad. Bye!"

Sam informed the others where her dad was and that he would call her again when they arrived at the object the next day. The climbing party of five reached the cabin in Glacier around 8 p.m. All they could talk about was their experience on the mountain. Art referred to the book he was reading and read the chapter on glacier rescue. He memorized the section on two-pulley rescue; his background in engineering made the technique easy to understand and remember.

Tim and Mikka looked at a relief map of Mt. Baker and realized the larger object was above Hadley Glacier on Mazama Glacier. Sam and Brian sorted through all the equipment in the garage closet and planned for their next climb.

CHAPTER 11

LEFT TO DIE

The Austrian group and Ranger Ashford camped on the mountain at about 8,000 feet that night. Tomorrow they would slowly ascend another 1,000 feet as they moved to the west on Mazama Glacier. The nine men set up their camp on a relatively flat area and used ropes to mark the safe zone around the three tents. They had packed a small propane stove on one of the sleds and were able to have a hot meal. One of the Austrians cooked for his friends and one of the other three men cooked for them. The Ranger had some hot chocolate and heated a plastic packaged meal in boiling water. He always carried several of the meals in his backpack. They were compact, high in calories and created little waste to carry off the mountain.

Ashford, Franz and another Austrian, Hans, slept in one tent. Otto and two other Austrians stayed in the second tent and the three French-speaking men occupied the third small A-frame. All nine men had been on the mountain since late morning, climbing on glaciers for nearly six hours. They were all dead tired and a couple of them were beginning to nod off after eating. Although it was still light out, almost all of them were asleep by half past eight. Franz and Glenn talked about the next day's activities for a few minutes and then went to sleep. Hans was snoring and didn't hear a word the elder climbers said.

"Franz. Please poke your countryman; he sounds like the start of an avalanche."

Franz elbowed Hans and the young Austrian rolled over. The irritating noise stopped.

"Thank you, Franz."

"No problem. He's known for his nighttime growling."

Glenn and Franz both woke up at five a.m. They started preparing breakfast and woke the other climbers. The team broke camp around seven thirty in the morning and started ascending the center of the glacier where few crevasses occurred. At nearly 9,000 feet, they began moving horizontally to the west, the ranger leading a group of four and Franz guiding the others. After two hours the two groups took a break to drink water and to snack on energy bars. Otto was the first to see what he thought to be the object.

"Ranger! Is that it?" asked Otto as he pointed to an oblong snowy bump with sharp corners.

Ashford stepped beside Otto and looked into the valley below and to the west.

"No, that's not it. I can't see Dawson's Butte from here. I think we're getting close though. As soon as we pass over the next rise we may be able to see it. I don't think it will be completely covered with snow."

One of the other Austrians, Karl, asked, "What is it that you are looking for?

Before Ashford could answer, one of the three outsiders, Amir, held up a piece of wrinkled paper. It was the napkin on which the ranger had sketched the hexagonal structure when he had talked with Franz and Otto back at the chalet.

He held it in front of Karl's face and snarled, "This is what he is seeking."

Seeing the napkin surprised Ashford. Glenn had wadded it up and thrown it in a wastebasket the day before.

Amir showed the sketch to all the climbers and said, "Please, gentlemen, watch for this object. We also want to find it."

Franz stepped beside the ranger and said, "I am feeling these guys know what is in the object."

The ranger replied, "I have the same feeling."

Franz's team of five would lead the climbers until they found the object. Highly suspicious of the three outsiders, the ranger hoped to control the actions of the group of three by having two of the three men in his climbing team. Hakeem would be in the second position, Khalil in the third, with Otto being fourth. Franz's team began moving west and slowed considerably as they began to encounter crevasses. As the five men began to move over the rise, Ashford's group followed in their footsteps. When the ranger reached the top of the rise, he looked into the valley far below and could see Dawson's Butte. He scanned the glacier above and below his position but could not see the aim of the search. Apparently, no one in the leading group had seen the object; they were still forging ahead moving across the glacier toward the next rise. Ashford's group was about two hundred yards behind Franz's assembly.

Franz stood on the top of the next rise and scanned the snow and ice surface that lay before him. As climber number two joined him, Franz pointed down the glacier, turned toward the ranger, waved his arms over his head and shouted, "We have found it!"

Franz and his Austrian teammate could see the partially snow covered black hexagonal shaped cylinder about eighty yards from them at a slightly lower elevation. Amir joined them and acknowledged that what they saw was the target of their search. Hans was the next Austrian to reach the top of the rise and stand upright to observe the object of the other climbers' attention.

Hans turned to Franz and asked, "Should we wait for the ranger?"

"I believe we should, Hans."

Glenn was excited when he saw the motions and heard the yelling from Franz. He felt like untying the rope that linked him to the other three men and rushing to the site, but he couldn't absolve himself of the responsibility for their safety. He set out following the trail left by Franz and his group. Glenn anticipated the contents of the object would be revealed in a few minutes.

The ranger could see the other climbers nearing the object and untying the rope linking them together. Franz must have surveyed the site and told his party it would be all right to move around independently. If the danger of falling into a crevasse were great,

Franz would never have allowed that to happen. Glenn wasn't aware that Amir had taken the leadership role from Franz. Amir had drawn a gun and instructed Franz to tell the others to untie the rope. Amir had enough mountaineering experience to recognize the object was dangerously close to the lip of a crevasse.

As Glenn approached the first group of climbers, he thought they were extraordinarily quiet, considering they had come upon the object first. He moved closer to the hexagonal structure. It was larger than he had expected, about four feet in diameter and ten feet long.

"That's far enough, ranger."

Glenn looked for the source of the voice and saw Amir holding a handgun, pointing it directly at him.

"Who made you in charge, Amir?"

Amir waved the gun around and said, "This put me in charge. Remove your rope and help free my men."

Ashford complied and Amir's two comrades, Hakeem and Khalil were released from the rope. Khalil moved toward the bottom of the object, which hung over the lip of a fairly large partially exposed crevasse. Khalil said something to Amir in Arabic and Amir said, "Ranger, help my man pull the baby carriage away from the hole."

Otto moved toward the object to help and Amir yelled, "Stop! Follow my orders!"

Ashford said, "He was just trying to help."

Amir said, "Let me show you what happens when you don't do what I say."

"Otto. Look at me!"

Otto stood frozen in place momentarily and then turned toward Amir.

Amir pointed his gun directly at Otto and fired one shot. A surprised look appeared on Otto's face; he said nothing, reached toward his mid section, stumbled and fell sideways into the chasm.

"What a stupid thing to do," uttered the ranger.

"Do what I say or you'll be next, ranger. Put a rope through the ring on the end of the baby carriage and help Khalil move the case away from the opening in the snow."

Ashford picked up the end of a rope and moved toward the object as he was told. But Glenn never got there. He wrapped his arms around Khalil and lunged toward the crevasse. Khalil attempted to resist the motion but was no match for the ranger. The two men tumbled sideways, broke through a weak snow bridge and disappeared into the crevasse.

Glenn was falling into the depths of the glacier still holding onto Khalil. The two men bounced from one wall of ice to the other and then suddenly stopped. The v shape of the crevasse had narrowed enough to stop their fall. Khalil was wedged above the ranger but the ranger's left arm and leg were trapped between the foreigner's body and the ice wall. Glenn looked down and could see the glacier opening narrowed and then began to widen out several feet below him. He estimated it was another fifteen- to twenty-feet to the bottom of the crevasse. The ranger could make out some rocks and hear a trickle of water beneath his position. Khalil did not move. He must have been knocked unconscious during the fall.

Ashford evaluated his position and realized if he could pull his left leg free, he would swing down so only his left arm was keeping him from dropping to the rocks and dirt below the glacier. Then, if he could free his arm, he could drop to the ground.

"Khalil! Are you all right?" yelled Amir from above.

Khalil could not answer and Amir yelled down again, "Allah is with you!"

Glenn then heard two shots fired and could feel the impact of the bullets hitting Khalil. Ashford thought, my god; what kind of people are these guys? They killed one of their own without even attempting a rescue. Glenn began flexing his muscles in his arm and gradually started to slip from between the ice wall and the body of the dead climber.

He guessed it had taken him about ten minutes to work his arm from the vise grip of the ice and the body. He suddenly dropped to the ground below and felt the pain of twisting his foot between two football size rocks as he hit the ground.

Glenn heard from above, "Ranger! If you are alive, have a nice life. You will freeze before the night is over."

Ashford had other ideas, however. Khalil's body was wedged overhead and the ranger had a coil of rope over his shoulder. He found an oblong rock and tied the rope around it. He threw the rock over the body above him giving the rope enough slack to return the rock to the ground. The ranger used the rope like a saw and was able to release the body from the glacier's icy grip. Glenn quickly stepped to the side as the body crashed to the rocks beside him.

"Ranger!"

Ashford was startled, at first thinking the voice had come from the body that had just dropped twenty feet to the ground.

"Ranger! Up here!"

Ashford looked a little farther up into the opening above his head and saw Otto's legs. He was firmly lodged between the icy walls of the crevasse; his crampons jammed into the ice.

"Otto! I thought you were dead!"

"Not yet, ranger. The bullet hit three layers of my harness and barely made it through my parka. I've lost some blood but I think I'm in pretty good shape. Can you help get me down?"

"Do you have and ice ax and pitons?" Ashford asked.

"I have an ax but no pitons."

"What about a pulley?"

"There's one in my backpack. I'll get it when I need it."

"Good. I'll get a couple of pitons for you. Can you drop me a line so you can pull up the pitons?"

"The rope is partially wedged between my body and the ice. I'll work the rope out and extend one end to you."

While Otto freed the rope, Glenn surveyed his surroundings. The ice had melted to create a cavern about ten feet high tapering to the ground five to six feet on either side of where he stood. In the center of the cavern, a little stream of water wound its way around the rocks. He limped to Khalil's body, checked for a pulse but found none. Then he began removing the dead climber's coat, pants, shoes and socks. The ranger dragged the body to the side of the void in the frozen water and pushed it up against the ice. He tossed the shoes aside, folded the clothing and piled it on the largest boulder in the cavern. He and Otto might have to rely on extra clothing to prevent hypothermia. There was no telling how long they would be under the glacier before being rescued or saving themselves.

"Ranger, I'm dropping the rope."

Ashford attached the two pitons to the rope and gave it a slight tug. The pitons disappeared above his head. About fifteen seconds elapsed and Ashford heard tapping of metal against metal as Otto drove the pitons into the ice above his head with his ax. The ranger suddenly remembered he had his cell phone with him, so he dialed Sam's number. Just as he expected, there was no signal. He placed the phone in his pocket and thought for a moment. *If I can get in touch with mountain rescue, they can send a chopper with a crew but they would be exposed to gunfire from the goons, or worse. The chopper could get shot down and everyone would be lost. Besides, it would take several hours to assemble a crew. If I can contact Sam, she and Brian can get here with less danger. The goons wouldn't fear some kids on a climbing expedition. Brian knows the mountain and would serve on the mountain rescue squad if he didn't live so far away.*

"Otto! Do you have a cell phone?" Glenn asked.

"Yes. I had it adapted with a signal booster for use in mountainous terrain."

"Great! I would like you to try to call my daughter. Here's the number."

Nearly one hundred feet above them, the baby carriage had been opened and six rockets had been extracted from carriage yokes. With guns drawn, Hakeem and Amir had instructed the Austrian climbers how to remove the rockets from their container. The babies were about six inches in diameter, nearly six feet long and had foldout fins for guiding the missiles. Each rocket weighed about sixty kilos or

130 pounds. The Austrians were forced to strap two missiles to each of the sleds they had brought with them. Amir checked the straps to be sure they were secure and the group set off toward Thunder Glacier and Black Buttes.

CHAPTER 12

RESCUE CALL

"Hello."

"Is this Samantha?"

"Yes it is."

"My name is Otto. I am with your father at the bottom of a crevasse on Mazama Glacier. He tried to call you on his cell phone but can't get a signal. I am above him and my phone has a stronger signal so I am calling you to see if you can help us. My friends from our climbing group have been forced to transport some rockets. The men with guns left us to die at the bottom of a crevasse."

"May I please talk to my father?"

"I'm sorry, but no. He is about ten meters below me and has a sprained ankle. I am trying to get down to him but we don't have enough equipment to climb out. We will need to be lifted out of the crevasse. Can you, Tim, Art and Brian rescue us? We will be all right for another day. We have some food and water and some extra clothing. We are where the large object was when you saw it with the telescope."

Sam wasn't sure whether to believe this voice so she asked Otto, "What are my brother's names?"

There was a pause and Otto answered, "Tom and Jim. And your mother's name is Donna. Are there any other questions? I'll ask your father for the answers."

"No. I guess you are who you claim to be. Tell Dad we'll get there as fast as we can. We'll try to get there by early morning tomorrow.

When we get closer we'll call you every hour. We'll start calling at midnight."

"All right. Thank you Samantha. Goodbye."

"Goodbye Otto."

Sam put the phone in her pocket and looked at her friends. They were just about to leave the cabin for another afternoon on Hadley glacier.

"Who was that?" asked Mikka.

Sam frowned, clamped her lips together and then said, "A climber named Otto. He and Dad are trapped at the bottom of a crevasse. We are going to rescue them. Let's get all the rescue equipment together and get started. It will take us all day to get close to their location. They're where the large object was. This is going to be a difficult climb. Brian will lead, followed by Tim, Art and me. Mikka, you will be our observer from Dawson's Butte. I'm thinking we may have some unwelcome visitors so Mikka can warn us. Tim, make sure Mikka can use the telescope. We'll take the SUV and the pickup to the parking area on Hadley as we did before. Mikka, you can go from there to the butte and set up the scope. Is that all right with everyone?"

Sam looked around and everybody nodded.

"Okay, then. Let's go save my dad and Otto. Oh! Before we go, everyone take their cell and this number so we will always have a phone available to call my dad. And Mikka, get everybody's number so you can be sure you can call us."

Tim had started toward the garage door and said, "Come on Mikka, let's make sure you can use the telescope."

"Okay. Tell me about the eyepieces."

Mikka jumped up from the sofa and followed Tim into the garage. She wanted to help Sam any way she could. Tim gave Mikka a quick demonstration of how to set up the telescope and then had Mikka do it alone. It only took about ten minutes for her to learn the operation of the scope. She asked Tim about gas for the truck and he told her the tank was full. As her three friends and brother packed their gear for climbing, she would get ready for an overnight stay on Dawson's Butte. Mikka went in the cabin for food, extra clothing, snatched her battery operated CD player and a roll of toilet paper. She would drive the pickup, with Art riding shotgun, to the parking lot on Hadley. After the gear for the climb was unloaded, she would drive to the butte and set up the scope.

The four young climbers packed three ropes 165 feet long, one for the ascent and two for the extraction of the men from the deep crevasse. Each of their packs carried enough food for two days, half a dozen carabiners, an ice screw, and eight feet of webbing. Brian suggested they take a sled in case they have to transport an injured man. Art packed a large equipment bag with a small stove, one of the long ropes, toilet paper and plastic bags for solid waste. Sam made sure they each carried a pocketknife, a bottle of water, and an extra pair of socks. Brian double-checked everything. The rescue team climbed into the SUV and pickup and sped off toward the Hadley Peak parking lot.

While the younger generation prepared for the rescue climb, Otto had driven a piton into the nearly vertical ice wall of the glacier about a foot above his head. He put a carabiner through the hole on the piton and attached a pulley. After threading one end of his rope through the pulley and attaching it to his harness, he dropped the rope to ranger Ashford.

"Ready Otto?"

"Ready!"

Ashford made a loop in the rope, put his left foot in the loop and applied all his weight to the rope. Otto felt the harness pull up but he didn't move. His crampons were lodged in the ice below out of reach.

"Ranger! I am stuck. My crampons are stuck in the ice. I can't reach them."

Ashford stepped down from the loop and thought for a moment.

"Otto, you are going to have to break away some of the ice around your feet. Is there room to swing your ax?"

"Yeah, I can do that."

"If that doesn't work, try peeing on your boots. That should loosen your crampons," laughed the ranger.

"I don't have enough room to do that. Remember it's cold in here and it's too short anyway," laughed Otto.

Ashford smiled and said, "No one can say we're not having fun!"

A fist size piece of ice fell from above and crashed on the rocks beside the ranger.

"I got my right foot clear, ranger; now for my left."

More ice began to fall but in smaller pieces. It took nearly ten minutes for Otto to get his left foot free. Though his movement was restricted, the Austrian was able to undo his crampons and drop them to the ground in the small cavern.

"Okay, ranger. You can let me down now."

Glenn had tied two prussic knots to the rope and was able to gradually lower Otto to the ground about three feet at a time. As Otto finally reached the ground beside the ranger they gave each other a bear hug.

"Thank you, ranger."

"Thank you, Otto, for not being dead. If my daughter and her friends aren't able to reach us, we might have to work together to get out of here. Let's start carving some hand holds into the ice, but let's look at your wound first."

Otto removed his harness, his lightweight parka, his shirt and undershirt. The lead slug had penetrated his skin and was lodged in the muscle of his abdomen. They didn't want to encourage further bleeding so they decided not to remove the slug. Ashford cut the dead climber's shirt into strips and they bound Otto's stomach as best they could.

The wound began to bleed again when Otto was being lowered to the ground. He was not going to be of much help carving handholds in the glacier walls. The ranger was going to be on his own.

Ashford climbed the rope to Otto's former position where he

began chipping away at the ice. After making enough grooves to move up about four feet, he removed the first piton and seated another piton in the ice. It had taken him nearly half an hour to move up the glacier wall a little more than a meter. Glenn calculated it would take him nearly ten hours to reach the surface if he worked continuously. The ranger realized he would be able to get out of the crevasse sometime tomorrow if Sam's rescue team didn't arrive as planned. He decided to move up another meter or so, and then return to the bottom to rest his arms, eat and talk to Otto. They faced another problem.

Glenn drove the piton into the ice, relocated the rope and then dropped down to talk to the wounded Austrian. Otto was the first to speak.

"Ranger Ashford, this hole is going to gradually increase in carbon dioxide concentration. There is no air circulating from above so we will have to both move up in the crevasse to obtain a supply of fresh air."

"That's exactly what I needed to talk to you about, Otto. As I was cutting handholds in the ice above, I realized the carbon dioxide, as a heavy gas, would build up in the cavern to dangerous levels. Have you any ideas?"

"I think we need to move up into the crevasse to avoid the concentration increase. Can you cut a shelf in the ice so we can stand on it to work on hand holds above us? I believe the carbon dioxide should continually go to the bottom of the crevasse. But that is all right if we are not there."

The ranger replied, "That sounds like a good plan. I'll chip out a shelf so we can stand on it. It is difficult to work hanging from a piton. As soon as I get a shelf made, I'll help you get to it. Make sure you put your crampons back on."

Otto waited about fifteen minutes while the ranger broke off chunks of ice, which fell to the floor of the cavern. Just as Otto thought Ashford was finished, more ice tumbled from above. Several times the Austrian thought the mound of ice on the floor was enough, but more ice fell to the pile. His anxiety was building; he wanted to get out of this crypt and start the climb to safety. Why was the ranger taking so long?

Otto finally heard Glenn call out, "Okay, Otto, tie the rope to your harness and I will start lifting you." Otto grabbed the end of the rope hanging from the ceiling and attached it to his harness. He wanted to assist the ranger but knew if he tried to pull himself up, his wound would open and begin to bleed again. He tried to relax and let the ranger do the work. He would be able to help cut grooves in the ice higher up.

"Okay, ranger. I am ready."

Otto felt the harness pull taut against his chest and he began to be slowly lifted off the ground. He moved up two to three feet at a time. Otto was trying to envision how the orientation of the ranger allowed him to go up in such large intervals. As soon as his head rose above the restriction in the crevasse, he could see what Ashford had done. The ranger had cut deep notches in both walls of the crevasse and was straddling the opening. Glenn could then lift Otto with his legs and not his arms. When Otto reached the level of the ranger, he placed his feet into a large groove cut into one ice wall and leaned back against the other surface. It was a rather comfortable position. He checked his wound and was gratified no more bleeding had occurred.

While Glenn and Otto were beginning to move up the interior walls of the crevasse, the rescue team had made it to the center of Hadley Glacier at the elevation they had reached the day before. Brian, as leader, was able to avoid occasional crevasses with ease. They were making good time, even though they were pulling a sled. During the first hour on the glacier, Sam pulled the sled. She switched positions with Art and he hauled the sled for the second hour. They stopped for a break at five o'clock to eat and call Mikka for directions to reach the object; unaware what remained was just a metal frame.

"Mikka. Can you see us on the glacier?" asked Sam.

"I can see four little specs in a line. Let me switch to a higher power. Okay, everybody wave," she laughed.

Sam told the group to wave and Mikka replied with, "You are

little ants standing with your antennae moving. I'm guessing you have to go quite a bit higher and move to my right; I guess that would be south, about that same distance. What's your elevation?"

Sam checked with Brian then answered back with, "We're at 6,700 feet."

Mikka said, "Based on the height of the mountain, you still have about 2,000 feet to go both vertically and horizontally. I can see the object, but its orientation is different than previously. How are you guys doing?"

"We're fine. I think adrenaline is helping us. Hopefully we won't crash until after we find my dad. Call us if you notice anything, okay?"

"Okay, roomy. Good luck!"

Mikka decided to survey the mountain in the vicinity of her friends. As she swept the telescope horizontally to the north, she noticed two other ants at a lower elevation. Mikka decided she would call Smash if the little spots got any closer to the rescue party.

The sun would set around nine p.m. There was still plenty of time to watch the movement of the other two climbers. She would eat and listen to music for a half hour and then take another look at the mountain.

CHAPTER 13

INTERVENTION

The rescue party encountered multiple crevasses as they moved diagonally across Mazama Glacier. The circuitous route they were taking significantly slowed their progress. However, extracting someone from a fall would surely delay their arrival at the object to rescue Sam's father and Otto from the deep crevasse. It had been a little over 30 minutes since talking with Mikka when Sam's phone rang.

"Sam, those two specks are getting closer to you. You might be able to see them. They are behind you about 1,000 feet. It appears they are following your tracks."

"Okay, Mikka. Thanks for the warning."

Sam told the guys about Mikka's call. They looked behind them but couldn't see anything. There were so many undulations in the glacier; the two people following were probably in a low spot hidden by a small ridge.

"The sun seems to be sinking toward the horizon pretty fast. We've only a couple of hours of daylight left, maybe less. When we have to use artificial light, we are going to slow down considerably," stated Brian.

"We might make it to the object before it gets dark, though. Don't you think?" questioned Tim.

"We won't make it there before dark if we stand here and talk about it. Let's go!"

"You're right about that Sam," Tim conceded.

They had just taken a few minutes to catch their breath but the irritation in Sam's voice was evident. They took a drink of water, shoved an energy bar into their mouths and pushed their pace to get as much accomplished before dark as possible. After another half hour, Mikka called again to tell them the two followers were getting closer but were still a significant distance away.

Brian said, "I think we should try to call your dad, Sam, even thought it's a bit early. We can see if Otto and him are all right and tell them our expected arrival time."

The ranger and Otto had decided to stop climbing the crevasse walls. They were both tired and it was getting colder and more difficult to see in the crevasse. They chipped out a cavity on one ice wall large enough for one person to sit on a ledge. After driving a piton into the ice above the cavity, they tethered Otto to it so he couldn't fall. He put on the dead man's parka and sat on the dead man's pants. He was going to try to sleep for a couple of hours and then Ashford would take his place. The ranger used the rest of the dead man's clothing to add more insulation to his parka and pants and tethered himself to the other piton. The two men talked for a few minutes and Otto fell asleep. Glenn reviewed the day's events and felt satisfied with their progress. They had climbed nearly halfway out of the deep crevasse, but had another 45 to 50 feet to go. When Sam arrived, he expected they would be pulled to safety in a relatively short time.

As he began to relax, his phone rang. Not Otto's but his own phone.

"Hello."

"Hi Dad. How are you and Otto doing?"

"We're doing okay. Otto's asleep and I'm just hanging around," he laughed.

"I know you just said that to keep me in good spirits, but I know if you can tell jokes, you're in pretty good shape. I wanted you to know we are at most a couple of hours from you. So, hang in there!" she laughed.

Sam decided not to tell her father about the two men following the rescue team. There was no reason for him to worry any more; he had enough to think about being stuck in a crevasse not knowing when he would be set free. They all knew hypothermia was a potential problem.

"Okay Sam. Be careful. We should be all right for four to six hours yet, maybe longer."

Amir and Hakeem were gradually moving the four Austrians and six rockets across the glaciers of Mt. Baker toward Thunder Glacier and Black Buttes. The party of six had dragged the sleds and their explosive cargo across Roosevelt Glacier and halfway across Coleman Glacier.

From the time Otto had been shot, the Austrian climbers had decided to cooperate with the two outsiders. The younger climbers followed the lead of Franz who did not want to lose another member of his team. He thought when the opportunity was presented; he would act and disarm these two misguided followers of Islam. These two men were certainly not good representatives of their religion, although he didn't know much about the teachings of Islam. Franz felt that treachery and disregard for human life surely was not part of the Quran's doctrine. If enough Muslims acted as these men did, the non-Muslim world would forever be suspicious of the followers of Islam. Franz theorized that World War III would not be a war between nations, but a war between religions.

The gap between Red and Blue and the four Americans was gradually narrowing.

The route for the two men was provided by the tracks the Americans left in the snow and ice. The pair moved steadily, not stopping for rest at any time. They had been chosen for this assignment because of their stamina. As they moved over the glaciers, they drank water and ate energy bars provided by Green. Red estimated they would catch the Americans within an hour. He wanted to overtake them as soon as possible. Night travel would make the tracks difficult to follow and would increase the risk of falling into a crevasse. They knew the dangers of a two-man team traversing a glacier and if one of them fell, he would have to be abandoned. They had an important mission; nothing would be allowed to get in their way.

The rescue party continued moving up the central portion of Mazama Glacier directly toward the summit. Brian called his sister to check on their position relative to the object.

"Hello."

"Hi Mikka. Can you still see us? I know the light is getting dimmer up here. The whites are turning to grays but we can still see the butte. How far do you think we are from the object?"

"I'm guessing you are about a thousand feet from it now. You need to go up and to the southeast. I can't see the climbers following you anymore. I just looked at the map. The ridge between Roosevelt Glacier and Mazama Glacier may be concealing them. When it gets dark I won't be able to see you any longer. Do you have lights?"

"Thanks Sis. We'll have some helmet lights but they aren't very bright. But I have some red flares and you should be able to see them after dark. I'll light one about fifteen minutes after the sun goes down and then every twenty minutes thereafter. I have ten flares, but we should be at the site before I use them all. Each flare is supposed to last twenty minutes."

"Okay Brian. Good luck!"

"Later, Mikka."

Brian related what Mikka had said and the group of four continued moving to higher elevations but began to encounter numerous small crevasses and irregular ice falls. Brian was using a probe to test nearly every step as he proceeded. After moving about a hundred yards, he stopped to rest. They were in the shadows of a ridge and the moisture from his breathing appeared as if he were exhaling smoke from a cigarette. The sun was plunging below the horizon and the temperature had suddenly dropped. The disappearance of sunlight seemed to contribute to a sudden wind chill.

Tim stood next to Brian and tried to look ahead but could see nothing more than a few feet in front of his boots where the ice and snow were dimly illuminated by Brian's helmet light. If it weren't for the company of the others, he would be frightened to be on the mountain. He had a feeling the object would be within sight if the sun were still out. He wondered how the ranger and Otto were doing halfway down a deep crevasse. Within the next half hour, they should be hauling the two men from the crevasse.

"What's holding you guys up?" quizzed Sam.

"Darkness," Tim replied.

"You're afraid of the dark? A big man like you?" Sam questioned.

"I won't lie to you, Sam. This place is a little scary."

"Don't worry. I know what you mean. I'm a more experienced climber than you and I don't like it either."

Art joined the others and said, "My arms are about to fall off. Tim, could you spell me with this damn sled?"

"Okay Art. Let's switch places. I'll take the rear…say; I've got an idea. Could you guys strap the sled to my back so I can carry it? Pulling it over these blocks of ice is not very efficient. The sled will get hung up and I will have to lift it repeatedly to get it free. What do you think, Art?"

"I wish I'd thought of that. Now I know why you're majoring in Physics. I'll carry the equipment bag and you carry the sled. I think the weights are about equal."

"That's a good idea too," acknowledged Tim. "Let's do that."

Five minutes later, the rescuers were on the move. Brian encountered a relatively smooth slightly inclined area and lit a flare. The ice in front of them was illuminated for at least twenty yards and they were able to traverse the frozen landscape at a fast pace. Just as the flare was burning out, Sam's phone rang.

"Hello?"

"Sam! I could see the bright red flare. You guys should be there! Don't go past the object. Light another flare and look around."

"Okay, Mikka. Thanks for the heads up. Bye."

Sam started to put the phone back in her unzipped pocket but hesitated and said to Brian, "Mikka said to light another flare and look around. We should be able to see the object. I'm phoning Dad. If we're close to the object, he should be able to hear us yell."

The ranger's phone rang once, twice, three times. Glenn had fallen asleep and was dreaming. Someone was beeping a car horn at him and waving as he walked down the street in Bellingham.

"Ranger!" Otto yelled. "Your phone is ringing."

Ashford woke up startled, but soon got his bearings. He reached into his pocket and withdrew his cell phone as it rang again and said, "Is that you, Sam? Sorry, I fell asleep."

"Dad, we're very close. Turn off the sound on your phone. Listen, we're going to yell."

Sam said, "One, two, three…" and they all yelled, "Ranger Ashford!"

"I heard you guys, Sam. You are very close. Your voices came from the north. Can you see the object?"

"Not yet Dad, but we should be there in a few minutes. We have some red flares to light the way."

Brian lit another flare and began moving south. He had taken only a few steps when he saw the black skeleton of the object faintly illuminated by the flare.

"There it is!" Brian cried out and pointed at the edge of the lighted snow and ice. He wanted to run but would have dragged Art with him. He had to continue to probe the ground for crevasses, so took his time. When he reached the object, he waited for the others to join him.

Art had investigated the skeleton network of the object and when Tim arrived he did also. Sam was looking for the crevasse, which had her father and Otto trapped.

Brian said, "Let's follow the skid marks in the snow. It looks like someone has moved the metal skeleton from its original position."

They followed the tracks and came to a large crevasse nearly ten feet wide.

"Dad!" Sam yelled into the chasm.

"Sam! You made good time! I hope you can get us out of here before long, we're getting cold."

"We have to set some anchors and we'll drop you a line. It will be a few minutes."

"Okay, Sam. I want you to bring up Otto first."

Brian had scraped away the surface snow and was pounding ice screws into the solid ice that lay beneath. He had instructed Tim and Art to follow what he was doing and they closely followed his example. After four screws were prepared, Brian went to the lip of the crevasse to make a pad for the hauling rope. They had doubled up the anchors to make sure the hauling rope would not give way. Art and Tim were attaching pulleys to make a Z system for hauling Ashford and Otto from the crevasse when they were interrupted by a voice from behind them.

"Stop what you are doing," ordered one of two men that appeared from the edge of the illuminated snowfield.

"Who the hell are you guys?" quizzed Brian scornfully.

"We have been following you for the past eight hours. Thank you for providing a trail through the glaciers. Your flares were easy to follow, too. You are going to help us with a little project. I am Mr. Red and my friend is Mr. Blue. That is all you need to know."

Sam walked toward the man speaking and said, "Why should we help you?"

"Because, if you don't, I will shoot you. If you try any tricks, I will shoot you. If any of you tries anything, I will shoot this girl. She is coming with us, but first, give me your knives. Line up right here."

Red pointed at the edge of the object's skeleton with his gun. He pushed Sam up against the cold black metal structure and motioned for the others to join her. Brian moved quickly to her right, Tim to the left and Art moved next to Tim. As Tim and Art were crossing in front of Sam, she whispered to Brian, "Give me your knife."

Brian pulled his knife from his pocket and held it in his left palm with his thumb. He slowly lowered his hand to his side. Sam took it from him and jammed her hands deep into her pockets as if her hands were getting cold.

Blue stepped up to Art, looked him in the eye scornfully and held out his hand. Art reached into his pants pocket, pulled out his old scouting knife and placed it in Blue's open hand. Tim already had his knife in his hand. He reluctantly dropped it in Blue's palm. Blue moved in front of Sam and ordered, "Open your coat, stupid girl!"

Tim thought to himself. Man! That was the wrong thing to say! This guy is going to have problems. Blue seemed comfortable with his actions. He was humming something Tim had heard before. He remembered where he had heard it before…in the grocery store. Rose Brannigan had been humming the same tune.

Sam slowly opened her parka and Blue reached in and groped her breasts. Sam recoiled at his touch and smashed down on his wrist with her forearm.

"Hands off, creep!" she yelled in his face.

Blue replied, "What is creep?"

"Look in a mirror, you dumb ass!"

Tim stepped between Sam and Blue and said, "Leave her alone, butt head!"

Blue swung his gun at Tim's head and knocked him to the ground. The barrel of the gun caught Tim above the left eye and opened an inch long cut. Tim, on his hands and knees, reached up to his forehead and looked at his hand. The index and second finger of his glove came away with blood on them. Tim shook his head, gathered some snow and applied it to the cut. Sam reached down, gripped his forearm and helped her friend stand up.

Red said to Blue, "Leave them alone. We have more important things to do."

Blue held out his hand and Sam dropped Brian's knife in his palm.

The creep stepped in front of Brian and held out his hand, palm up.

"I don't have one. I lost my knife somewhere on Hadley Glacier,"

Brian informed Blue.

Red said, "Search him!"

Brian thought if this guy didn't have a gun with backup from his friend, I'd break him in half. Brian stood quietly and let Blue search through all his pockets and pat down his body. When he completed the search, Blue turned toward his compatriot, shrugged, and uttered, "He has no knife.

"All right, you come with us."

Red pointed at Sam, but she just stood there between Tim and Brian.

"Did you hear? What if I shoot one of these guys?!"

Red pointed his pistol at Tim.

Sam stepped forward, zipping up her parka. Reluctantly, Sam said, "Okay, I'll go with you."

CHAPTER 14

CUNNING, NOT STUPID

Red told the men if they interfered, the stupid American girl would be shot. If they stayed where they were, the girl would remain unharmed. Brian, Tim and Art had no choice, Red and Blue had guns. The two gunmen roped themselves together and told Sam to rope to them. She would be in the lead. As Sam and her new "friends" began to move away from the object, Sam said, "Brian. Please call my dad and tell him we'll talk later."

Red told Sam in which direction to proceed. He held some sort of device with an attached antenna, which he swept from side to side and then pointed across the glacier with his gun.

"Stop!" Red said as he pulled on the tether attached to Sam. He approached Sam and handed her two flares that he had taken from Brian. "These should be enough; we are close to our goal. Go that way," he demanded and pointed up the glacier.

As Sam moved away from the dimming red light of the flare near her real friends, she removed the cap and struck it on the exposed end of the flare, which burst into flame. She was delighted to be able to see things in front of her so well. She hoped her plan was going to work. Moving uphill, Sam had traversed about forty yards when her scanning eyes saw what she was looking for. Shadows about fifteen yards in front of her indicated a crevasse with sagging snow bridges was present.

She was hoping her weight of about 135 pounds, including all her gear, would not cause the bridge to fail. When she neared the bridge, she took short steps, probed through the snow and felt the rod easily pass through the thin bridge. She carefully stepped on the snow bridge, ready to leap forward if it gave way. She felt her foot sink into the snow but the bridge held under her weight. Her second step was as tentative as the first but she then proceeded with her natural walking pace. Two more steps and Sam felt a change in her footing. Solid ice was beneath her feet.

Now for the test, Red followed in Sam's footsteps and crossed the bridge successfully. Sam crossed her fingers when Blue stepped on the bridge. After his second step, he dropped out of sight, crying out.

Red yelled, "Blue fell through the snow!"

The rope connecting Red and Blue suddenly became taut and started pulling Red toward the opening in the snow bridge. Sam watched as Red dropped his weapon and reached into his pocket. He withdrew a knife and started to cut the rope.

Sam yelled, "No! Don't cut it! We can pull him up! Lean toward me and hold his weight. I'll make an anchor to hold you both."

"You'll help us?" Red questioned.

"Sure. American climbers always help those in trouble."

Under normal circumstances, Sam had told the truth, but not in this case. Sam scraped the top half-foot of loosely packed snow from the harder surface underneath. She cut a horseshoe shaped groove into the ice about two feet in diameter, but instead of sloping the groove toward the fallen climber; she cut straight down into the ice. She told Red she would have to release her rope to tie it around the groove and he agreed, not knowing Sam's plan. Sam's bollard had a major flaw, but she used her ice ax to hold the rope in the bend of the bollard temporarily. When the anchor rope was under tension, she could pull out the ax and the bollard would fail. She tightened the rope from the bollard to Red and yelled to him, "You are secure now! You can relax."

Red sat down near the lip of the crevasse and spoke to his countryman; the tension on his harness released.

"We'll have you up in a few minutes, Blue."

Sam had reached under her parka and pulled her knife from

under her belt. Several years ago, she had made a pocket of leather attached to her belt to hold a thin blade. She disliked having a knife in a pocket. It was too easy to lose.

Red was exhausted from holding Blue for the ten minutes Sam had taken to prepare the ill-shaped bollard to anchor the men. He sat with his back to Sam and was unaware that Sam was cutting the rope. When the rope parted, Blue's weight dragged Red from the lip into the crevasse. Red was taken completely by surprise; he didn't utter a word. He just disappeared.

Sam got up from sitting on the surface of the glacier and using light from the flare, peered into the crevasse. She couldn't see anything. There was no point in wasting any more time trying to see the two men; both creeps were gone. If she hadn't been able to cut the rope, she was going to pull her ax from the bollard and the bollard would have failed. This dumb girl had planned two ways to get both men in their icy graves. She activated the second flare just as the first one burned out, picked up the gun Red had dropped and headed back to help haul Otto and her father to safety.

As Sam was returning to the crevasse that was holding her father captive, Otto had been pulled to safety and was sitting on the sled wrapped in a blanket. He had noticed the bright red flare Sam carried was getting brighter and said, "Someone is coming."

When Sam arrived, centered in the flare's red glow, the men looked up from their hauling task and noted she was alone. Tim was especially relieved to see her without Red and Blue.

"Where are your buddies, Sam?" Tim inquired.

"They took the down elevator and didn't return," Sam replied without a smile. "I'll fill you guys in on the details later."

Brian, Tim and Art were gradually lifting her father to safety. There was nothing for Sam to do but make something warm to eat for the two men that had been in the deep crevasse for nearly twelve hours. She thought, which soup should I make, minestrone or chicken noodle? Sam removed the cook stove from the equipment bag and set it up. In a couple of minutes, just as her dad was nearly out of the chasm, the snow had melted in the pan and the water had come to a boil. Chicken noodle always made her nose run so she opened a packet of minestrone and poured the dry contents into the water.

The first few words uttered as the ranger appeared above the lip of the crevasse were, "Do I smell soup?"

Sam ran to her dad and they hugged each other. She didn't want to let go.

"I'm so glad you're all right, Dad."

"It's so good to see you, Sam. We're just a little cold. I've got a sprained ankle and Otto has a bullet in his stomach, so, I guess we're all right…we're not frozen, just cold. I want to thank all of you for coming to get us."

Ashford shook hands with his three rescuers and said, "What was going on up here before you pulled us up?"

Sam handed her dad and Otto a Styrofoam cup of soup, smiled and said, "Let me tell you a bedtime story, Dad."

She told them how she planned Blue's fall into a crevasse and how she managed to force Red to join him. She commented that on the way back, she wondered how they would retrieve the human garbage at the bottom of the crevasses.

"That is quite a story, Sam. You are a very clever, young lady. What a heady thing to do," commented her proud father.

Sam smiled and said, "Oh! Before I forget, here is a present I picked up for you. One of my former friends dropped it."

She pulled a gun from her parka pocket and handed it to her dad. He checked the ammunition, made sure the safety was on and slipped the cold metal into his pocket.

"That might come in handy. I wonder how many more of these guys are around?"

"I think I know," contributed Tim.

Everyone looked at Tim questioningly.

"There is one more member of this team, a Mr. Green. When I was getting groceries, Mrs. Brannigan was humming the same tune that Blue was humming earlier. She said the guy's name was Mr. Green. So, there were red, blue and green which can be combined to make white light, but I don't know what, if any, significance that has. Remember the three helicopters? I think they were the pilots."

They all relaxed and found things to munch as Ashford told them what had happened the previous day. The ranger extracted the last couple of meals from his backpack and everyone had something hot to eat. Otto prepared some tea that he had brought from his homeland, but the tea was not grown in Austria, the tea had originated in China. When the group sat drinking tea, Art happened to pick up one of the unused flares. He laughed when he read from the label, "Made in China." Just about everything is made in China, especially if it is related to fireworks.

The ranger asked the group, "Do you think those two men were looking for the unit containing the electronics?"

"I think they must have been. If they felt it was that important, we should try to find it and see what it's for," answered Sam.

"And what should we do about the rockets?" quizzed Tim.

The ranger, sitting on the sled beside Otto, leaned forward and said, "Okay, here's my plan. Sam, you and Tim will try to recover the electronics package. Brian and Art will follow the Austrians, Algerians and the rockets. I'll give Brian the gun in case they have a problem with the two Algerians. Otto and I will start moving down the glacier to lower elevations where we can get him to a hospital. I'll pull him on the sled but my sprained ankle will slow us down. Fortunately, we'll be going downhill. Sam and Tim will follow us down the mountain with the electronics package if they find it. Are there any suggestions?"

The tired, but driven, members of the group looked at each other and then Sam stated, "I think Art and Brian should put their phones on vibrate so they can't be heard by the Algerians. They might have to sneak up on them." Sam smiled, "That's all I can think of, except, be careful!"

Before anyone else was ready to go, Sam looked at Tim and said, "Hey, get off your butt and let's go. We have to hook up first."

Tim's mind was filled with fantasies when Sam said hook up, but he knew she was talking about roping themselves together. The thoughts passed through his mind in an instant. As his exhaled water vapor condensed, it appeared pink in the light from the flare. He stood up, moved his leaden legs, and hoped this whole episode would soon be over.

Sam handed Tim the end of the rope, he attached it to his harness and Sam started moving along the route she had taken before. Tim judged her speed and moved off trailing her keeping slack out of the rope. When the red light from the campsite grew very dim, Sam ignited one of the three flares she had gotten from Brian. They arrived at the down elevator crevasse in less than ten minutes. Sam avoided it by going around the end and they continued about ten yards to a similar opening in the glacier.

Tim joined her at the lip of the crevasse and they peered over the edge.

"There it is, Sam! We found it!" Tim shouted.

They both smiled and Tim put his arm around Sam's shoulders and gave her a hug. Tim was thinking they might be able to join Otto and the ranger before the two men leave the campsite.

Sam replied, "And it's not very far down, only fifteen or twenty feet. I can get it if you anchor the rope. I'll walk down the ice wall, attach a rope and come back up. Then we can pull it up together. We don't know how heavy it is."

Tim cut a bollard in the ice and Sam inspected it. She thought to herself that Tim's bollard was as good as she could have made. She secured her rope and walked to the edge of the crevasse. Tim attached the rope to himself as a backup and Sam dropped over the lip of the crevasse and descended to the container housing the electronics.

Sam looked into the circuitry and yelled to Tim, "The red lights are still glowing. I'll attach a rope to the module and you can start hauling me up."

"Okay. Start pulling, Tim," directed Sam.

Tim hauled Sam out of the chasm with ease. When she stood beside him, she looked into his eyes, smiled and said, "Thank you."

Tim said, "My pleasure, ma'am." And then he kissed the back of her gloved right hand and held onto it for a moment. He was trying to make her blush and it worked! Sam was completely disarmed and wasn't sure what to say.

She came to her wits and said, "You know, I think the altitude is affecting my brain. Let's get that thing up here and be on our way."

Tim began pulling on the rope but couldn't get the module to move. He moved several steps to the right and then the left and gave a couple of tugs from each position.

Sam said, "Let me try."

She took Tim's original position, pulled hard and the module came loose. She reeled in the rope as Tim watched. As the electronics reached the lip of the crevasse, Sam smiled and said, "See how easy that was?"

She knew Tim had loosened the ice's hold on the object but thought, for fun, she would rub it in. She was really getting to like this interesting guy, or was it some strange emotion that appeared at 9,000 feet above sea level on a Mt. Baker glacier?

Tim didn't say a thing. He stepped next to Sam, knelt by her feet, reached for the object and lifted it over the edge of the fissure. He gave it a quick inspection, could see the red LEDs and stood up. Standing beside Sam an internal voice said, "Kiss her!" But another voice said, "Don't mess up your relationship. You could destroy everything, you fool!" The other voice said, "You may not get another chance." Tim deferred to the conservative voice and looked out into the valley below. He could see the flickering lights from the small towns and off in the distance the glow in the sky above the larger cities.

Sam was looking, too, and said, "Isn't that beautiful?"

The flare burned out and they stood in darkness for a couple of minutes. Tim looked up at the stars. The North Star, Polaris, was brilliant and the big dipper was truly a beautiful sight. In fact, Tim had never seen starlight so intense.

Sam asked as she pointed, "What constellation is that containing the big "W"?

Tim didn't need to look, he just answered with "Cassiopeia." She was the wife of Cepheus and the mother of beautiful Andromeda. He was totally lost thinking of the majesty of the universe and the stars in our galaxy. How puny he felt on top of this mountain. Strangely, he wasn't cold. He enjoyed a feeling of warmth throughout his body. Perhaps it was because of the company? This was the first time he felt warm and fuzzy all over since he was a little boy. The feeling of contentment came over him when his mother put him to bed and kissed him good night.

Tim suddenly was struck by an overwhelming reality attack. I've got to get serious. We have to get this module off the glacier and investigate its properties.

"Sam, light another flare. We have to get out of here and catch up to your father and Otto."

"I was just about to say the same thing, Tim. You beat me to it."

Sam removed the cover from another flare and struck the end of the flare on the cap. It burst into flame throwing a few sparks into the snow. They gathered up their ropes, linked themselves together, tied the module to Tim's back and started down the mountain. When they reached the rocket cradle skeleton, everyone had gone, but the sled marks were easy to follow. In less than thirty minutes they could see Sam's dad pulling the sled. He was limping badly but had traversed a good distance down the glacier. The sky in the east was becoming lighter and it wouldn't be long before the sun would rise on a new day.

CHAPTER 15

PURSUIT

Brian and Art, with only two flares, moved as rapidly as they could before darkness prevented them from going further. Just as the second flare burned out, Brian looked at his watch and realized they would only be delayed for about forty-five minutes before enough sunlight would allow travel to proceed. They sat down and Brian called Mikka.

"Mikka, are you still observing the mountain?"

"I'm freezing my butt off, but I'm still watching flares moving slowly in opposite directions. There are two red lights fairly close together to the north and a single red light far to the south. The lights are nearly at the same elevation. There was another light, about in the middle, but it went away."

"The one in the middle was from Art and me. Our last flare burned out. We are waiting for the sun so we can see where to go. Get in the truck and run the heater!"

"Okay brother, be careful! Call me if you need me. Bye."

"Bye Mikka."

Sam and Tim had overtaken the ranger and Otto. They talked for a few minutes while taking a look at the electronics. Otto said he could read French but the light was too poor to see all that was written on the circuit boards. Sam unlashed the device from Tim's shoulders and back and they placed it on the sled with Otto. They all could see some numbers and Otto said he could see the words for activate and fire. Tim commented that it looked as if there was a panel that slid away from the electronics but perhaps they should wait for better light for further investigations.

The module was tied to the sled and Otto was able to use the housing as a handhold for his ride down the glaciers. Tim and Sam took over the sled from the ranger so he wouldn't risk more injury to his ankle. Sam placed a call to Mikka and brought her up to speed with all that had transpired.

Toward the end of the conversation, Mikka said, "Should I stay up here with the telescope?"

Sam answered, "Please do, but you can take a nap. As soon as we get to the parking lot, we'll drive over to the butte to watch Brian and Art track the rocket team ahead of them. Relax and get some sleep. It will be at least three or four hours before we arrive. We'll wake you up."

"Oh, thank you Smash. I've worried about you guys all day. I'm really pooped. See you later."

Sam had to smile when Mikka said she was pooped. Mikka was probably more tired than any of the rest of the group since she didn't have their physical activity to lessen the tension.

The first hints of dawn brought enough light to the mountain for Art and Brian to continue following the tracks of the overweight sleds and the six men ushering the rockets across the glacier. They crossed Mazama Glacier rapidly and scaled Bastile Ridge. Nearly running, they were guided by the tracks descending the ridge and crossing Roosevelt Glacier.

After nearly two hours of exertion, they took a few minutes to scarf down some energy bars and drink some water. Art had remembered what Rose Brannigan told Tim; drink plenty of water.

As soon as Art had caught his breath, the two men set off at a more leisurely pace than before. Brian realized Art wasn't in great physical shape and too much exercise at this altitude could have undesirable consequences. Crossing Roosevelt Glacier was not difficult. The glacier had few dramatic changes of hills and valleys. The transition onto Coleman Glacier was seamless as they continued to follow the deep tracks in the snow and grooves cut into the ice. Another hour passed and Heliotrope Ridge loomed in front of them.

Mikka's brother knew this area of the mountain well, having been in the area three times previously. The first time, when he was a Boy Scout, one of the young climbers broke his leg and the other scouts transported him off the mountain to a waiting ambulance. The other times were less eventful but very memorable. Brian had made friends with climbers from New Zealand, Canada, and Switzerland. He enjoyed the camaraderie and the various accents exhibited by foreign climbers. Some of the foreigners kidded him, trying to speak with an American accent, which always brought laughter to the assemblage of climbers, especially when they tried too hard to speak American.

Brian had abruptly left the trail they were following and began to ascend the glacier moving directly south instead of southwest. Art considered yelling at his partner to ask what he was doing, but Art knew Brian would not deviate from the well-defined trail unless there was a good reason. Art kept his mouth shut and continued to follow the more experienced climber.

About twenty minutes later, Art saw why Brian had diverted from the larger party's trail. It was much easier to negotiate Heliotrope Ridge by going up and around rather than climbing straight up and then going straight down on the other side. The ice and snow on either side of the ridge was a rugged and dangerous route. Surely, the men with the rockets had to carry the projectiles over the ridge one at a time. It must have taken them several hours to accomplish the task.

At the top of Thunder Glacier, laying on the other side of the ridge from Coleman Glacier, Brian and Art stopped to look down and across the icy expanse.

"Crouch down!" Brian said as he jerked on Art's parka.

"What's going on?" responded Art, a surprised look on his face.

"I guess you didn't see what I did. The guys we've been following are just below the ridge about a hundred yards below us. It looks as if two of the rockets are pointing in the air. I think they are ready to launch. Take a look, but just peek over the blocks of ice in front of us. Fold your dark parka hood back."

Art slowly raised his head and looked where Brian had indicated. Sure enough, there were six figures standing beside two rockets pointing skyward. As he watched, the men began moving directly south across Thunder Glacier. A climber was pulling each sled and another man was roped to the back of the sled to keep it from getting out of control. Two other men were following behind the sleds. Art guessed the two following men were the ones with the guns. Art ducked down and told Brian to watch the distant group.

After Brian observed the group's progress for a couple of minutes he said, "As soon as they're out of sight, we'll go down to the rockets and tip them over. Let's see if we can dismantle or break the fins so no steering is possible. The rockets will just burn out on the glacier if they're ever fired. Then we'll call Glenn and tell him what we've done."

Art and Brian had to wait nearly twenty minutes before the six men were out of sight. The young men began descending through rock and ice but found their speed was much slower than before. They weren't following the tracks of others now and had to make their own way through the large ice boulders. But, as long as they remained near the edge of the glacier, they could ignore the possibility of falling into a crevasse.

When Brian and Art reached the rockets, they discovered the missiles had been positioned with struts that would fall away when the engines ignited. The metal braces weren't very securely attached to the rock and ice below them and didn't offer much resistance to Brian's strong arms and shoulders. He rocked the missiles sideways a few times and pushed them over so their noses were digging into the ice and snow. Art helped fix them in place with large chunks of ice and rock. As planned, they were able to bend the fins so guidance would be impossible. Art was bending one of the fins and it broke off in his hand. When it snapped off, he laughed and said, "Probably made in China!"

Their handiwork complete, they looked at the tracks made by the two sleds and six climbers. It was going to be easy to follow them.

They had to be careful to make sure the men with guns were unaware of their presence. At some point Brian and Art would have to change their route to avoid being seen by the two men carrying firearms. Franz's men surely would not disclose that Art and Brian were near if they saw them. How could the two trackers reveal their proximity only to Franz? Perhaps that would be impossible.

Brian flipped open his cell phone and called Glenn.

A woman's voice answered, "Hello." It was Sam.

"Hi Sam! Can I talk with your dad?"

"Sure. Here he is."

"Hello Brian. Where are you and Art?"

"We're just over Heliotrope Ridge on Thunder Glacier. We disabled two of the rockets that were set up and ready to launch. We watched six men pulling two sleds move out of sight. They're moving southwest at about 7,500 feet. We're going to continue to follow them and hopefully damage more rockets. How are you and Otto doing?"

"We're okay. Sam and Tim are going to take us into Glacier to a doctor and then they'll join Mikka on the butte. They want to watch you with the telescope and warn you if they see you might be in danger. They'll call at the hour, starting in about an hour, maybe two. It will depend on how quickly they can get back to the butte."

"Okay, Glenn. Are Sam and Tim all right?"

"They're both fine, just a little tired. See if you can contact Franz or one of the other Austrians so they can help you take care of the goons. Be careful. Remember, they have guns."

"Okay. We thought of contacting Franz. It might not happen though. We might have to act alone. I'm sure the Austrians will help if they can. See you later."

CHAPTER 16

CAPTURED

Brian shut his phone off and looked at Art. Art's eyes were closed and his breathing was slow. He looked very relaxed, apparently asleep, and Brian couldn't resist the impulse to play a little trick on his friend.

"Time to get up, Arthur!"

"Okay, Mom. What's for breakfast?" replied Art.

"Snow-cones, dirty socks and coffee." answered Brian.

Art opened his eyes and said, "Come on Brian. You can do better than that. Did you really think I was asleep?"

Brian answered, "Yep. You sure had me fooled. I thought you were getting some Zs."

"That would be great but we have some rockets to disable. Let's get out of here."

Art ripped the covering off an energy bar, bit it in half and put the entire thing in his mouth.

"Jeez Art! Have you no manners?" Brian laughed. "What else can you get in there, your foot?"

Art chewed and swallowed for nearly a minute before smiling and saying, "If your sister were here, I could probably get my foot in my mouth, too."

Brian had started after the men pulling the sleds and just as all the slack was being taken out of the rope, Art grabbed for his water bottle and stood up. As he began moving he swallowed several gulps of water to wash the energy bar down. They were moving across the glacier horizontally and after thirty minutes, Brian stopped. When Art caught up to him, Brian said, "We're starting around Lincoln Peak and our vision will be obscured by some ridges, so be on the lookout. Try to look ahead and watch for the goon squad, I'll keep us from falling into a crevasse. If we don't deviate from their tracks, we should be all right."

The tracks began rising in elevation and not far in front of them, maybe thirty yards, was an expanse of exposed rock surrounded by ice and snow. Nestled between the rocks in a relatively flat spot were two more rockets, pointing skywards. One of the missiles pointed southwest and the other to the east. The two men probed the glacier with their eyes but could see no one. The goons had vanished with the Austrians and the last of the rockets. They would be able to move faster now. Each sled would carry only one rocket.

As before, Brian worked the explosive containing tubes free of their supports and knocked the rockets to the ground. Art pounded the exhausts shut with a large rock and broke off the guidance fins. Brian picked up the metal pieces and hid them in the rocks.

As Art finished breaking off the triangular metal fins he said, "Damn, that felt good! We've got four out of six completely screwed up; they'll never fly."

Franz and his fellow climbers were exhausted. They must have dragged the sleds and their heavy cargo over three miles of ice and snow of all types. He was getting tired of watching the white and gray surface for signs of crevasses. The two gunmen were of little help, they considered the Austrians as their slaves, unworthy of breathing since they weren't Islamic. If the two goons hadn't pledged to carry out this act of terrorism, they would not have lifted a finger to help pull the sleds. They were truly the selected ones, the perfect warriors. Franz felt nothing but contempt for these two mislead misfits.

Franz wondered if the ranger and Otto were actually dead or just injured. He had seen injuries from falls into crevasses before and most were pretty severe. Without the experienced ranger and Otto, his best climber, Franz was nearly powerless. He didn't know his fellow countrymen well enough to know how and if he could depend on them in a time of crisis. He felt frustrated not being able to help the Americans protect their beautiful country. He wondered what he could or would do if this disregard for people and resources were taking place in Austria.

As they trudged on, he began to consider what was going to happen to him and his men when the final two rockets were in position. For some unknown reason they were ascending again making a steep climb up the western flank of Black Buttes. They ascended for thirty to forty minutes and reached the crest of the buttes. They could see the large expanse of Deming Glacier sloping to the east. As the group began to descend, Hakeem was the last to start over the crest. He looked below toward Thunder Glacier and spotted two climbers making their way around the southwestern flank of Lincoln Peak.

"Amir!" he yelled. "Someone is coming; two men."

Art and Brian could not see Hakeem only a hundred feet above them. Just the head of the goon would have been visible above the rocks. The irregular skyline helped hide his presence. Hakeem stood in full view, but like a chameleon, his dark clothing hid him amongst the rocks.

"Hakeem! Wait for them and bring them to me," ordered Amir. Hakeem climbed over the crest and sat down against some large rocks and waited with his gun ready. He was out of sight of anyone coming over the ridge until they were standing on some flat rocks at the top. Hakeem would take the climbers by complete surprise and remove any weapons they might possess.

Sam and Tim had taken Sam's father and Otto to a doctor in Glacier and rushed back to Baker Butte to assist Mikka with the telescope observations of Art and Brian on the mountain. Sam and Tim climbed out of Sam's SUV and walked over to the telescope.

"Can you see them, Mikka?" Tim asked.

"I could until about ten minutes ago. They went behind this peak area."

Mikka pointed to the relief map she had folded so only the appropriate area was showing.

"That's Lincoln Peak. I wonder what is going on up there?" inquired Sam.

Tim looked at his watch and said, "It's time to call them. Let's see if we can find out what they're doing."

Tim flipped open his cell phone and placed a call to Brian.

"Hello?"

"Hi Brian. How are you guys doing? Tim inquired.

"We're okay…a little tired. We've messed up four rockets so they can't be launched. Art and I are behind Lincoln Peak so we're out of sight. We've got about 50 feet to go to reach the top of the ridge. When we get over the ridgeline, we might not be able to get a phone signal. Call us again in about an hour, okay?"

"Okay, Brian. Good luck! Talk to you later."

Art and Brian continued up the rocks, occasionally encountering small snowy areas exhibiting footprints. Some of the jagged rocks offered handholds and they quickly scaled the remaining volcanic rocks to the top of the ridge. Brian reached the top first.

He turned to assist Art, extending his hand to pull Art up the last few feet. When they turned to see where the men they were following had gone, Brian and Art saw Hakeem, instant trouble, with a gun.

"Good afternoon, gentlemen. Where you going? Why you follow us?"

Brian answered instantly, "To the summit. We thought your group had a new route to the peak, so we decided to follow you."

"Have you weapons?" Hakeem asked, shaking his handgun at them.

"We found this gun near the bottom of Mazama glacier," replied Brian. He didn't want to tell the goon that Red had dropped the gun just before falling into a crevasse.

"We couldn't figure out how it got there." Brian handed the gun to Hakeem, who turned it over and looked at the handle below the grip.

Hakeem put the gun in his jacket pocket and said, "Go down this hill. I am right behind you. Don't try anything or I shoot."

From their vantage point, Brian and Art could see the party they had been following. The five men were slowly moving down Deming Glacier, towing two sleds, each carrying a rocket. Each sled had a lead climber and one man following, roped to the sled to keep it from coasting out of control. Although Brian and Art didn't know Franz, the Austrian climber was leading the group and a goon was following with a gun in his hand.

Brian, Art and Hakeem quickly descended the rocky area and emerged on the ice and snow of the glacier. They were able to move rapidly, following the jumbled tracks of the climbers in front of them. In less than ten minutes they had overtaken the larger group. Hakeem joined Amir for a short conversation. Amir looked at the gun Hakeem had taken from Brian and returned it to Hakeem. Amir approached Brian.

Amir stood in front of Brian, who was at least six inches taller. Amir frowned and said, "Where you get gun?"

"Just as I told your friend, we found it near the bottom of Mazama Glacier. It might have come down the mountain in an avalanche, there was one earlier."

"You saw no one?"

"Not on the glacier."

"Somewhere else?" Amir asked.

"Yes. We saw two men being put in an ambulance in the Hadley Peak parking area." Brian wanted Franz and the other Austrians to hear that the ranger and Otto were going to be all right. He didn't want the goons to know the whole story.

"What they look like?"

"They were both big guys, I think one was called Otto. We didn't know them; we just watched for a few minutes and then started up the mountain. We followed tracks so we moved very fast."

"When?"

"Yesterday evening."

Brian had to remember his story. It was full of lies but he wanted his tale to be consistent with their movements on the mountain.

Amir stepped back from Brian and said, "Hakeem, search them."

When Brian had mentioned that Otto and the ranger would recover, the Austrians looked at each other in amazement. Otto was alive and so was ranger Ashford! Franz moved closer to Brian and Art, hoping to hear more clearly.

"Franz! Step back!" Amir warned. Franz turned and walked back to his three countrymen.

Brian and Art now knew which climber was Franz.

Hakeem searched the young Americans but found no weapons. He took their cell phones and dropped them in the snow. Amir motioned for Art and Brian to join the other climbers.

"It is nice for you to join us. Makes things easier," commented Amir with a sinister smile. Amir pointed at the first sled and then at Franz and Brian with his gun. "You take this sled." He pointed at Tim and Gunner and at the second sled. "You take this one. Hakeem, go with the others in front."

Amir talked with Hakeem for a moment, pointing down the glacier to a relatively flat area. Hakeem talked with the two Austrians and told them where to lead the climbing party. The distance they had to cover was about 200 yards, almost entirely downhill, to a saddle point between Portrait Rock and Lee Promontory. Brian began pulling the sled containing one of the rockets. The movement was too rapid and Franz was knocked off his feet and dragged.

"Stop!" Amir yelled. "What are you doing?"

"Franz! Tell this stupid boy what to do," Amir ordered angrily.

Franz walked over to Brian, about ten yards away from Amir, laid his hand on his shoulder and said, "I assume you did that so we could talk. If not, I will have to tell you how to pull the sled."

Brian looked at Franz and pointed at the sled as if he were following Franz's instructions. Then he said, "When we stop, we will probably have to lift the rocket and carry it. I will cough and drop the rocket; then we attack. I'll knock Amir down and you control the gun. The other guys will have to take care of Hakeem. Okay?"

"Okay." Franz was turned away from Amir, smiled and raised his voice, "When you pull the sled, don't go so fast!"

Amir seemed satisfied with Brian and Franz's conference and said, "Let's go!"

An hour had passed since Tim had talked with Brian. Sam placed the call this time. The phone rang but she got no answer. She gave Tim and Mikka a look of concern and said, "No answer. I'll call Art's phone." She dialed and again, no answer. "Both phones rang but no one answered. I wonder if something's wrong."

Tim said, "I hate to say this but it looks as if they were taken prisoner. But I'm not worried, both Brian and Art are quick thinkers and tough dudes. They'll call us as soon as they can." Tim really was a little worried but didn't want to alarm Sam and Mikka.

Amir looked at his GPS indicator and stopped the party's movement at a predetermined location. Brian and Franz were ordered to untie the rocket and remove the rocket struts from the sled.

Amir pointed at Brian and Franz and said, "Bring baby over here!" He marked a position in the snow where the glacier's surface was relatively flat.

Franz got near the tail of the rocket and Brian took a position near the tip. They looked at each other and nodded. The two climbers picked up the rocket, moved about five feet and then Brian coughed and dropped his end of the projectile. Franz released his hold also and the rocket skidded in front of Amir.

"Idiots!" Amir yelled angrily. "Pick it up!"

As Brian bent down and began to pick up the rocket, Amir hit him in the head with the gun and Brian fell in the snow.

"See what happens to fools!" Amir shrieked.

Brian started to get up but pivoted on his arms and kicked, hard. His crampons slashed into Amir's legs like a grizzly's claws, shredding his pants leg and ripping into the thigh of his left leg and the shin of his right. Amir cried out in pain and fell to the ice. But he still held the gun. In the moment it took for Amir to fall and look at his bloodied legs, Franz jumped and grabbed Amir's gun arm and twisted it behind the goon's back. Amir pulled the trigger and shot a round into the glacier. At the moment Amir was kicked, the Austrian climbers swarmed Hakeem and took his gun before the goon had a chance to pull it from his belt.

Brian stood over Amir looking at him with disgust. Blood running down Brian's forehead added to the mean look he gave the goon on the ground. Amir and Hakeem were tied up and Franz inspected Amir's leg wounds. Although there was a significant amount of blood from the lacerations, no arteries were involved. Franz made some bandages with a shirt to minimize the bleeding.

Brian rubbed his head and commented, "I think we all know who the fools are around here. Let's tie these stooges to the sleds and get a phone. We need a ride out of here."

Art took Hakeem and Amir's phones and called Sam.

"Hello!"

"Hi Sam! We've got them! We captured the last two goons and their rockets."

"That's awesome, Art!"

"Everybody is safe except for the goon, Amir. He has some deep gashes in his legs. Brian pretended he was a bear and mauled him," Art grinned. "Would it be possible to get us flown out of here? Maybe your dad can arrange for a chopper to pick us up? We're at the 6,200 ft level of Deming Glacier near Lee Promontory. We're tired and need hot food, relaxation and a warm bed."

"I'll call dad and we'll call you right back. I'm so glad you guys are all right. We couldn't get you to answer your phones."

"Yeah…the idiots took them from us on the butte and left them up there in the snow. Tell Mikka that Brian got hit again but he's okay. He made it possible for us to disarm the goons."

"Okay Art. We'll call you back in a few minutes. Bye."

"Bye Sam."

While Art was on the phone, Brian and the Austrians were disabling the rockets by burying the tips of the missiles two feet deep in the ice and breaking off the fins. One Austrian used his ice ax to deform the exhausts of the rockets.

About fifteen minutes elapsed and Art's phone rang.

"Hello?"

"Art?" quizzed Tim.

"Yep! Hi buddy! Are we getting a ride?"

"You bet. It will be about 30 minutes and a chopper will pick you up and take you to the lodge. We'll see you tomorrow. Okay?"

"Thanks Tim. See you tomorrow."

CHAPTER 17

FIREWORKS

Tim and Mikka prepared the telescope for traveling and Sam policed the area around the vehicles. They didn't want to leave any garbage on Dawson's Butte. They returned to the cabin and collapsed in the overstuffed furniture in the great room. It was eerily quiet for a few minutes; the three weary climbers were all exhausted. Now they could relax, the saboteurs were taken care of and the rockets were disabled. Brian and Art would return to the chateau in the morning. June would probably be remembered as the most eventful time of their lives.

Tim was the first to say that he was hungry. He went to the kitchen and got some ice cream and chocolate sauce. Sam followed him into the kitchen and said, "You're kidding me…you must be pregnant!"

Tim grinned and said, "I haven't had any regular food in two days Sam!"

"But you're eating cold stuff right after coming off the mountain! That gives me the shivers!"

"All that snow looked like vanilla ice cream, but no calories and no taste! I need some calories to feed my brain."

"Well, I'm going to shower, have some hot food and go to bed," Sam remarked.

Mikka agreed, "Me too!"

Sam and Mikka returned to the great room in pajamas with towels wrapped around their heads. Tim had started a fire in the fireplace and was in the kitchen frying hamburger.

"I've got to call Dad and find out about his ankle," stated Sam.

She flopped down on the giant sofa, grabbed a cell phone and called the doctor's office.

"Hi. I'm Samantha Ashford. How is my father?"

"His ankle is broken and is in a cast. Would you like to come pick him up?"

"Sure. I'll be there in about 15 minutes. Bye."

Sam dropped the phone on the sofa and ran upstairs. She came running back down the stairs just as Tim was taking a big bite out of his burger. He couldn't believe Sam could have gotten dressed that fast. His experience with women indicated they took forever to get dressed. She probably set a record.

"What's going on, Sam?" Mikka asked.

"I've got to pick up my dad…and probably Otto at the doctor's office. I'll be right back."

"Need any help?" Tim asked after swallowing hard.

"Maybe when we get back. Dad has a cast on his leg; he broke his ankle. I've got to go."

"Okay, we'll be waiting for you," replied Mikka.

Sam rushed out the door and it slammed shut. Mikka and Tim could hear car wheels spinning and gravel being thrown as she sped off in her little SUV. Tim took his hamburger into the great room and sat across from Mikka. He suddenly said, "Damn! We didn't get them all, Mikka. We forgot about Mr. Green!"

Mikka reacted with, "Where do you suppose he is?"

"Jeez, I don't know, but he's got to be around here somewhere. Course, he could have taken off since all his buddies are dead or in jail."

"How would he leave the area?" quizzed Mikka.

"He'd have to hitch a ride or take a bus. If he flies around in a little chopper, he'll just get in trouble. The police know about it now.

When Sam's dad gets here, let's ask him about it, okay?"

"Okay. Say, could you please make me a hamburger?"

"Sure. Want some cheese on it too?"

"No cheese, thanks. Do you have some bacon?" she laughed. "For some reason, I want the taste of bacon."

Tim grinned and said, "Maybe you're pregnant!"

"Tim! That is ridiculous as well as impossible!" Mikka nearly yelled.

"I was just trying to be funny."

"That wasn't funny!" Mikka was peeved at his remark. She was tired and wasn't in the mood for teasing.

About five minutes later, Tim called out, "I'm sorry, Mikka. Your burger's ready with bacon…two slices." Tim put the sandwich on a plate and got out the mustard and ketchup. Mikka came in the kitchen, squirted some ketchup on the meat and took a big bite. She chewed for a moment and said, "That is really good, Tim. Thank you!"

"Am I off the hook?"

"No," Mikka pouted.

Tim had just decided to shut up when the door opened. It was Sam. She pushed the door open as far as it would go and her dad came in on crutches. Otto followed the ranger walking slowly.

Otto was introduced to Mikka and they all sat down, except Mikka, who took her hamburger into the kitchen to finish it.

"Dad, would you and Otto like something to eat?"

"We sure would," answered the ranger looking at Otto. "How about it, Otto?"

"Yes, please. I could eat a horse…a small one that is," he grinned.

"Tim and I will cook for you, if that's all right," Sam offered.

Mikka set the table and helped in the kitchen and in about twenty minutes they all sat down for dinner. Mikka and Tim didn't eat much, having already had a hamburger, but they joined in the conversation. As they finished dinner, Otto asked, "Do you still have the circuit board module that was with the rockets? I'd like to look at it again."

"It's out in the pickup. I'll get it," answered Tim.

Tim brought the unit containing the circuit boards into the cabin and set it on the floor next to Otto. Tim hadn't looked at it since they were in the parking lot near Hadley Peak and now he could get a much better view. He scanned over the electronics and noticed a lever that was holding a control panel in place.

Otto was looking at the lever also and said, "The lever isn't connected to any wires; you can release it."

Tim flipped the lever and the control unit slid out into his hands.

"Otto, what are these words next to the push buttons?"

"Let's see…this one says launch and this one says self destruct." Otto pointed at the two buttons.

Tim posed a question, "I wonder if the electronics would work from here? What do you think, Mr. Ashford, should we try the self destruct button?" Like a small boy, Tim wanted to press that little red button just for the fun of it but he waited for the ranger's response. Besides, the rockets could be out of range of the transmitter.

"I think not. We don't know if anyone is on this side of the mountain and an explosion might get someone injured. I'll check tomorrow. We can go to Dawson's Butte and push the button…in the evening when it's dark, so we can see what happens."

Mikka looked at Sam and said, "Maybe we'll have some fireworks on the first of July?"

Friday was a cool but bright sunny day. The birds, squirrels and other small animals were up early and out seeking nourishment. They were starting out a new day with complete disregard for the calendar. The interior of the cabin remained quiet until around ten o'clock.

Otto had slept in a large recliner so he wouldn't move around much and disturb the stitches in his abdomen. Glenn Ashford had gone to bed on the giant sofa. There was a small extra bedroom upstairs, but he didn't want to climb the steps using only one leg. He refused to be carried.

Sam had gotten up first and turned on the coffee maker. The odor of the coffee permeated the cabin causing everyone to stir. Tim and Art joined Sam in the kitchen and started making breakfast. A few minutes later Mikka and Brian joined the others.

Mikka said, "Hey guys, it's too crowded in here for all of us. Let Sam and I take care of the kitchen. Join the men in the great room."

It didn't take much to get them out of the kitchen. They each took their coffee and left the kitchen to the women.

"Very effective, roomy," Sam commented with a smile.

Mikka asked in almost a whisper, "What do you think of the guys, Sam?"

Sam knew immediately what Mikka was getting at. She answered with, "I like Tim…a lot. He's smart, fun and brave. I don't know if he's a good kisser though." She grinned and then laughed with Mikka.

Mikka volunteered, "I really like Art. He's a great guy, just like Tim. Brian said he was a quick learner and very dependable. He's strong and has a good sense of humor."

Sam looked at Mikka and said, "I'm glad we don't have to fight over them."

They both laughed again.

The men heard the laughing and Brian said, "What are you guys laughing at?"

The two girls responded in unison, "Oh, nothing," and they laughed again.

Otto smiled and said, "They sound like teenagers."

Glenn replied, "They are."

During the afternoon, Glenn called Ranger Headquarters and found that no one would be on the mountain after dark. Otto and Glenn inspected all the climbing gear from the garage closet and threw out some items, a few carabiners and some rope that had seen better days. Tim sat down with the older men and discussed the missing terrorist, Mr. Green. Ashford had alerted the police about Mr. Green when he and Otto were at the doctor's office the day before.

Sam called her mom and told her that Glenn had a broken ankle. Donna wanted to know all about it but Sam told her she should get the story from the horse's mouth. Donna decided to get a sitter for the boys and take the bus to Glacier. She would arrive from Bellingham around dinnertime.

Sam inquired, "Tim. Where is the bus depot? I noticed it wasn't where it was before. There's a Pizza place where the bus depot used to be."

"It's at Brannigan's Market. Rose takes care of the tickets and luggage."

"My mom's coming by bus this evening. I have to pick her up. I guess she will have to sleep with me."

"I have a better idea, Sam. Your mom and dad can have my room and I'll take the couch. Everyone will sleep better that way. The couch is about the same size as my bed in the dorm, but much softer."

"That's very nice of you, Tim. You're so sweet."

"Yeah, I know," Tim grinned.

Cards, board games and basketball kept the younger generation busy all afternoon. The two old guys talked and slept most of the afternoon, interspersed with a little TV. Otto was interested in American football but had to have some lessons to comprehend some of the finer points. Glenn was happy to oblige.

Plans for dinner started about five o'clock. Mikka and Sam needed to visit Brannigan's, get some steaks and pick up Donna Ashford when she arrived on the bus. The ladies were gone for nearly an hour. Meanwhile, beer, pretzels, cheese and soft drinks were served. The ranger chose to save the wine for dinner.

When Sam and Mikka returned with Donna, the men were absorbed in watching a Mixed Martial Arts fight. Otto was the first one to stand and say hello to Donna. When he stood up, the others were drawn away from the bout, stood and said hello to Donna. She rushed over to Glenn and gave him a hug and kiss.

"Otto, I'd like you to meet my wife, Donna. Donna, this is Otto Mohr, my friend from the crevasse."

"I can see why you wanted to get out of the crevasse so badly, Glenn. It's nice to meet you, Donna."

"Thank you, Otto. Please sit down. I know you were shot. It must hurt."

Otto held up a plastic bottle and rattled the container.

"It's not too bad. The doctor gave me these, but only one per day," he smiled. "I took one last night before bed. The pill makes me sleepy."

Dinner began around six o'clock and was dominated with discussions of the details of the events on the mountain. Dessert was ice cream, which Tim relished, and wine for the adults. At eight o'clock they finished dinner and prepared to go to Dawson's Butte. Mikka warned everyone to wear a heavy jacket.

Otto decided not to go. He thought it would be smarter to allow more healing of his wound to take place. He wanted to return to Austria with the rest of his group when they left July 6th. Glenn didn't want to go either and neither did Donna. So, it was left to the young people to see what happened when the self-destruct button was pressed.

They piled into the SUV and the pickup and went to the butte. Tim and Art had wrapped the electronics module with a blanket and tied it to the telescope pedestal to keep it from being jolted too much as they drove over the unpaved roads. Sam had remembered to bring a camera with her and took several pictures of the group on Dawson's Butte. The module was removed from the pickup, unwrapped and placed on the tailgate. It was completely dark at 9:30 p.m.

Tim said, "I think Sam should press the button, she was responsible for a large part of the effort made to retrieve the module."

Sam replied, "Art and Brian did more than I did. They disabled the goons and their missiles."

Brian said, "I'll defer to Art, he's younger."

Art said, "I'll defer to Sam, she's even younger."

Mikka said, "Okay, Sam. Let's see if you can light up the mountain."

Sam stepped over to the module, Tim illuminated the button with his flashlight and Sam pressed the red button. Nothing happened…for a few seconds…and then there was a thunderous explosion that reverberated throughout the area. As they watched the mountain, they could see the light from three fires high on the glaciers.

"It worked, Sam!" shouted Mikka.

As the fires burned brighter, they grew over a larger area and it began to look like lava was being emitted from the glaciers and cascading down the ice.

Brian said, "Wow! Will you look at that! Those flames would have set the whole county on fire."

Tim and Art were both wondering how long the flames would burn but after watching for about five minutes the burning area began to recede.

Sam said, "You know, I would never have believed in glacier fires, but I set them off."

Tim smiled and remarked, "And you did an awesome job, Sam."

Sam giggled and was joined by Mikka, and then everyone started laughing. Sam said, "Sometimes you come up with some really funny stuff, Tim."

"Well, let's get out of here. Our work is done," Brian commented.

Back at the cabin Donna, Glenn and Otto had been doing some planning. Donna would drive Glenn and Otto back to Bellingham the following day. There was limited space in the car with three adults and climbing equipment that had to be returned to Bellingham. Sam would return home on the bus. She had a summer job at a veterinary clinic and her vacation break was over. Donna was also thinking of Tim's parents. They were expected to arrive at the cabin on July 3rd. There were too many people in the cabin already.

Sam wanted to stay at the cabin a little longer, at least until Art had to leave for Walla Walla. When Art left, Mikka and Brian would return to Bellingham. Art was slated to leave on July 5th, according to his mother's orders.

As the group discussed their plans for the coming few days, Art glanced at the TV. The sound was muted but a red bulletin was scrolling across the screen. Art pressed the mute button and the sound for the newscast returned.

"Reports of fires on Mt. Baker glaciers have been coming into the station for the last half hour. We have contacted the Ranger Station and they confirmed the fires. They have been testing new flares to be used for rescue efforts and no one should be alarmed. The glaciers themselves are not burning."

Glenn smiled and said, "Can you imagine that? They are testing flares on the glaciers." Everyone laughed.

CHAPTER 18

GOING HOME

It was a bright and sunny Saturday morning. There were a few clouds in the sky obscuring the mountaintop but the weather report indicated the sky would clear by noon.

By ten o'clock, Donna, Glenn and Otto said their goodbyes and squeezed into Sam's SUV. Sam watched her little car disappear around the bend of the cul-de-sac. Her parents and guest would be in Bellingham an hour later.

Sam had given her parents a hug and shook hands with Otto. Donna would pick up Sam at the Bus Depot at 1:00 p.m. Sam packed her bags and they all talked about what they would be doing the rest of the summer. Tim helped Sam load her things into the pickup. Mikka and Sam gave each other a big hug and with a few tears, said goodbye. Sam gave Brian and Art a hug and jumped in the pickup. Tim shook his keys and climbed in the driver's seat. Tim didn't know what to say to Sam as they made the short drive to Brannigan's so he kept his mouth shut. Sam felt the same way so they made the drive in silence.

Brannigan's was busy. Tourists were coming and going and Rose was pretty busy selling groceries, maps and bus tickets. Sam bought her ticket and sat on her suitcase on the long covered porch of the market.

Tim looked down at her and said, "Got everything?"

Sam looked up and said, "I think so. Oh, I was going to get some Reese's, the little ones."

"Just a minute, I'll get some for you."

Tim stepped back into the market and grabbed two packages of chocolate and peanut butter candy. He took them over to Rose and she said, "Hi Tim! That will be four dollars, please."

Tim gave her a five-dollar bill and she rang up the sale and handed Tim a dollar bill. Rose was humming again, as before, when Tim was in the store.

"That's the same melody as before, isn't it, Rose?"

"Yes. It happened again," she said.

"What happened, Rose?"

"That Mr. Green was here a few minutes ago. He bought a ticket for Bellingham."

"Rose, call the police, that guy is a terrorist. What does he look like?"

"He went outside. He's wearing blue jeans and a yellow jacket."

"Okay! Rose, call the police…right now! Tell them a guy got on the bus with a gun."

Tim went outside and gave the candy to Sam and said, "Whatever you do, Sam, don't get on that bus when it arrives. Wait until everyone else gets on."

"What?"

"Please do as I say. Mr. Green is going to get on the bus. He bought a ticket to Bellingham."

"What does he look like?"

"Rose told me he's wearing blue jeans and a yellow jacket."

The bus pulled up to the bus parking area to the front and right of the market. The door opened and at least a dozen people got off. Some of the passengers were greeted and some went into the market. Tim followed a couple of people and walked over to Rose.

"Are the police coming?"

"Yes, they're on the way. Sheriff Richardson said they would come to the back of the store."

"Okay. Thanks Rose. I'll go out back and wait for them. I told

Sam to stay off the bus until we take care of Mr. Green."

Tim went behind the counter and out the back door. Just as he stepped outside, the sheriff's cruiser pulled up. The sheriff and a deputy climbed out and approached the back door.

"Sheriff, I'm Tim Morgan. I've got an idea to get the guy so no one gets hurt. Watch me from the store and when I give you a yell come on the bus and grab the guy. I'm going to grab his arms and pin him to the seat. I'm afraid if he sees you get on the bus in uniform, he might pull his gun and someone will get hurt. Okay?"

"Okay, son. We'll try it your way. Go ahead."

The three men went into the store and Tim went out to talk to Sam.

"Did you see the guy get on the bus?"

"Yes. He's about halfway back on the other side."

"Okay, Sam. Wait right here. The police are inside. When I yell they're going to climb on the bus and grab the guy."

Tim walked over to the bus and started to get on. The driver stopped him at the door.

"Ticket, please."

"Oh. I'm not going on the bus. I need to tell my friend something. I'll get right off, just a second or two."

"All right. Make it snappy. I've got a schedule to follow."

Tim got on the bus and slowly walked back to the suspect and sat down beside him. They looked at each other and nodded. As soon as the man looked away, Tim grabbed him in a bear hug and yelled, "Sheriff! Come and get him!"

The man, Mr. Green, tried to pull away, but Tim just tightened his grip.

"What you doing?" he snapped.

The goon was trying to get to the gun from his belt behind his back but Tim swung him against the bus window and pinned him to the seat. The Sheriff reached behind the man and pulled a gun from the suspect's belt. The deputy grabbed one of Mr. Green's arms and twisted it behind his back. Tim crawled out of the mass of bodies and got off the bus.

Sam ran over to Tim. "Are you all right?"

"I'm just fine. We got him. He did have a gun."

They watched as the deputy led the man in handcuffs from the bus.

The Sheriff stopped to talk to Tim.

"You did really good, son. Thank you for the assistance. You say he's a terrorist?

We'll take care of him until the FBI comes calling. We've got a nice little room for him at the jail and we won't leave the light on for him."

The Sheriff smiled and helped the deputy usher the man to the patrol car.

"All aboard for Bellingham. We've got a schedule, you know."

Tim picked up Sam's suitcase and carried it to the bus. Sam turned to Tim and standing on her tiptoes, kissed him on the cheek.

"Bye Tim."

"Bye Sam. I'll see you at the UW-WSU football game. Okay?"

"Okay. It's a deal. You've got my email address, keep in touch."

Sam got on the bus and sat down next to the window where she could see Tim.

She made sure Tim was watching her and she mouthed the words, "I'll miss you."

Tim was watching and wanted her to say, "I love you." But deep down he knew that it was too soon for those words. He mouthed "I'll miss you, too," and waved goodbye. Sam waved and as the bus pulled away, Tim thought there was always a possibility the nerd would get the pretty girl.

Ornaments
of
Value

CHAPTER 1

Holiday Preparation

City traffic typically caused pedestrians irregular periods of waiting on street corners anticipating for that lighted hand signal. Evan could use that time for planning, but he couldn't afford to think of anything but making his way to his shop. He certainly wasn't as spry as he was when younger. One misstep and he could be on his way to the hospital, or worse, his eyes closed permanently. A few years earlier, he was deep in thought and stepped off the curb prematurely. Fortunately, his wife grabbed his shirt and pulled him back, saving him from a collision with a deliveryman on a bicycle. Now he watched the lights and the traffic like a hawk. Today, however, unusual cooperation from the traffic lights allowed the five city blocks to be traversed quickly. He felt that today was going to be his lucky day, even though his legs had experienced some wear and tear.

Evan had started with a brisk stride but slowed after a few blocks. He wore a bright blue down-filled coat and a yellow stocking cap. He wasn't a tall man. The last time his height was measured he was five feet eight inches tall. Over the years he had shrunken some. Brown leather work-boots that laced halfway to his knees protected his feet from hot and broken glass at his shop. His well-worn jeans and plaid shirt were nearly concealed by his long coat. Nothing was more remote from Evan's mind than being a fashion icon. A comb never touched his short, thin silver-gray hair. He kept it short so combing wasn't necessary. Always anxious to get to work, he occasionally forgot to shave. That happened today.

Within a few minutes of 2:00 p.m., Evan Finley opened his shop. As he slid the key into the lock, he looked straight ahead at the gold letters painted on the glass. The sign on the door read, *"Hours 2-6 p.m. Mon-Sat."* A somewhat bare but dusty window display, a front sales counter, always spotless, and behind that, a large wooden desk made up the front of the shop. Small bits of paper, some with addresses and orders and a few with sketches were scattered on top of a desk organizer. A desktop computer ran 24/7 so orders and supplies could be obtained using the Internet. Adjacent to the desk, a small laser printer sat atop a wobbly TV tray. Most of the remainder of the 700 square foot business contained a large annealing oven, workbenches, a glass furnace, a fume hood and several large tanks of compressed gases. Next to the rear entrance was a rack of glass rods and tubing and two five-gallon cans partly filled with broken glass. A small bathroom occupied a back corner of the shop.

Finley intended to buy some new office furniture, but most of the money he had saved and much of his social security had paid for his shop equipment. Some of his apparatus was second hand from universities but he had to buy a new annealing oven. A big expense, his credit card was nearly paid off after three years. The money made from the glass shop supplemented his social security benefits and small investments in annuities he made twenty years ago added a few extra dollars to his bank account. At the end of each month, he had a little left over and having good health, he felt secure.

Finley's Glass Shoppe was written across the top of the storefront windows in large block letters. The letters were gold outlined in black. This was the third year of the elderly gentleman's retirement from working for the city's two universities as a scientific glass blower. His forty years' experience was now being put to good use making decorative glassware. Christmas was his special time of year. Anyone visiting his store could see he loved what he did. He made glass sculptures of everything relating to Christmas. Some of the objects he had produced, but had slight imperfections, adorned his window display and shelves in the front of the shop. Finley wouldn't sell pieces with defects. His income in December was the largest of any month of the year.

The store was always warm. The annealing furnace was kept on standby and it produced more than enough heat to warm the interior of the shop. Finley derived the most enjoyment from making Christmas tree ornaments. Angels and cherubs were very popular. He expertly added colored glass to make facial expressions on his creations. Ornamental bulbs were produced in a variety of colors and sizes. He charged $2 each for his bulbs or a dozen for $20. Angels and cherubs were a little more expensive. Right after Thanksgiving, Mr. Finley set up a small artificial Christmas tree to display an assortment of his ornaments. The glass bulbs were put in just the right places to transmit and reflect the multicolored LED tree lights. Many holiday shoppers passing by would drop in the shop to look closely at the decorations. Some of the shoppers would place orders for at least a few of his ornaments. Occasionally, someone would splurge and buy an entire Nativity scene. When a scene was ordered, he worked late into the night to finish the project. Most of the time he worked late so he wouldn't be disturbed. Finley climbed out of bed between ten and eleven in the morning and therefore opened the shop in the afternoon.

Mrs. Finley, Eveline, had passed away a year after Evan had retired. She had suffered heart arrhythmia for many years and a massive stroke resulted in her death. She hadn't suffered; it was all over in less than 24 hours. At Christmas time Eveline had made cookies and set up a CD player in the shop to play carols and other holiday music. She had also taken care of the front window displays. One fond memory Evan had of Eveline was kidding her about kissing him. He teasingly told her his hands and lips were of extreme importance for blowing glass. She had to be careful when kissing him so not to injure his lips. She threatened to never kiss him again and he said she didn't need to go that far. They had a good laugh about it. Now there wasn't much life in the shop. Aside from a few customers entering the store, the only activity was Finley quietly creating decorations behind the front counter at his workbench.

It was December 1, a Wednesday. Work at the shop started out as usual. After about an hour, Finley took a break and made a cup of tea. He sat down at the counter in the front of the store to enjoy the beverage and watch people passing by. A tall pretty young woman

with three children stopped in front of the store to admire the glass decorations. She pointed at the artificial tree in the window adorned with glass ornaments and said something to the children. The biggest child, a girl, appeared to be about six or seven years old. The second, a boy, was maybe four and was about six inches shorter than the girl. The young woman was holding a small child on her hip. Finley guessed the little boy was about two years old.

The woman pointed at the door of the shop. Finley could tell she was taller than he was. She could easily see over the lettering on the door. The little girl opened the door and all four entered the store.

"Hello!" Mr. Finley greeted them.

"Hi. Are you Mr. Finley?" the woman inquired.

"At your service. What can I do for you?"

"I'm Karen Ekstrom, and these are my children, Susan, Larry, and John."

"It's a pleasure to meet such a nice looking group," Finley replied.

"We were looking in your window and I wondered if I could help you with your display. I'm an out of work artist and need to make some money for Christmas. I could paint some winter scenes on your windows and I think your display could use some artificial snow."

Finley sat on a stool behind the counter. His left elbow was on the counter and he leaned forward and placed his chin in the cup of his hand. He could feel the stubble on his chin and realized he had forgotten to shave.

"Hmm, I hadn't thought of that. Those are good ideas."

"I could do it for $50. I have all the materials I need."

"What would you put on the windows?" Finley asked.

"How about some children decorating a tree and a snow covered cabin with Santa on the roof?" she suggested.

"That sounds fine. When can you start?"

"Tomorrow. Oh, I'll have to bring the kids. I don't have money for a sitter."

"That's okay. I'll set up a card table and the children can color

and draw. I think I have a jigsaw puzzle they could work on. It's a Christmas scene of a family gathered around a fire opening presents."

"All right, but not the puzzle. I'm not sure what I will have for them for Christmas. I'll bring some things to keep them entertained."

"That sounds like a plan. See you tomorrow at 2:00. It was nice meeting you and your children, Karen."

"It was nice meeting you, Mr. Finley. Thanks so much for the job!"

The next day, Finley had a card table, three fold-up chairs and some snacks for the children. At 2:00 p.m., he set up the table and got right to work. Several orders had been received from the Internet and he was anxious to get the ornaments finished and shipped. Three o'clock came and went. It was nearly four o'clock when the phone rang.

"Hello. Oh! Hi Karen. I was wondering what happened to you."

'I'm sorry I couldn't come today. My landlord told me I had to pay my rent by the end of the week or we would be evicted. I went to the bank to try to get a loan.'

"Did you get a loan?"

'No. I really need that $50 for doing your windows. We'll be there tomorrow.'

"Okay Karen, I'll see you tomorrow. Thanks for calling. I was a bit worried about you and the children."

CHAPTER 2

Artwork and Snacks

Karen and the children were waiting at the shop when Mr. Finley arrived carrying a plastic bag full of things from a supermarket.

"Good afternoon everyone."

"Hello Mr. Finley," the family answered in near unison.

Finley opened the front door and ushered the family into the warm shop. He noticed the children were not dressed for the low temperatures. They lacked warm coats but were dressed in several layers of clothing. The children pealed off one layer of clothes and piled the garments on the floor. They needed some freedom of movement and would be warm in the cozy shop. Karen got the kids working on projects at the card table. Finley retrieved a coat rack from the back of the store and hung up the children's clothing. He then sat down at the computer to check his website for orders received over night.

The preparation for the window decorations started with measurements of the windows. Karen showed drawings of what she envisioned to Mr. Finley. He was impressed with the pencil sketches so he told her to go ahead. Karen untied the drawstrings on her canvas bag and pulled out a small tape player.

"It is all right for us to have some Christmas music, Mr. Finley?"

"I guess so, but not too loud please. I have to be able to think while I work."

"Okay. Let me know if it's too loud. The kids and I like Christmas carols."

"You don't have one of those new CD players with earphones?"

"No Mr. Finley. Too expensive when children need to be fed."

"Oh yes, I understand. Say, if you don't mind me asking, where is your husband?"

"He was killed in a traffic accident about two years ago. I was pregnant with Johnny then. Marcus was a freelance writer and we didn't have much money or any insurance. I'm always looking for work to keep us afloat."

"That's too bad. I lost my wife about that same time. She had a massive stroke."

"I'm sorry. So you live alone now? No children?" Karen replied.

"That's right. I have an apartment a short walk from here. I have a female cat named Mystery."

"Kids, did you hear that? Mr. Finley has a cat named Mystery."

"What color is she?" quizzed Susan.

"She's brown, white and black. When she was a kitten, we thought she was lost but we found her in a small suitcase in the closet. It was a mystery how she got there," answered Finley with a smile.

"Karen, I don't recognize an Eastern accent in your voice."

"That's right. I'm from Montana."

"How'd you happen to come to a big city in the East?" Finley inquired.

"My husband and I met at the university. I was a junior and Marcus was a first year graduate student. We dated until I graduated and then we married. My mom didn't want me to marry him. She didn't think he could support a family as a writer. But I didn't listen. We decided to come to the East Coast where there were more opportunities for a writer. Mom gave up on me. I haven't talked to her in a long time, seven or eight years.

She hasn't even met the kids yet. I don't know if we'll ever go back to Montana."

"Maybe you can go back for a visit sometime. I'll bet your mother would love to see the children."

"Maybe. I kind of miss the open spaces and the smell of cow poop," she grinned.

Karen turned back to the window, began applying paint and watching people on the sidewalk observing her winter scenes being created. One little old lady tapped on the window and said she would come back tomorrow to see the finished decorations. A particularly handsome young man caught Karen's eye. He moved as if he were a corporate executive. He had a determined look on his face and walked quickly. He was nicely groomed and wore a tan suit and overcoat with a dark brown fur collar. The man's wavy blond hair gave him the look of an actor. He appeared to be in a hurry and hardly looked at the store windows. It occurred to Karen that some people were out of her class in a different part of society. Still, she wondered what he did for a living.

As four o'clock approached, Mr. Finley took a break and opened the plastic bag he had brought to work.

"Karen, is it okay for the kids to have a snack?"

"Maybe. What do you have?"

"I've got oatmeal raisin cookies and some apple juice."

"That would be perfect, Mr. Finley. How nice of you."

Finley came around the counter with the cookies and juice. John looked up from playing with his toys and started crying. He dropped his toy car and ran for his mother. Mr. Finley was astounded.

"Mom, I think John is afraid of Mr. Finley's dark glasses," commented Susan.

"Gosh, I think you're right Suzy."

Mr. Finley took off his glasses and walked over to the little boy. He offered John a cookie. John wiped his eyes with his shirtsleeves, took one and smiled.

"What do you say, John?"

With a bite of cookie in his mouth, John looked at Mr. Finley and said, "Tank you."

"Good boy John. I'm sorry I scared you."

Finley gave each of the children a small plastic glass of apple juice and a multicolored festive paper napkin.

"Take a break Karen. Have a cookie and some juice; it will energize you."

Karen put down her paints and brushes and joined Mr. Finley at the counter.

"You wear sunglasses to protect your eyes, Mr. Finley?"

"That's correct. If you watch me heating glass with the torch you will notice a bright yellow light. It comes from the sodium in the glass. If I don't shield my eyes I'll get a bad headache. And Karen, you can call me Evan."

"Thank you, Evan, but I think I'll stick with Mr. Finley. I don't want the kids to start calling adults by their first names." She turned toward the windows and said, "I'm more than half finished with the windows. I'll complete them tomorrow. Would it be okay if I watched you work for a few minutes? You are a real artist with glass."

"Thank you Karen. Sure, you can watch from a distance. I'm making a snowman, an angel and some multicolored bulbs. They were ordered on the Internet; already paid for."

"Not many paying customers come in from the street Mr. Finley. People come in but don't seem to buy much," Karen observed.

"Yes, today was a slow day. It will get better as Christmas approaches. I'm making duplicates of this order. These decorations are very popular."

Karen watched Finley for about five minutes. She marveled at how the glass turned into little sculptures in the flame. The children were getting a little restless, so she turned her attention to cleaning up her brushes and sealing the bottles of paint. In a few minutes she was ready to get the kids dressed for the trip home. John put his little sweatshirt on backwards but Karen didn't care, it was only about seven minutes to the apartment and then the outer clothing would come off again. Besides, John didn't like to be helped with his clothes. He was a big boy and wanted to show his independence. Karen checked the older kids and a minute later they were out the door.

"Thank you for the snacks!"

"Bye Mr. Finley!" came from Karen and the kids.

"See you all tomorrow," Finley answered from the workbench.

He heard the door close and the muffled sounds of kids talking as Karen and her little tribe walked away from the store.

Ten minutes later, the jingle of the bell above the door caused Finley to look up from his work.

"Good afternoon. May I help you?" he asked.

"Good afternoon. I'm just looking right now. I need to see what you have."

"Okay. Let me know if you would like to order something or purchase something I have on hand."

The gentleman was about six feet tall and very well dressed. He had wavy blond hair and looked to be about thirty years old.

"I see you're having your windows decorated."

"Yes. I'm having a local artist paint some winter holiday scenes. Hopefully they will help my Christmas business," Finley answered.

"May I ask who the artist is?"

"Her name is Karen Ekstrom. She lives in the area with her three children. She's a widow…a very nice young woman, smart as a whip."

"I'd like to buy a dozen of the Christmas tree bulbs, please. I'd like the opaque ones."

"I'll have to make some for you. I don't have a dozen right now. I just have some transparent ones on hand. I can have the opaque bulbs for you tomorrow about this time if you like."

"That will be fine. I'm Robert Hathaway. I'll come back tomorrow."

The young man left the shop and Finley got back to work. A small coo-coo clock on the wall above his workbench announced six o'clock. That little bird had been very reliable for many years. Finley walked to the front of the store and locked the door. He turned the sign hanging in the door around so it said CLOSED and went back

to his bench.

At seven o'clock, Finley took a break to have some soup and cheese and crackers. As he ate he looked around the store and noticed the front floor could use some sweeping. Tidying up took only a few minutes; most of the material on the floor was where the kids had been. Cookie crumbs and bits of paper seemed to be most of the rubble.

Finley turned toward the front windows and noticed Karen had forgotten her little tape player. He picked it up and took it back to his workbench. As he sat it down, his finger hit the play switch and Christmas music started playing. He decided to listen for a few minutes but got involved in his work and lost track of time. Finley caught himself humming along with the music and it surprised him. He hadn't done that since his wife passed. Karen and her children seemed to have injected some holiday spirit into him.

Finley was enjoying the music as he made bulbs for Mr. Hathaway, but after about a half hour the music started slowing down. The player's batteries were getting weak. He took the back of the player off to determine the type of batteries needed. He would get some new ones and bring them to the store tomorrow.

CHAPTER 3

Sketches

Saturday arrived; it was December 4. It had warmed up a bit and many people were out shopping. A cool breeze didn't indicate that snow was on the way. Finley got up at ten o'clock and had some cereal and coffee. After feeding Mystery, he was out the door. He bought a package of batteries, more juice and cookies and stopped by an electronics store and looked over the new CD players. At a clothing store, he looked at winter coats in the children's department. He was thinking of buying Karen and her kids some Christmas presents.

Two blocks from his store, Finley walked past a tall building housing Abbott and Finnegan: Architects. He could see people entering the building, some stopping at the large directory next to the four elevators. Finley saw the man that had visited his shop the day before. Robert Hathaway was talking to two other men and entering one of the elevators. Finley wondered if Mr. Hathaway was an architect.

Mr. Finley expected Karen and her children to be waiting at the entrance to his store, but when he arrived, no one was there. He unlocked the door and turned on the lights. Finley removed his coat and donned his work apron that was hanging on a hook behind the counter. He ignited a torch as Karen and her daughter entered the front door.

"Hello ladies!" greeted Finley. "Where are the boys?"

"They're staying with my younger sister, Mr. Finley. She

volunteered to baby sit for a few hours today. She's correcting some papers and said she could watch the boys for me. I took the boys to her apartment so Suzy and I are a bit late."

"Oh, your sister's a teacher?"

"Jen's a graduate student in Chemistry. She's much smarter with math and science than I am."

"But you are an artist. That takes a different kind of intelligence."

Karen smiled. "I guess you're right. Jen can't draw, but she is a good teacher."

Susan was busy taking off her sweater and Karen laid down a cardboard cylinder on the floor near the front windows.

"What have you got there, Karen?" Finley asked.

"Oh, just some sketches. I'll show them to you later."

Karen climbed into the window display, opened her paints and grabbed a brush.

She was adding faces and expressions to the children in the window painting.

Finley opened his shopping bag and replaced the batteries in Karen's tape player.

"Karen, you left your tape player here last night and I ran down the batteries. I bought you some new ones."

"Thank you Mr. Finley. When we got home yesterday, I remembered I forgot the player, but I couldn't recall where I put it."

Finley looked at Susan and said, "How old are you, young lady?"

"I'm six. I'm in the first grade. I'll be going back to public school in January.

Mom is home schooling me now."

"Boy, you are full of information. Could you help me?" Finley questioned.

Susan looked at her mom and said, "Can I help Mr. Finley, Mom?"

"Sure, just be careful."

"Let me show you what to do."

Finley led the little girl to his workbench and handed her a small empty cardboard box. He picked up a small piece of packing material from a large bag.

"This is packing material called peanuts. I put it in the box to keep the ornaments from touching each other and breaking during shipment."

He continued, "Put a layer of peanuts on the bottom of the box, then three or four ornaments. Then, put some more peanuts in and repeat the process until you have twelve ornaments in the box. Put enough peanuts in so the bulbs don't touch each other. Okay?"

"Okay Mr. Finley."

"Oh yes. Just use the opaque bulbs, not the transparent ones. The opaque ones are the ones you can't see through."

She held up one of the bulbs and inspected it. "Okay. Boy, these are pretty."

Finley watched as Susan followed his instructions. When she finished, she looked up at the elderly gentleman.

"Very good work Susan. Thank you."

"You're welcome, Mr. Finley. The bulbs are beautiful."

"Thank you. Here's something for helping me."

Finley handed Susan a dollar bill.

"Oh! Thank you."

Susan put the dollar in her pocket and returned to her coloring in the front of the store. Finley checked his web site and printed out several orders. Business seemed to be picking up. The elderly woman who said she would be back to see the finished window returned and entered the store.

"My, young lady, the windows look beautiful. The eyes of the children just sparkle. I don't know how you do it!"

Karen smiled and said, "Thank you."

The woman walked over to the artificial tree and looked at the

angel ornaments.

"I think I'll get some of these."

"Could you help me dear?" she asked Karen.

"I'm sorry, you'll have to ask Mr. Finley. I'm just painting the window. I don't work here."

Finley walked over to the lady and said, "May I help you?"

"Yes. I'd like to buy two of the little angels."

"Come over to the counter and you can pick out two you like."

There were about a dozen angels in the ornament box Finley showed the short chubby lady. She pointed at two ornaments. Finley packaged them and put the money in his cash box. A short time after the lady left the store, Karen put the finishing touches on the windows.

"There Mr. Finley, I'm finished," Karen stated.

"Okay, let me take a look from outside."

Finley stepped outside and inspected the window paintings. Karen watched him as he looked over her work. Finley was all smiles when he came back in the store.

"You did an amazing job, Karen. The windows look fantastic."

"Thank you Mr. Finley. I'm glad you like my work. I'll show you what I have in the cylinder now."

Karen unscrewed the metal cap on the cardboard cylinder and extracted several large sheets of coiled paper from the tube. She moved to the counter and unrolled the paper to expose a pencil sketch of the front of Finley's store prior to the decorations. The second sheet of paper was the same as the first except the block letters **"Finley's Glass Shoppe"** had been changed to *"Finley's Glass Sculptures"* in script curving over the front door. The third sheet was a picture of Finley working at his bench. Karen had added watercolor washes over the acetylene flame, the workbench, Finley's dark brown skin color and his blue and brown clothing. The color enhanced the three-dimensional quality of the sketch, already drawn in perspective.

Finley was studying the sketches so intently he fell silent. At first Karen thought he was going to react negatively, but she was relieved and delighted when he exclaimed, "These are wonderful!"

Karen beamed.

"Oh, I'm so happy you like them. I've been experimenting with the line and wash technique and you working at your bench made a perfect subject."

"I really like the new look of the storefront. Can you redo the lettering for me?"

"Sure I can, but I was thinking that I should wait 'til after the holidays. What do you think? Do you like the change in the name?"

"I think you should get started right away. The store's new look could be good for business. I like the new name. It's more sophisticated and might encourage a new clientele with deeper pockets," Finley smiled.

Finley added, "I'd like to frame the sketch of me working and hang it on the wall in the front of the store. The details are wonderful. You must have a photographic memory."

"Well, the idea came to me when I was watching you work yesterday. I started sketching as soon as I got home. We had a quick hot dog dinner and I put the kids to bed early. I finished the sketches early this morning."

"I'm going to give you $100 today. That's for the windows you've done, this sketch and an advance for the new lettering. How does that sound, Karen?"

"That sounds awesome, Mr. Finley."

Karen was delighted to have money for her rent payment and a few dollars left over for food.

Finley took out his wallet and counted out five $20 bills. Karen folded the money and put it in the right front pocket of her jeans.

"Well, Susan and I have to pick up the boys from my sister. We'll see you Monday, Mr. Finley. Come on Susan, let's get the boys from Jen."

"See you Monday, ladies."

"Bye Mr. Finley!" Suzy exclaimed.

As the door opened, the bell jingled, and sounded again as Karen and Susan left the shop. Finley got back to work and listened for the shop door to open, but no one came in. Mr. Hathaway didn't show up to get his tree ornaments. After locking the door, Finley got busy preparing the Internet orders for shipment. He left for home about midnight.

CHAPTER 4

Hathaway Returns

Finley woke up Sunday morning to find Mystery a couple of inches away looking him right in the face. The cat had never gotten so close to him on the bed before. Finley reached over and stroked his little buddy a couple of times.

"Now what do you want Mystery? Are you hungry?"

Mystery stood up, stretched, and moved to the foot of the bed. The cat picked something up with her mouth and dropped it beside Finley's pillow. It was a dead mouse.

"Mystery! Is that a present for me? Thank you girl. I'll get you some extra food for that. You're the best mouse trap I've ever had."

Finley got out of bed and used a paper towel from the kitchen to pick up the mouse carcass. He walked into the bathroom, lifted the hinged lid and flushed the dead body down the toilet.

"Goodbye mister mouse."

Finley took a shower, washed his sparsely distributed hair, returned to the bedroom and got dressed. After starting some coffee in the kitchen, he sat at the table, put on his glasses and made a list of things to do. First on his list was to find a nice picture frame for the beautiful picture Karen had made of him working at his bench. He knew of a nearby furniture store that had some nice frames. He also needed to buy a short, sturdy ladder for Karen to use while painting the new window lettering. He fed Mystery, had a quick breakfast and set out for Colton's Furniture and Appliances.

Colton's was about three times the size of Finley's shop and only a couple of blocks from his apartment. The store was open every day till Christmas, even on Sundays. After Finley looked at nearly a dozen frames, he found a wooden frame with glass that was just what he wanted. He asked about a ladder and they were able to supply that too. The sturdy aluminum ladder was about four feet tall. Now he could hang the framed sketch on the shop wall. The ladder was light and easy to carry. Finley went directly to his shop from the furniture store, the ladder in one hand and the frame in the other. He only had to walk three blocks but his arms were strong from years of manipulating glass blowing equipment.

Finley had been in his shop only a few minutes when he heard someone tapping on the glass in the front door. He recognized Mr. Hathaway. Finley walked to the front door, unlocked it and let the man in.

"Thanks Mr. Finley. I was out getting some exercise and I saw you come in the store. I couldn't get here yesterday, I was busy with legal problems."

"Legal problems?" Finley quizzed.

"Yes. I'm a lawyer. I work for Abbott & Finnegan, the architects."

"I know the building. I wondered what you did. I saw you over there the other day getting in an elevator. I thought you might be an architect."

"You were in the building? I didn't see you."

"I was just walking by and saw you through the window."

"May I pick up the ornaments I ordered?" asked Hathaway.

"No problem, I'll get them."

Finley went behind the counter and retrieved the box Susan had prepared. The bill was taped on top of the package.

Hathaway glanced at the bill and pulled a $20 bill from his wallet. Finley wrote, "Paid in full" on the ticket and removed the pink copy for his records. He put the money in a slot so it would fall into the cash box under the front counter.

"The windows really look nice Mr. Finley."

"Thank you. Karen will be pleased to hear that."

"If you don't mind me asking, could you describe Karen for me?"

"Well, she's about five-eight, has short brown hair and is very pretty."

"Is her daughter five or six and her two sons, about four and two years old?"

"That's correct. You know Karen?"

"No, but I saw her in our building about a week ago. She was looking for a job as an illustrator. Unfortunately, we already have illustrators on staff."

Finley said, "When she came in here she was really in need of a job. She and the kids were going to be kicked out of their apartment if she couldn't make a rent payment."

"Do you have her address or phone number? I have some contacts and they might have some work for her. She appears to be a very talented."

"Sorry, I don't have a way to reach her. But, she'll be in on Monday to redo the lettering on the front windows. Let me show you what she created for me."

Finley unrolled the sketches Karen had left with him. He was very enthusiastic about the illustration of him working.

"I bought a frame for this one. I'm going to hang it on the wall right over there."

Finley pointed to the wall in front of the counter.

"I was just going to put it in a frame and hang it up when you tapped on the door window."

"That's a beautiful piece. It will add some character to that barren wall," commented Hathaway.

"Do you know if she has any paintings for sale? I need to find something for my office."

"Hmm, I don't know. I'll ask her when she comes in. Why don't you come by and I'll introduce you?"

"Unfortunately, I'm required to be available for consultation at

my office until 6:00 p.m. But, if I can get off early some afternoon, I'll drop by. Ask her to bring some of her work, especially oil paintings. I'm looking for something about three feet by five feet, or a little larger, for a large blank wall. I'm partial to animals and mountain scenes but I would consider an abstract. Expense is not a problem."

"She'll be glad to hear that," smiled Finley.

"I'll get her phone number and address for you on Monday, Mr. Hathaway."

"I'd appreciate that. Well, I'd better get out of your hair and let you get back to work."

"Have to get home to the family?" Finley quizzed.

"No, I'm a bachelor. I haven't found the right woman for me yet. I've never been very good at the dating game. I don't care for women that visit bars and I rarely go to church."

"Well, don't worry. You're still young and there are a lot of fish in the ocean," Finley commented.

Hathaway understood, but laughed. He couldn't help making a further comment. "I'm not a very good swimmer, either. I've gone trout fishing a few times but never had much luck. Bye Mr. Finley." He waved and gave Finley a sly grin.

"Goodbye, and thanks for the business."

Finley followed Hathaway to the door, let him out and relocked it. As he went to his workbench he smiled about what Hathaway had said. This lawyer fellow has a good sense of humor.

CHAPTER 5

No Oils

Karen and the kids arrived at Finley's shop promptly at 2:00 p.m. on a dreary Monday. Finley was already at work. He remembered where his wife's CD player was stored and brought it with him. He found a few CDs of Christmas music and inserted three of them in the player. All the buttons on the front of the player were a bit confusing but he saw one marked random. That seemed a good idea, so he pressed it and music flooded the shop. He tried to adjust the volume and went to work.

As Karen and the kids removed their second layers of clothing, Karen raised her voice and nearly shouted, "Mr. Finley, the music is too loud."

Finley replied, "Can you turn down the volume for me?"

Suzy was already at the player adjusting the sound to a more reasonable level.

Finley commented, "Kids these days know more than adults do. The digital world seems easy for them to grasp."

Karen was setting up the card table for the kids and Finley brought the little fold-up aluminum ladder to the front of the store.

"I have something for you, Karen."

Karen saw the ladder and said, "Oh, that is great! I was thinking I would have to stand on a chair and a stack of phone books to do the lettering."

"Before you get started, I want you to help me hang the picture.

I purchased a frame for it."

Finley showed Karen the framed picture.

"What a nice frame! Where do you want to hang it?"

"Well, I thought it would look nice right over here."

Finley walked to the wall and held the work of art over his head.

"What do you think?"

"I think that's a good spot for it."

"Okay. I'll get a hammer and nail."

Karen got up on the ladder, found a solid spot and put the nail in the wall. Finley handed her the picture and it was now prominently displayed.

Finley stepped back and looked at the picture.

"Boy, that really looks good!"

Karen smiled. "I think so too." She was proud of her depiction of Finley at work. She took the ladder over to the window and got out her cleaning supplies.

The kids were busy at the card table, singing and humming with the music. Karen climbed to the top of the ladder and started removing the old lettering from the windows.

An hour later, Karen had the old block letters removed and had washed the windows. She was ready to mark the windows for the new cursive letters. Finley was taking a break and he walked out to talk with Karen.

"Have you any oils for sale, Karen?"

"No, I don't Mr. Finley. Why do you ask?"

"A customer came in and asked me to find out if you had any oil paintings for sale. Your window paintings impressed him. He is looking for a picture about three by five feet for his office wall. He said he liked mountain scenes, animals and maybe an abstract. Oh yes, he said expense is not a problem." He really likes the windows.

"Oh my gosh! I've been hoping for something like that to

happen. My window decorations have generated some interest in my work."

"That seems to be the case."

"I don't have any oils but I do have a few fairly large acrylics. I can't do oils in an apartment with kids and other tenants around. The odor would cause some problems, plus the kids might get the paint all over the place. I need to find a small inexpensive place to use as a studio."

"Well, what about right here in my shop? My customers could see your work develop day by day and you could display some of it on the walls. We might consolidate some of my things in the back to give you a little more space."

Karen's eyes sparkled as she smiled with enthusiasm. The excitement showed in her voice.

"And, I could give you a commission on what I sell; kind of like paying rent."

"That sounds like we have a deal then."

Finley extended his hand and they shook on the deal.

"Oh yes, can I get your phone number and address for the gentleman? His name is Robert Hathaway. He's a lawyer for the architects over on Grand Avenue."

"Not a lawyer! I hate those guys! When my husband died, a lawyer took most of the money we had after I paid the Funeral Home and the Cemetery. That shyster was supposed to settle any contracts my husband had with publishers. It should have been an easy thing to do. Marcus didn't have many things going on at the time and he hadn't received any advancements. And you said his name is Robert?"

"That's right, Robert Hathaway. If you have art that he would like to purchase, you could double your regular price and get some money back," Finley said half kidding.Karen was serious. "No, I don't want to do that. I don't want to be as underhanded as that lawyer was. I'll sell at the normal price. Besides, he might be one of the good guys."

"Let's hope so," Finley replied.

A jingle of the bell on the front door announced the appearance of a customer.

"I'd better get back to work. Thank you Mr. Finley. Let me think about giving the lawyer my address. I cancelled my phone service two months ago."

Before Karen could even get the lettering started on the window, her two boys were arguing over one of their toys.

"Boys, I think you need a nap. You got up early this morning so you need to lie down for a little while and then we'll have a snack."

Karen opened a small blanket she had in her backpack and spread it out on the floor next to the card table. She coiled up some of the clothes they had removed and made pillows for them. In a couple of minutes, both boys were asleep.

"Wow, am I lucky today," Karen exclaimed.

Suzy hadn't made a peep. She was immersed in coloring and humming to the Christmas music.

In the meantime, Finley had waited on the customer and gotten back to work.

It took about twenty minutes for Karen to draw the outlines for the new lettering on the glass, make a few changes and get out her paint and brushes. As she worked, Karen thought how nice it would be to leave her supplies in Finley's shop and not have to carry things back and forth. She could only think of three paintings she had at home that might interest the lawyer. She would bring them to the glass shop so he could look at them. But first, she would have to attach one of her business cards with a reasonable price to each of them.

The silver-outlined white letters flowed from her brushes with little effort. Her arm moved deliberately but smoothly. When she finished "Finley's", she went outside to look at her work. She could see a couple of spots that needed touching up but that could wait 'til after the rest of the lettering was finished.

She had made up her mind. She did not want Robert Hathaway to know where she lived. Karen went back inside and spoke to Mr.

Finley, "I don't think I want this guy Hathaway to know where I live. If he wants to look at my acrylics, he will have to come here to the glass shop."

"I understand, Karen. Maybe after you know more about Hathaway you can give him your address, but it is entirely up to you. I don't think any of my customers know where I live. I wouldn't want any of them dropping by my apartment."

"Well, this is a big city. One doesn't know what kind of creeps are around. I don't have a gun and I sure can't defend myself with paintbrushes or dirty diapers. The kids and I have to watch out for ourselves, so I like to be cautious."

Karen resumed painting the new letters until an elderly gentleman entered the shop. He was immaculately attired and carried a small cardboard box. The man had a look of concern on his face. He hesitated at the doorway and then proceeded to the counter.

Finley got up from his workbench and said, "May I be of assistance."

"I am Horatio Secor. I work for Mrs. Womack. I have a bit of a problem. I was cleaning the light fixtures in Madam's library and I broke one of the glass shades in a chandelier. It was purely accidental, of course. I have one here just like the one I broke.

Do you think you could make a replacement for me? I know they are not made any more; they are very old."

"I'm sorry, but who is Mrs. Womack?" Finley asked.

Finley knew who Mrs. Womack was but he thought he would have some fun with Mr. Secor.

"Sir, do you not read the society pages?"

"I read the sports pages, the comics and look for coupons; never pay much attention to the society pages."

"Mrs. Womack throws the biggest parties in the city. She knows everyone that is anybody. She runs charity benefits all the time."

"I know who she is, Mr. Secor. I was just pulling your leg."

"Very good sir. You had me there for a moment. Let me show you the glass lamp shade I need to have you make."

Secor took the ornate glass lampshade from the box and gave it to Mr. Finley.

"Hmm. Yes, I can do this. When do you want the copy?"

"Could you have it tonight? Madam will return to the estate this evening from Washington. I don't want her to find out I broke something. I might lose my job."

"I'm sorry sir, that would be impossible. The glass has to anneal in the oven for 24 hours or it will crack."

"Oh, no. What will I do?"

Karen had been listening to the conversation as she painted. She had an idea.

"Mr. Secor, may I make a suggestion?"

Horatio turned around toward the window.

"Do you have a solution, young lady?"

"Maybe. Why not take down all the glass shades and tell her you are cleaning them and will put them back up tomorrow? It wouldn't be a lie."

"Well, what a clever idea! Thank you young lady. I'll do just that."

"Mr. Finley, how much will it cost me?"

"Normally I'd charge fifty dollars, but since it's the holiday season, I'll charge you forty dollars."

"Splendid! I'll be back tomorrow to get the shades. Thank you, both of you."

"I'm glad we could be of assistance, Mr. Secor."

Horatio left the shop with a smile on his face.

"Karen, that was a good idea. Very smart of you to think of that."

"Thank you Mr. Finley. All in a day's work," she said with a proud smile.

Suzy had fallen asleep with her little head on her coloring book. Karen looked at her kids thinking she would have to wake them and walk home in the cold. They would be unhappy campers. Finley was observing her looking at the children.

"Karen, do you and the kids like Chinese food?"

"We sure do."

"Okay. I'll place and order and it will be delivered. After eating, it will be dark so I'll call a cab for you."

"Mr. Finley, you are a very generous man. Thank you! I should be able to finish the lettering if we do that."

It was about 5:30 when the food was delivered. Karen woke the kids and had them wash their hands. Suzy and Larry sat at the card table and John sat on the blanket leaning against the wall. Karen and Finley sat at the counter and talked as they ate.

Everyone had a fortune cookie. Karen's fortune read "Small things sometimes harbor big rewards." She read it, laughed and tossed it in the garbage. Karen remembered reading something like that when John was born.

After the sticky fingers and mouths were wiped clean, the kids put on their outer layers and Finley called a cab. A taxi showed up in front of the store in about five minutes. Finley paid the cabby and Karen and the kids were on their way home.

Not ten minutes later, Hathaway showed up and knocked on the door. Finley let him in the store and they talked for a couple of minutes. Finley explained the situation with Karen's phone and address. He also told Hathaway that Karen would bring in some acrylics for the lawyer to look over but she had no oils.

"Well, I'll take a look at the acrylics. She might have something I'll like."

"I forgot to tell you; Karen is going to use my shop as a studio so you won't need her address. Also, she doesn't like lawyers," explained Finley.

Hathaway thought for a minute before he said, "Maybe I can change her mind about lawyers. Thanks Mr. Finley."

"You're welcome."

"Oh! I almost forgot. I told my aunt about your ornaments and she wants to order a dozen of the transparent bulbs. You'll have to ship them to her. I'll be back in a day or two. I'll give you her address then."

"Okay. I'll make them tomorrow. I have a special order to work on this evening. Thanks for the order."

"You're welcome. Bye Mr. Finley, see you in a couple of days."

Finley let Hathaway out of the shop, locked the door and adjusted the sign so CLOSED was showing. He dimmed the storefront lights and began to work on Horatio Secor's flashy glass lampshade.

CHAPTER 6

Hathaway's Investigation

The following day Hathaway called his secretary into his office as soon as he got to work.

"Janet, I'd like you to call the Gotham Detective Agency and arrange for a female investigator to meet with me this afternoon, if possible. Please schedule the meeting when I am free, probably about three o'clock. Have the agent meet with me at the commissary. Give the agency my description so she will recognize me."

"Okay, I'll get right on it. Mr. Hathaway; is this company business?"

"No, personal. Thank you, Janet."

Hathaway finished with a meeting around 2:45 p.m. and went to the commissary to get a sandwich and some coffee. He had been there about ten minutes when a middle-aged woman approached him. Not pretty, not ugly, the woman was just average. She was going to be just right for what Hathaway had in mind. She was forgettable.

"Are you Mr. Hathaway?" she quizzed.

"Yes. Are you from the agency?"

"That's correct. My name is Judy Dixon. How may I help you?"

"I would like a woman followed so I can find out where she lives. I have a plan to give her family some assistance anonymously, so I need to know her address. She is working at Finley's Glass Sculptures on Bartlet Avenue. It's only a few blocks from here."

"Yes. I know the store, but I've never gone in."

"Her name is Karen Ekstrom. She's an artist and has three

youngsters, a girl and two boys. She has been decorating the windows at Finley's."

"Okay. That's enough information. As soon as I determine her address, I'll report back to you."

"Thank you, Miss Dixon."

"You're welcome. It's Mrs. Dixon. Most people think I'm single," she smiled.

Hathaway looked at his watch and stuffed the last bite of sandwich in his mouth.

"I've got a meeting in five minutes. I'd better go. See you tomorrow?"

"Probably," Mrs. Dixon answered.

Mrs. Dixon went to her car and drove within a block of Finley's. She was lucky to find a space that near the destination. She got out of the car, buttoned the top of her coat and walked to a position near the glass shop. Observing from across the street from Finley's, she could see a woman in the window with what was apparently an artist's brush. Dixon walked to the corner, crossed the street and began walking toward the shop.

It appeared as if she was admiring the painted windows, but she was looking into the shop to see who was there. She noted three small children, a man behind the counter talking on the phone and a pretty woman, in all probability, Karen. Now all she had to do was watch the store and follow where the kids went when they left the store. She went to her car, changed her coat and put on a scarf. She didn't want to be too noticeable to Karen who had seen her from the store window. A department store across the street from Finley's offered a good site for Mrs. Dixon to observe the glass shop. She could wander around the department store as if she were shopping, but keep an eye on Finley's, watching for Karen and her kids leaving for home.

Meanwhile, across the street in Finley's, Karen finished the new lettering and cleaned her brushes. She had brought one small painting with her to mount on the interior wall but decided to lean it against the drywall on the window exhibit floor. She had attached a card with the title of the painting and the price. It was an acrylic of a

puppy and a kitten playing together and was entitled "New Friends."

Mr. Secor returned to the store and picked up the glass lampshades and paid his bill. He had difficulty telling which shade was the new one. Finley had done a magnificent job.

At 4:00 o'clock, Jen arrived to take the kids for a snack. They got bundled up and were out the door by 4:10. They weren't going far, only a block to a mom and pop grocery store to get some cookies and juice. While they were gone, Karen was going to rush home and grab a few things, including a larger painting and return to the store.

Judy Dixon focused her attention on Jen and the kids and followed them down the street. She had assumed Jen was Karen. Jen was wearing a scarf so Dixon couldn't see that her hair was not as short as Karen's. In the meantime, Karen was going in the opposite direction. When she arrived at the apartment, Karen filled a bag with paints and brushes and picked up one of her larger acrylics. She left the apartment and reached Finley's before Jen and the kids returned.

The kids were excited when they got back to Finley's. It was nearly 5:00 p.m. and getting dark. However, with all the Christmas lights on in the stores, there was a festive mood in the air. The kids had really enjoyed looking at all the decorated windows in the stores near the glass shop. One of the windows in the department store across the street had a model train running through a winter scene. The two little boys were entranced and would have watched the train for an hour if Jen hadn't insisted they return to Finley's. Suzy was drawn to another display of an animated ballerina dancing around a Christmas tree. All three children had to tell their mom what they had seen.

As soon as they were back in Finley's, the children all starting talking at once.

Karen put down her brush to give them her full attention and Finley came to the counter to hear of the expedition.

"There was a tunnel!" John almost yelled.

"The train went into a town made of Lego's," added Larry.

"Mom, the dancing doll was beautiful!" Suzy commented.

"Well, it sounds like you guys had some fun. Did you thank your Aunt Jen?" Karen quizzed.

"We did," answered Suzy.

"Karen, I want to tell you something I noticed when we were looking in store windows."

"What's that, Jen?"

"Maybe I'm paranoid, but I think someone was watching us. I saw reflections in the store windows of a woman that seemed to be following us."

"She wasn't just shopping?"

"No. Everywhere we went I could see her as a reflection or directly about one or two store fronts behind us. She was wearing a red scarf and a dark gray overcoat. She didn't have a purse."

"Well, when the kids and I leave for home, you can wait and follow us. We'll ask her what is going on?"

"That sounds like a good plan," replied Jen.

"I don't know if that's a good idea," commented Finley. He added, "I'll go with Jen so there won't be any altercation, okay? She might have a gun in her pocket. We'd better be cautious."

"Okay Mr. Finley, you can be our escort and bodyguard," quipped Karen.

"Yep, I can do double duty," Finley said with a big smile. Then he added, "I hope I don't have to run. I'm getting too old to dodge bullets."

Karen and Jen both laughed.

Finley had one more customer and then the plan was set into motion.

Karen and the kids left Finley's and walked about a block. They stopped to look at Christmas displays in a couple of store windows and then continued on. Jen and Finley closed the glass shop and followed about one block behind and watched for anyone that might be following the family. Jen spotted the woman she had seen in the reflections and pointed her out to Finley.

Mrs. Dixon followed Karen and the kids at a fairly constant distance; however, Jen and Finley had nearly caught up to the investigator. By this time, Karen and the children were entering their apartment building and could no longer be seen. Dixon began to run to catch up.

"Here we go!" Finley announced. Running was just what he didn't want to do.

Finley surprised himself and Jen too. Finley was able to keep up with Jen as they ran to the building. They had only run about a block, but Finley was nearly out of breath.

Finley was realizing that walking was good physical activity but it doesn't build much endurance. His forty-year younger companion was not even breathing hard.

Jen went up the stairs and Finley used the elevator to the fourth floor. When the elevator door opened, Finley spotted the woman standing in front of Karen's apartment door, writing in a small notebook. Jen was walking down the hall on the other side of the woman. They had her trapped.

Jen spoke first, "Excuse me, who are you and why are you following my sister?"

Dixon was caught off-guard and had to come up with an excuse for following Karen and her kids. She thought quickly.

"I'm currently assigned to a clothing company. It's donating coats to children this winter. When I was downtown, I noticed the children that live here don't have warm coats for the winter. I need to get their names, sizes and their address, so I've been following them."

"Why didn't you just stop them on the street and get the information?" asked Jen.

"My employers want to be anonymous so they suggested I get the information without contacting the recipients. That way it would be a surprise. I need the first names and sizes and their favorite color. Normally, I would ask some of their neighbors for the information I need. The coats will arrive wrapped as Christmas gifts."

"Mr. Finley, what do you think?" said Jen.

"I think we should see some ID," Finley answered.

Judy Dixon pulled out her wallet and showed them her ID from the detective agency.

"Well, I'm sorry we were so suspicious, Mrs. Dixon."

"That's okay. You didn't know what I was doing."

"I'll give you the information so you don't have to interrupt Karen and the kids," Jen volunteered.

"Thank you, I'd appreciate any help you can give me," Dixon replied.

Finley escorted Mrs. Dixon out of the building and went back to his shop. Jen knocked on Karen's door and told Karen what had transpired in the hallway. Following a short discussion with Karen and saying goodnight to the kids, Jen went back to her apartment near the university campus.

CHAPTER 7

Hathaway's Plan

Mrs. Dixon called Hathaway's office in the morning and was asked to meet the lawyer as before, in the commissary at about 3:00 p.m. Hathaway and Dixon served themselves coffee and sat at a table.

"I had a bit of a problem getting Karen's address," confessed Dixon.

"A bit of a problem?" queried Hathaway.

"Yes. Karen has a sister who spotted me watching the children. She and Mr. Finley confronted me in the apartment building. I made up a story and I'll need some money to buy winter coats for the three kids."

Dixon told Hathaway her concocted story. The lawyer told the investigator what she thought was a problem really wasn't. He would gladly provide the money for the coats. He didn't realize the kids needed basic things like winter clothing.

"But you got the address?" he asked.

"Oh yes. It's 1204 Lincoln, apartment 4-D," she replied.

Hathaway wrote the address in his little book he kept in an inside pocket of his suit coat.

"Great! Send the coats and bill me for your expenses. Thank you for your help."

"You're welcome, Mr. Hathaway. I'm sorry about the added expense."

"Think nothing of it. I'm happy to provide something they really need. And I'm doing it anonymously. Just what I wanted."

After work, as Hathaway drove to his condo, he remembered he had to go to Finley's to pick up the ornaments his mother wanted. Even though he was nearly home, he turned his BMW around and went to Finley's store.

He tapped on Finley's window as he had done before but Finley didn't appear at the door. He waited a few minutes and Finley showed up, unlocked the door and they entered the shop.

"How are you, Mr. Hathaway?" Finley asked.

"I'm good, thanks. And yourself?"

"Pretty good. I'll be better after I have some Chinese. I went down the street to get some food."

"Smells good."

"I'd offer you some, but I only bought one order."

"That's all right, thanks anyway. I came to pick up the ornaments for my aunt."

"Oh, yes. I have them right here. Karen has two paintings for you to look at. They're at the side of the window display."

Finley pointed to the paintings and Hathaway walked toward them.

He commented, "The smaller is very cute but not for my office. However, the larger one of the waterfall and the mountains is just what I am looking for. It will look great on my office wall. How much does she want for it?"

"There's a tag on the bottom right corner. It gives the title and the price," answered Finley.

"That's a good price Mr. Finley. Should I make out a check to Karen?" asked Hathaway.

"I'm sure that would be fine. She will be pleased to have sold some of her work."

Hathaway wrote out a check for $275. He took out his wallet and gave Finley a $20 bill for the ornaments and the gave him the check for the painting.

"Thank you Mr. Hathaway; I'm sure Karen thanks you too."

"You're welcome. Tell Karen I'll leave some names of contacts with you by the end of the week. Oh, I almost forgot. Here is my aunt's address."

Hathaway took out his address book, tore out a page and handed it to Finley.

"Bye Mr. Finley."

"Bye now. I'll see you later in the week," Finley replied.

Hathaway picked up the large painting and left the shop. Finley relocked the shop door and went back to work, taking a few minutes every once in a while to eat a few bites of his Chinese dinner. To keep the food warm, he would occasionally direct the torch flame on a piece of aluminum foil containing the food. A second or two of heat from the torch was all it took.

When Hathaway got home he opened the closet and hung up his coat. He took the box containing the opaque Christmas tree ornaments from the closet and went to the living room and sat down next to the coffee table. The metal ring and wire spring were easily removed from each ornament. He extracted his wallet from his left rear pant's pocket and removed the currency. Earlier in the day Hathaway had gone to the bank and picked up ten $100 bills.

"Now for the difficult part," he said out loud with a sigh.

He took a $100 bill, rolled it up very tightly and tried to insert it in the bulb. The bill was too stiff and wouldn't go all the way in the bulb.

"Okay. Let's try Plan B."

This time, after folding the bill a number of times, he bent it into a circular shape.

Hathaway retrieved a pair of tweezers from the bathroom and went back to the sofa.

He poked the bill into the hole and pushed it with the tweezers to get it completely in the hollow glass bulb. Then, he replaced the spring and metal ring restoring the ornament to its original outward appearance.

"Ah, success!" he said proudly.

"Well, this is going to take longer than I thought."

Hathaway spent at least half an hour putting the money in the bulbs. He sat on the sofa thinking about the last two bulbs being empty. He decided to put a one-dollar bill in one of the empty bulbs with a little note saying Merry Christmas and in the last bulb a one-dollar bill with a note saying Happy New Year.

He repacked the box with the ornaments and peanut packing to prevent breakage.

It occurred to him that Karen and the children wouldn't know to look inside the bulbs without some kind of clue. Hathaway labeled a sheet of paper with "INSTRUCTIONS". Then he wrote the following: "Hang them with delight

Secrets out of sight

If dropped they will break

Insides will make

Your holiday bright"

Hathaway wasn't a poet, but he thought it was cleverer than telling them that money was inside the bulbs. He placed the instructions page inside the box and taped it carton shut. Wrapped with Santa Claus wrapping paper and red ribbon, the box was transformed into a pretty Christmas present. Hathaway wrote "To Karen and the kids" in a small greeting card and taped it on the outside of the present. Now, all he had to do was deliver the Christmas box anonymously.

He decided to wait until early the next week before delivering the package. In the next couple of days Hathaway would make a list of people that might show an interest in Karen's artwork. Before putting any names on the list, he would have to get in touch with the people to ask their permission. He hoped to get at least a half dozen people for Karen to contact.

CHAPTER 8

Mr. Funny

Thursday was a dismal day in the city. The sky was gray and a slight wind was blowing snowflakes in little whirls as they dropped between the buildings into the streets and alleys. The wet snow was becoming slush and little puffs of steam occasionally rose from holes in manhole covers. The temperature was a little above freezing and the snow wasn't sticking to anything; it was just melting and sliding off surfaces onto the ground.

Karen and the children walked to Finley's as usual. The kids got their feet wet from the brown slush and puddles of very cold brown water. As soon as the Ekstroms were all in the store, Karen said, "Good afternoon, Mr. Finley."

"Good day, Ekstroms!"

"We need to dry out some shoes and socks. Do you think it will be all right for the kids to go barefoot for a little while?"

"Sure. It should be okay as long as they don't come behind the counter. There might be some pieces of broken glass on the floor back there. I'll hang up their shoes and socks near the oven and they should be dry lickety-split."

"I haven't heard that expression in a long time, Mr. Finley," smiled Karen.

"Also, if they need the potty, we'll carry them," stated Finley.

Finley took the footwear and socks and hung them on metal hooks on the wall near the annealing oven.

The kids got out their craft materials and other toys and were already busy playing when Karen noticed the large acrylic was missing from the front window.

"Mr. Finley, what happened to the large acrylic? Did someone buy it?"

"Oh, I forgot. I have something for you."

Finley walked over to Karen and handed her the check from Hathaway and another $50 check for the remainder of the payment for the window lettering.

"Oh! Thank you! Now we can pay this week's rent and have a good amount left over for other things. I might even put a little in the bank."

She looked at Hathaway's check and remarked, "Hmm, he has nice handwriting. I was thinking that lawyers were like doctors, their handwriting almost illegible. That's why they always have secretaries, isn't it?"

Karen folded the two checks and put them in her shirt pocket. She knelt on the floor in front of the window display area and pulled out a drawer to access her painting supplies. After attaching a new canvas to the easel she had brought from home, little John had to go pee. She picked up the two year old and carried him to the bathroom in the back of the store. Before returning to the front of the store with John, Karen stopped momentarily to look into the alley. She pushed the lever on the steel door and opened it. The snow was falling vertically without any swirls, the lazy flakes settling randomly on the asphalt. She suddenly had an idea for her next painting.

Finley's voice broke her train of thought, but the idea was firmly lodged in her mind.

"Say, Karen, do you have a Christmas tree?" Finley asked.

"No we don't, but I've been thinking about getting a small artificial one."

"Would you like this one?"

Finley pointed toward the tree in the front of the store.

"I've been thinking I should get a real tree this year. A real tree in

the front of the store would smell good. I think customers would like it. You and the kids could decorate it for me. And, you could have the kids decorate the artificial one at home. Is that a good idea or what?"

"That's a good idea, Mr. Finley. Marcus and I used to always have a real tree, but with my present financial situation, I was thinking a tree wouldn't be practical this year. Thank you very much."

"All right then. I have a box for the tree in the back of the shop. We'll take the tree apart before you leave and it can be reassembled at home. I think you and Susan can carry it. If not, I'll carry it over tomorrow night. Tomorrow I'll bring a real tree here and the kids can decorate it. They should enjoy decorating two Christmas trees this year."

"What do you think, kids? How would you like to decorate two Christmas trees?

Doesn't that sound like fun?"

The kids answered "Yes," but not quite in unison. Suzy was absorbed in coloring and her "Yes" followed that of the two boys by a second or two.

Karen started working on a sketch of her idea for the painting. After a few minutes, she ripped the page from her sketchbook, wadded it up and dropped it in the wastebasket. She had to do some more thinking about the mental image she had when looking out the door to the alley. The creation in the mind was sometimes difficult to present on paper or canvas. Three-dimensional ideas did not always develop with ease on a two-dimensional surface. Trial and error had made art both interesting and intriguing for Karen. She rarely just started painting without a clear idea of what she wanted.

Snowflake shape was based on hexagons, but how would she represent the city in the snow? Maybe she should reverse the sizes? She would make some large overlapping semi-transparent snowflakes with the city buildings and multicolored Christmas lights shining through. With her enthusiasm increasing, she began a new sketch.

Finley had taken a few minutes' break and noticed Karen engrossed in thought.

"Hey kids, let's take the ornaments off the tree and put them in this box."

Finley came around the counter with a small cardboard box and the kids got up from the table and moved over to the artificial tree. The three children watched Mr. Finley remove an ornament and place it in the box.

"Okay, it's your turn."

John pulled an ornament from the tree, turned toward the box and dropped the glass angel from about two feet above the container. Karen heard the glass breaking, as did Mr. Finley and the other kids. Larry continued removing ornaments and gingerly placed them in the box.

"Mom, John broke one of the angels," reported Suzy.

"Oh, oh. John, you'd better tell Mr. Finley you're sorry."

John moved over to Mr. Finley, looked up and said, "I sorry Mr. Funny."

Karen smiled and Suzy laughed.

"Mom, he said Mr. Funny!" Suzy laughed again.

"John, his name is Mr. Finley," Karen instructed.

John tried again, "I sorry, Mr. Finney."

Karen looked at Finley, smiled and said, "I guess that's close enough."

"That's okay John. I can make another one," smiled Finley as he patted John on the top of his head.

"John, you have to be more careful. You have to be tender with the ornaments."

"Okay, Mommy."

The kids finished removing the ornaments without any more breakage. Suzy carried the box over to the top of the counter for Mr. Finley. Finley had gotten the box for the tree and started removing the detachable limbs. He used some rubber bands to keep each tier of the branches clustered together. The box filled quickly. After the trunk pole and the stand were in the box, he folded the tabs together and sealed the box with some wrapping tape.

"There we go. It's ready to travel."

Finley picked up the box and realized it would be too heavy and awkward for Karen and Suzy to carry.

"Karen, this is too heavy for you to carry. I'll take it over to your apartment tomorrow evening, if that's all right with you."

"Sounds good to me. Thank you Mr. Finley."

CHAPTER 9

Finley gets sick

When Finley got up mid-morning on Friday his nose was plugged and he was getting a sore throat. Was he going to go to work today? If he did, he would expose Karen and her children to a cold virus. That made up his mind for him. Before noon he would go to his shop and put a note on the window with instructions for Karen.

The medicine cabinet had several cold remedies. In his mind, it was questionable if any of the drugs would do any good. However, he took an aspirin to help reduce any fever he might have. He drank a large glass of orange juice and took a long hot shower.

Now he could breathe through his nose again. After getting dressed he put on his heavy coat and headed to his shop.

When he got to the shop he wrote a note and taped it to the front door. It instructed Karen to see Mrs. Clausen two doors down in the antique store. He wrote a second note to Karen and taped a shop front door key to it. Finley locked the front door and went to the antique store. He left the note and key with Mrs. Clausen and gave her instructions to give them to Karen. As Finley walked home, he remembered he had forgotten to feed Mystery. He hoped he would feel better by Monday but he knew he couldn't blow glass shapes if he had a cough.

Karen and the kids got to the glass shop a few minutes after 2:00 pm. At first Karen didn't see the note taped to the glass but she saw that the lights weren't on. As she tried to open the locked door, she saw the note.

"Come on, kids, we have to go to the antique shop to see Mrs. Clausen."

"Who is Mrs. Clausen?" asked Suzy.

"I guess she runs the antique store," replied Karen.

Karen took John's hand and they walked to the antique store. When they entered the store, a two-tone doorbell sounded. A middle-aged woman wearing glasses approached Karen. Her black and gray hair was pulled back into a ponytail and held tightly with a rubber band.

"I'm Mrs. Clausen and I'll bet you are Karen," she stated with a pleasant voice.

"Yes. How did you know?"

They shook hands and Karen said, "It's nice meeting you, Mrs. Clausen. Where is Mr. Finley?"

"Mr. Finley described you to me this morning. He has a cold and is staying home today. He gave me this note and the shop's front door key. He wants you to run the store this afternoon."

"Oh. It was nice meeting you. If I ever have some extra money in my budget, I'll come back to do some shopping. I love to look at antiques. Thanks for the note and key."

Karen and the kids retraced their steps to the glass shop and Karen opened the door. Finley's note gave instructions about the store lights and the cash box. She should follow the price schedule on the counter top if anyone wanted to buy ornaments. She was to keep the key after locking up and return it on Monday when Finley hoped to be back. He said he would surely be back on Tuesday. Mr. Hathaway might come to the shop to leave a list of potential clients for her artwork but he usually came by around six p.m. She might not want to stay that late. She folded the note and put it in her pocket.

"Well, I guess I'll meet Mr. Hathaway today. I can't afford to pass up potential clients for my work. Christmas will be here shortly."

"Who are you talking to Mom?" asked Suzy.

"Nobody, Susan. I'm just thinking out loud."

Before any customers came in, she got the kids busy with Christmas wrapping paper, ribbon, scissors and glue. She was having them use little pieces of wrapping paper and ribbon to make presents around a Christmas tree she had drawn on a piece of her sketch-pad paper. She had Suzy cut some shapes for John so he could glue them to the paper. Suzy and Larry did their own cutting and gluing.

Customers drifted in during the afternoon and Karen sold nearly fifty dollars worth of ornaments. One customer ordered a Santa in a sleigh but Finley would have to make it when he came back to work. She wrote down the order and gave a rough estimate of the cost based on other items on his list.

Karen made good progress on the painting she had envisioned in the brainstorm the day before. It took her most of the afternoon to complete the background of city buildings and colored lights. She searched the Internet for enlarged photos of snowflakes and found several pictures that gave her good ideas. She would have to experiment a little with the application of the snowflakes over the background buildings. She wanted the flakes to be translucent and distort the background into somewhat fuzzy shapes. She wasn't sure how to capture the refraction of light by the snowflakes.

A blanket brought from home was folded to provide a cushion for the boys to lie on for their nap. As she had done before, rolled up sweatshirts and sweaters were used as pillows. When 5:30 rolled around she took some time and reflected on the work she had accomplished during the afternoon. She had been able to run the store, keep the kids busy and make major progress with her painting. Karen had done a day's work in three and a half hours. It was time to clean up and give the kids a snack. They would have dinner a little later than usual today.

Suzy cleaned off the card table and got some cookies from Mr. Finley's supply. Karen poured some drinks and they all sang to the Christmas carols emanating from the CD player. Just as Karen was standing to go to the front door to lock it, the heavy glass door opened and the man she had seen before from the window stepped in. It was the nice looking guy with the wavy hair, the one she had seen over a week ago. She almost tripped over her own feet. Karen

reached out to steady herself by grabbing the edge of the card table.

"Hello. You must be Karen. I'm Bob Hathaway."

His captivating smile disrupted Karen's thought processes. Karen was thinking he is taller than she had originally thought. She smiled back and said, "Hi Mr. Hathaway. I'm Karen Ekstrom, and these are my three monsters, Susan, Larry and John. Thank you for buying my painting."

"You're welcome. I've had several positive comments from people meeting with me in my office. They really like the picture. Did the idea come from Yosemite?"

"Yes. My husband and I used to go to the National Parks for inspiration."

Hathaway stepped over toward the children and shook hands with each of them.

Suzy was first. When he got to John, Suzy was at Karen's side pulling down on her mom's right hand. Karen bent down to hear what Suzy was saying.

"Mom, he really smells good," whispered Suzy.

Hathaway looked at Karen as if to ask if there was something wrong.

"My daughter said you smell really good."

Karen got nearer to Hathaway and leaned toward him then stood up straight.

"She's right, you do smell good," Karen smiled and laughed.

"Well, I'm happy I passed the smell test," Hathaway grinned.

Hathaway reached into his coat pocket and pulled out two sheets of folded paper.

"This is what I came over to deliver. These are some people you can contact. They might want to commission you to do some artwork for them. You will have to call them or meet with them to find out what they would like."

He handed the papers to Karen and asked, "Where is Mr. Finley?"

"He caught a cold and is staying home until Monday or Tuesday.

The kids and I are keeping the store open until he returns."

"That speaks well of you. He trusts you to take care of the store. I hope he get over it quickly. This is a bad time for him to get sick. I imagine it is hard to blow glass without full use of one's lungs."

Karen saw the box containing the artificial tree lying on the floor against the wall under Finley's picture. She thought of something that would give her an opportunity to get to know Hathaway a little better.

"Could I impose on you to do something for us?"

"Sure. How can I help?"

"That box contains an artificial Christmas tree Mr. Finley gave us. I can't carry it home and still manage the kids on the city streets. If you have time, could you carry it home for us?"

"Better yet, I'll give you, the kids, and the tree a ride home. It will be quicker and you'll be warm and out of the weather. My car isn't parked far from here."

"That would be wonderful. Thank you."

"There are some parking spaces real close. I'll get my car if you are ready to go. It will take me about five minutes to move my car."

"Okay, we'll be ready."

Hathaway left the shop and Karen locked the door.

"Let's get ready to go home, kids. Mr. Hathaway is going to give us a ride. We don't need to walk or call a taxi."

Karen helped the kids get into their heavier clothing and pushed the box containing the tree over to the door. She put away some of her painting paraphernalia, donned her coat and was ready to go. She poked the papers Hathaway had given her into her coat pocket. Hathaway was outside and tapped on the window. Karen unlocked the door and let him in.

"My car is two spaces to the left of the store. It's the blue BMW. Let me take the tree first and I'll come back for you."

Hathaway picked up the box with ease, carried it to his car and put it in the trunk.

When he took the box, Karen shut off the lights, got the kids outside and locked the door.

They walked to the car and Hathaway helped the kids get in the back seat. He opened the front passenger door for Karen and helped her in. As they pulled away from the curb, Hathaway apologized for not being able to put the kids in safety seats.

"I'll drive slowly and be very careful."

"We have total confidence in you because you smell so good," Karen laughed.

"Tell me where you live, or maybe you better just give me directions. I don't know all the streets around here."

Hathaway knew her address but he didn't want her to be aware of that. When they got to her apartment, there was a note on the door.

The pink note stated "Attempted Delivery" and "see Mrs. Sifuentes in Apt. 4-C."

Karen unlocked her door and they entered her apartment. Hathaway set the Christmas tree box on the floor away from the door.

"Mr. Hathaway, could you please watch the kids for a few minutes? I want to check out the note on the door."

"No problem, I'll help them remove their outer layers."

Karen pulled the note from the door and went down the hall to Apt. 4-C. She had met Mrs. Sifuentes in the elevator once but no friendship had developed. Karen guessed the lady was in her eighties. She was tiny, maybe five-three, and frail looking. She had curly white hair. Karen knocked on the door and waited. She could hear someone walking and the door opened an inch or two until the security chain stopped it.

"Oh! It's my neighbor. Come in Dear," her initial surprised look changed to a smile.

The door closed momentarily and then opened wide.

"Come in. Come in. I have some packages for you. A deliveryman tried to leave the packages with you but you weren't home. He knocked on my door and asked if I could give them to you. I was

hoping you would get home soon. I'm going to bed early tonight. I need my rest. I don't want to get that virus that is going around."

"Thank you for accepting the packages. I appreciate your kindness. Let me take the boxes to my apartment."

"What do you think is in the boxes, dear?"

She noted the advertising on the boxes. "I think they might contain winter coats for the children. My sister said we would be getting some packages."

Karen picked up the boxes and left the elderly lady's apartment.

"Thanks again, Estelle."

"Good night, dear."

"Good night," Karen replied.

Karen carried the three large packages to her apartment and tapped on the door with the toe of her shoe. Suzy opened the door and exclaimed, "Wow, look at the boxes!"

Larry was right behind her and said, "Who are the boxes for, Mommy?"

"I think they are for you guys. Let's take them in your bedroom and open them."

Hathaway took two boxes from the stack Karen was carrying and followed her and the kids into the bedroom. The kids crawled up on the bed looking at the boxes.

Karen removed a card from one of the boxes. The small white card was addressed to John and Merry Christmas was printed in green ink.

"This one is for you, John."

Karen handed the present to John and he began ripping off the paper as the others watched. He had trouble getting the unwrapped box open so Suzy helped. John folded back the white wrapping paper and saw a new green winter coat. He wasn't sure what it was but he said, "It's gween!"

"John, that is your favorite color. It's a winter coat, John. Now you will be nice and warm when we go outside. Let's see if it fits.

Try it on."

Suzy was next. Her new coat was pink with a white fuzzy collar and white mittens in the pockets. The last box was Larry's. His coat was blue with purple trim. Inside one of the pockets was a small transformer toy. When John saw the toy Larry had found, he picked up his coat and looked in the outside pockets. He was disappointed when he didn't find anything. Karen thought that was strange considering what Suzy and Larry had found in the pockets of their coats.

"John, give me your coat. Let me look."

John dragged his coat over to Karen and she looked in the outside pockets. When she looked in the empty right hand pocket, she felt a hard object inside the coat. There was an inside pocket containing something.

"John, there's a pocket on the inside of the coat! You didn't look in there. Check and see what's in the inside pocket."

John put his little hand in the pocket and pulled out a Batman figure. When he moved one of the arms of the figure the head tilted back and a flashlight was activated.

"Look Larry! It's a light!"

Hathaway said, "Isn't that clever! A Batman flashlight."

Karen explained to Hathaway how they had gotten the winter coats, not knowing the true story and that Hathaway was the benefactor. Hathaway was happy to see that his plan was working and Karen apparently had no suspicion that he was involved. He suddenly realized that the note with the ornaments was in his handwriting. Karen could conceivably compare the writing on the note with his writing on the check for the painting and realize Hathaway was responsible. In his way of thinking, he would just keep it a secret forever. As soon as he got home he would use the computer to write the note and print it with his laser printer.

"Mr. Hathaway…Mr. Hathaway?" Karen repeated herself.

"Oh. I'm sorry. I was thinking of something I have to do when I get home."

"I guess we're keeping you from something," Karen observed.

"No, it's nothing immediate. The interaction with your kids reminded me to send a contribution to the Make a Wish charity." He was already starting to regret these little lies.

"Well, what I was going to say is we forgot about the tree in your trunk."

"Oh yes! I'm glad you reminded me. I'll go get it."

Hathaway went to his car and Karen made sure the new coats fit the children.

The coats fit perfectly so Karen made room in the bedroom closet to hang them up.

A tap on the door announced Hathaway's return with the Christmas tree. Suzy opened the door and let him in.

"Can we put up the tree tonight, Mom? Maybe Mr. Hathaway can help?"

Suzy looked questioningly at Hathaway and he said, "I'd be glad to help with the tree Suzy. Do you think I'm smart enough to figure it out?"

"Sure Mr. Hathaway. You have to be smart to smell so good."

Karen looked at Hathaway and they both started laughing. Hathaway took off his coat and tie, loosened his shirt collar and rolled up his sleeves. Suzy had already ripped the tape from the box and was opening it by the time Hathaway joined her on the floor. The boys were playing with their new toys and didn't show much interest in setting up the Christmas tree.

"I'm going to get some dinner ready while you two assemble the tree," Karen announced. She smiled at Hathaway and said, "Do you need me to help with the tree?"

Hathaway grinned. "I think Suzy and I can figure it out. We both smell good."

Hathaway smiled at Suzy and she giggled.

"Can Mr. Hathaway stay for dinner, Mom?" queried Suzy.

"If he wants to, we're having spaghetti and meatballs," Karen answered.

"That sounds good to me. I'd like to stay."

After dinner, they finished assembling the tree. Karen found several strings of multicolored lights on a shelf in her bedroom closet, which they draped around the tree limbs. It was about 8:30 pm when Hathaway said, "I think I'd better go now. Thanks for the dinner and letting me help with the tree. I really enjoyed being here."

Hathaway draped his tie around his neck, put on his suit coat and moved toward the door.

"We enjoyed having you for dinner and thanks so much for the ride home and helping with the tree. Good night."

"Good night, Karen. Good night, kids."

He looked at Karen, smiled and said, "Please call me Bob."

"Good night Mr. Hathaway," Suzy and Larry said in unison.

John was silent. He had fallen asleep on the sofa, his Batman flashlight clutched in his right hand.

Ornament Mystery

Late Friday night it began to snow again. When the Ekstrom kids got up Saturday morning and looked out the windows, there was a blanket of white covering everything they could see. Few vehicle tracks could be seen in the snow. The snow had stopped falling and it was cold and windy. The usual activity of the city had slowed to a crawl. Many people had decided to stay home and avoid trying to get around in the snow. City crews were out plowing and sanding the streets.

About half past one Karen had the kids put on their new coats and they left to make the trip to Finley's shop. Karen opened the shop and immediately picked up the phone to call Finley. After three rings a gravelly voice answered.

'Hello.'

"How are you, Evan?"

'Oh, hi Karen. My voice is not very good but I'm feeling better. My throat is sore but the fever is gone. I have a bit of a cough.'

"I'm glad to hear that you're getting better. We're doing fine at the store and hope to see you Monday. You have some orders to fill."

'Okay. Thanks for calling, I'll see you Monday."

"Bye Mr. Finley."

The children had taken off their coats and piled them on the floor. Karen picked them up and hung them on the coat rack behind the counter. Larry and Suzy were busy playing at the card table. John

was looking at everything in the front of the store with his flashlight. Karen envisioned getting a new battery for Batman before long.

The afternoon went rapidly. A few customers came in but the bad weather limited the number of people out shopping. Karen progressed with her snowflakes but her success was constrained. She decided to do some trials on an old canvas before she committed to painting over the buildings on the large canvas. She wished Mr. Finley were present so she could devote more time to her work.

At 5:00 p.m. Karen bundled up the kids, locked up the store and went home. A customer had told her a blizzard was on its way and was to arrive in the early evening.

It was good that she had closed the store an hour early. By the time they got home and took off their coats, snow had started to fall and the wind was blustery.

"Suzy, turn on the TV so we can check the weather."

A meteorologist from one of the local stations said the edge of the storm was just hitting the city. Twelve to fifteen inches of snow were expected with winds of 30 miles per hour. People were advised to stay home. Street crews would try to keep the snow routes open during the night.

Hathaway didn't leave his office until 6:00 p.m. He learned of the approaching blizzard conditions from his car radio. When he got to his condo, he picked up the package of Christmas bulbs and drove to Karen's. He had taken out the handwritten instructions and replaced them with a page from his laser printer the night before.

He climbed the flights of stairs to the fourth floor and looked down the hallway.

No one was present so he walked to Karen's apartment and leaned the package against the door. He stood up, checked the hallway once more, rang the bell and ran to the stairwell. He watched down the hallway to make sure someone from Ekstrom's got the package. The door opened, Suzy picked up the box and went back in the apartment.

Hathaway was satisfied that the bulbs containing the money were in the right hands. He gave a little sigh of relief, returned to

ground level, got in his car and drove home. As he was driving, the wind seemed to be blowing harder. The intensity of the storm was increasing. Hathaway's condo was on a side street only half a block from a snow route. The snow was about an inch deep in the street and starting to drift when he turned off the street to his underground parking spot.

"Who was it?" asked Karen.

"Nobody was there, Mom, just this package."

Suzy walked toward Karen holding out the package.

"Mom, it has our name on it."

Karen read the card. "It sure does. Our name is printed on the card."

"Can we open it?"

"I guess so. Let me get some scissors."

Karen got up from the sofa and went into the kitchen. Suzy and Larry started ripping the wrapping paper off the box and had opened it before Karen could get back with the scissors. The directions paper slipped out of the package and slid to the floor under a magazine rack next to the sofa. The kids didn't pay any attention to the paper; their primary goal was to see what the package contained.

Karen came back with a pair of scissors but she placed them on the coffee table when she saw the package was already open.

"Boy, you guys sure got in that package fast!"

"Mom, they're ornaments from Mr. Finley," Suzy blurted out.

"But Mr. Finley is home sick and that is not his printing on the card. It must be from someone else," commented Karen.

"Maybe he had someone deliver it for him," Suzy suggested.

"Was there a note inside the box, Suzy?"

"I think a small piece of paper."

Suzy looked around on the floor but couldn't see the paper she barely recalled. "I don't see it now," she stated.

"Boys, did you see a piece of paper that was in the box when Larry and Suzy opened it?"

Larry and John both said, "No, Mom."

"Can we put the ornaments on the tree?" asked Suzy.

"Sure. Just be careful, they're made of glass, not plastic."

The box of ornaments was depleted quickly. Larry and John reached for the last bulb. John got his right index finger in the wire loop and Larry wrapped his fingers around the glass bulb.

"Let go, John!"

John said, "Mine!" and they each pulled. The metal cap and hanging loop came off the bulb in John's hand. Larry had the glass ornament in his hand.

Larry was first to speak. "John, you broke it!"

"You boke it!" John replied.

"All right boys, no fighting. Give me the pieces, please," instructed Karen.

Karen squeezed the spring wire together and tried to insert it in the hole of the ornament. She knew how to fix the problem because of experience from past Christmas tree decorating. However, this time the little wire spring would not go into the bulb.

"John, please get me your Batman flashlight."

John scanned around the room and saw the flashlight lying on the floor next to the magazine rack. He walked over, picked it up and gave it to his mom. Karen turned on the light and shined it into the glass ornament.

"Hmm. There's something in the bulb."

"Suzy, would you please get me the tweezers from the bathroom?"

Karen used the tweezers and pulled a small piece of paper from inside the ornament. She unrolled it and read the printed words, "Merry Christmas." She smiled and told the children what the piece of paper had written on it. She again directed the beam of light into the bulb and could see something else. She carefully extracted it. She unfolded a dollar bill.

"Well, that was kind of exciting."

While Karen was investigating the contents of the ornament, John had gone back to the magazine rack. When he retrieved the flashlight, he noticed a piece of paper under the rack. He squatted down and squeezed his fingers together on the piece of paper and pulled it out. He stood up holding the note and walked over to his mom.

"Mommy. Paper."

"What is that, John?" Karen quizzed.

"Paper!"

Karen took the piece of paper from her little boy and read the typed message.

"Oh, thank you John. That's the paper I was looking for! What a good boy!"

Karen kissed John on the forehead and reread the little poem.

"Kids! Bring me all the ornaments you just put on the tree. I think they all have something inside."

As the kids brought the ornaments to her, Karen took the caps and springs off and investigated the contents. She couldn't believe it. Ten 100-dollar bills, two one-dollar bills and notes saying Merry Christmas and Happy New Year were found in the ornaments. She reassembled the ornaments and had the children put them back on the Christmas tree.

"I don't believe this! Who would give us all this money?"

Her immediate thought was Mr. Finley, but she almost immediately dismissed that possibility. Finley didn't have enough money to give away a thousand dollars. Whoever it was, they wanted to be anonymous. Except for the bulbs being from Finley's, there were no clues. Karen wondered how many people had purchased a dozen opaque bulbs from Finley this year, or even last year. She would have to ask him Monday. She would also ask him if he could remember who had purchased the ornaments.

Then, Karen thought of Mr. Hathaway, but she and the kids barely knew him. He certainly had enough money to give away

a thousand dollars. But Hathaway was a lawyer. Would he do such a nice thing? Could she collect some evidence to determine if Hathaway was the guilty party? She looked at the notes with Merry Christmas and Happy New Year written on them. They were printed. She would have to get an example of Hathaway's printing. How would she get him into printing Merry Christmas and Happy New Year so she could make a comparison with the printing on the notes? She would have to enlist the help of the children, primarily Suzy.

She thought perhaps she should just accept the money and not try to be a detective. But, she would always wonder who had been their benefactor. Karen decided to talk it over with her sister. Would Jen see the situation the same way?

The storm ended Sunday afternoon. More than a foot of snow had fallen and many of the streets were impassable. The TV news said all the snow routes would be open by 6:00 p.m. During the day, Karen and the kids baked and decorated cookies and played games. For the first time in two years, Karen asked the kids what they wanted Santa to bring them for Christmas. Although she didn't want to be extravagant, she wanted them to remember this Christmas.

In spite of the snow, Monday was a workday and Karen and the kids would have to trudge through some of the deep white stuff to get to the glass shop. Karen needed to use Finley's phone and call at least one of the people on the list Hathaway had given her.

Maybe she would get lucky with the first call.

CHAPTER 11

Match Makers

Karen stuck one of the hundred dollar bills in her pocket, got the kids in their heavy coats and they set out to Finley's store. The trip wasn't as bad as Karen had imagined. They only had to walk though deep snow for about a block. Karen had to carry John; he couldn't move in the snow, it was too deep. When they reached the sidewalks in front of stores, most of the snow had been removed. Karen put John down. He was getting too heavy for her to carry very far. A few store owners were shoveling or using snow blowers, but the majority of the sidewalks were clear of snow. Most cars along the sidewalks were buried, their identity concealed. The plows had thrown snow off the streets and covered the vehicles. As they got closer to Finley's, trucks and front loaders were still working to clear the streets. Some cars were being towed.

They arrived at Finley's a few minutes after 2:00 pm. Finley had just finished removing snow from in front of the glass shop. Everyone stomped their shoes on the sidewalk and entered the store.

"How are you feeling, Mr. Finley?" Karen asked.

"Pretty good, thank you. I have the remnants of a cough, but I can handle it."

"That's good. I put the orders on your workbench. There are about a half dozen."

"Thanks Karen. How are all of you doing? Do you like the snow?"

"We're all fine. I hope the snow melts soon, although it's pretty right now."

The children had removed their coats and hung them up. John had handed his coat to Suzy who hung it up for him. They busied themselves at the card table. John was using his flashlight to look under the counter. He discovered two pennies.

"Mr. Finley, something happened over the weekend. I would like your opinion."

Karen related the ornament mystery and asked Finley if he could remember who had purchased opaque ornaments recently.

"Well, I've sold ten to twelve sets of opaque ornaments since Thanksgiving.

I can't give you a list of people because most people paid cash for the bulbs. The only name I remember is Robert Hathaway. You know, I think he likes you and the children. The first time he came in to the store he asked me if you were the artist that painted the windows. Why don't you ask him if he left the ornaments for you?"

"I don't know. Maybe I shouldn't say anything? I think I'll talk to my sister."

Karen set up her painting materials and stood looking at the canvas. She couldn't get that thousand-dollar sum out of her mind. She looked over at Finley; he had begun working on the orders from Friday and Saturday. The phone was not in use, so she pulled the folded papers from her coat pocket and moved to the phone.

"May I use the phone, Mr. Finley?"

"Go right ahead Karen," Finley answered without looking up.

The first name on the list was Mrs. Olivia Ostrum (wife of the architect firm's CEO). Karen dialed the number and a woman answered the phone after the second ring.

'Hello.'

"May I speak to Mrs. Ostrum?"

'This is she.'

"This is Karen Ekstrom, the artist Mr. Hathaway told you about. What type of project were you considering?"

'Oh, I'm glad you called. I need to talk to you in person. Can I meet

you somewhere?'

"Certainly. I'm at Finley's Glass Sculptures at 619 Washington. The cross street is Hawthorne. I'll be here with my children until 5:00 p.m."

'All right, I'll be there in about 30 minutes. Goodbye.'

"See you soon. Goodbye."

Karen hung up the phone and went back to her painting. She wondered why Mrs. Ostrum had to talk to her in person. As Karen worked on the snow effect she was looking for, she was thinking about calling her sister. Jen was teaching a lab and wouldn't be in her office until after four o'clock. She would call Jen after meeting with Mrs. Ostrum.

Mrs. Ostrum arrived just as she said she would. The middle-aged woman entered the shop and looked at Karen, the children and Finley.

She approached Karen and said, "I'm Olivia Ostrum. You must be Karen."

Olivia Ostrum was dressed in a light blue exercise outfit and was nicely groomed. Karen reached out and they shook hands.

"Yes, I'm Karen Ekstrom. It's nice to meet you. What did you want to talk about?"

"I would like you to paint a picture of my three grandchildren so I can give it to my husband for Christmas and his birthday. His birthday is on December 28. I want the picture to be a surprise."

"I haven't done many portraits but I will try my best. I'll let you decide what to pay me. How old are the children?"

"Sharon is seven, Chad is four and Sarah is two and a half. Judging from what you painted on the store windows, I think you'll do a fine job."

"They're almost the same ages as my three. I'll need to take some pictures of them. I have a digital camera at home."

"I was going to take the children to the museum tomorrow afternoon. Why don't we take all the children? I can watch them

and you can take the photographs you need.

The children are looking forward to seeing the dinosaur exhibits.”

“That sounds awesome! My kids will love that! I don’t have any transportation though, Mrs. Ostrum.”

“Don’t worry about that. I’ll pick you up at 1:00 p.m. tomorrow. Okay? And please call me Olivia.”

“All right. I’ll give you my address. We’ll be waiting for you.”

Karen wrote her address on a piece of Finley’s notepad paper and handed it to Mrs. Ostrum.

“These glass decorations are lovely. I think I’ll order one of Santa. It will look great on our mantel.”

Mrs. Ostrum went to the counter and ordered a Santa and sleigh decoration from Finley before she left the store.

“Bye Karen. I’ll see you tomorrow.”

“Bye Olivia. Thank you!”

Karen spent about 15 minutes with the kids, worked on her painting for a half hour and then called Jen.

“Hi Jen, it’s me. I’ve got to get your opinion on something that happened last Friday night.”

Karen related the story of the money in the ornaments and told her of the suspicion she had that Hathaway was involved.

‘I think Hathaway has the hots for you, sis. He sounds like a good man to me. Don’t mess with a good thing. If this lawyer is making things easier for you and the kids and the relationship develops into something, he will eventually tell you everything. Unless, of course, he is dishonest or just afraid of how you will react.’

“Well, okay. I wanted your opinion. Thanks Jen. How are things at school?”

‘I’ve been studying for a cumulative exam. It’s on Friday. Let me know if the lawyer asks you to marry him.’

“Jen! Goodbye and good luck with your exam.”

‘Thanks! See you later.’

Karen hung up the phone and looked at Finley. Finley had a funny look on his face.

"What?" Karen quizzed.

"I think you and Bob are going to be an item. If he asks you out, you'd better go."

"Mr. Finley, have you and my sister been talking?"

"Nope. We both just recognize a good thing."

"Okay, kids, put on your coats. We have to go now so we can see where we're walking."

Karen helped her children get ready to go outside. It was getting colder and she wanted the kids to get out of the cold as soon as possible.

"Mr. Finley, we're leaving for home now. Tomorrow the kids and I won't be here. We're going to the museum in the afternoon so I can take pictures of Mrs. Ostrum's grandchildren. She wants me to paint a portrait for her husband's birthday."

"Yes, I overheard your conversation. Have fun with all the kids. I hope you live through having six children at the museum."

"Well, I'll have help. We'll see you again on Wednesday. Bye Mr. Finley."

"Bye Ekstroms!"

Suzy was the last to leave the shop and she yelled, "Bye Mr. Finley!" and slammed the door.

Finley smiled and continued working on the orders Karen had taken on Friday and Saturday. At 6:00 p.m., Finley locked the door, dimmed the display lights and snacked on chicken noodle soup and crackers. His wife had always said that chicken noodle soup would help get rid of a cold. How that would help fight a virus, he didn't know. He looked at his workbench and decided he would finish one more Santa, go home and relax. He could feel his cold tightening up a little and he didn't want to miss any more workdays; Christmas was only twelve days away.

As he moved toward his bench, he heard a familiar tapping on

the front door window. It was Mr. Hathaway. Finley opened the door and let the lawyer in.

"Hi Mr. Finley. How are you today?"

"A little under the weather, but I'm getting better. How have you been?"

"Great! I had a good weekend."

"Yes, I heard."

"Oh? What did you hear?"

"Well, Karen is on a quest to find out who left the ornaments at her door. She thinks it might have been you."

Robert thought quickly. He wanted his involvement with the ornaments to stay a secret a little longer.

"What ornaments are you referring to?"

"Some ornaments that I made were left at her door. There were hundred dollar bills inside the ornaments."

"Hmm. I guess I have some competition! I was hoping Karen wasn't seeing anyone, but I guess that was wishful thinking. She is a very smart and pretty woman, and her kids are great."

"I don't think she is seeing anyone, Robert. She talked with her sister about it and her sister encouraged her to go out with you if you asked."

"Well, that's good to know. I was going to ask her to the firm's Christmas party.

It's going to be a dress up affair at the firm's vice president's home this coming Sunday evening. I'll come by tomorrow before she leaves and ask her."

"Robert, she won't be here tomorrow. Mrs. Ostrum and Karen are taking the kids to the museum so she can get photos of Ostrum's grandchildren. She is going to do a painting of the grandchildren for Mr. Ostrum. It's supposed to be a secret, so don't let it slip to Mr. Ostrum. Karen should be back on Wednesday though."

"Oh! That's even better. My entire Wednesday afternoon is clear. The main reason I came here tonight was to see you. You are invited

to a Christmas party at the Architecture Building on Christmas Eve afternoon, Friday after next. It's a come as you are party. Everyone that works in the building and their families will be there. We'll have a Santa for the children. I hope Karen and her kids will come too."

"Thank you, Robert. I'll be there."

"Great! I'll see you Wednesday when I come over to see Karen. Bye!"

"Bye! Don't freeze your tuchis, it's getting cold out there."

Hathaway laughed and waved as he went out the door. Finley shut off the gases to his torch and turned off the lights. It was time to go home. Finley put on his heavy coat, wrapped a long yellow scarf around his neck and chin, locked the door and set off into the cold evening. Tuesday was going to be a rough day. Karen and the kids wouldn't be there to liven up the shop.

CHAPTER 12

Museum Pictures

Karen was anticipating Tuesday to be a long and busy day. As usual, home schooling the children in the morning went well. She tried to teach things they could investigate more fully at the museum. She did her best to cover dinosaurs, art and astronomy between 9:00 and 12:00 noon. After lunch, Karen helped the kids get ready for the trip to the museum.

Karen checked her camera to see if the batteries were going to be a problem. All the functions on the camera worked fine, but she put more batteries in her pocket just to be sure nothing would go wrong. At 12:55 p.m. she locked the door and herded her tribe to the ground floor. As they walked down the approach from the building to the street, a Suburban pulled up and honked.

Olivia got out of the big white vehicle and opened the doors to the back seats. She had thought of everything. The seats had restraints for all the children. She had a double stroller and a picnic basket. Olivia had on a down filled pink parka, a pair of jeans and athletic shoes. Olivia didn't look as if she were the wife of an executive of a lucrative business. Karen, however, appeared about the way an aspiring artist might be expected to look. She wore a long brown heavy coat with deep pockets, an old pair of jeans, a sweatshirt, and an old pair of loafers. But Karen had never cared much for fashion; she just wanted to be comfortable.

The two women made sure the kids were all seated securely. Children of about equal age were seated together. After introductions were performed, Olivia drove to the museum. When they got out

of the car, the children were very orderly. When they got in the museum, it was a different story. The youngest children were in the stroller, so they were easy to control. The older kids started to run off as if a bomb had exploded. After Karen and Olivia told them how they had to behave, the kids told the women where they were going to be. After Karen got a group picture, the eldest pair went dinosaur hunting.

The four-year olds went to the hands-on science center to explore.

The women followed the children for nearly two hours as the kids visited nearly every exhibit in the three-story building. Karen took numerous pictures of all six children so she would have many views of their facial features. When she painted the portraits of Olivia's grandchildren, she wanted to paint her three also. In fact, she was going to do her kids' portraits as practice for those of Olivia's grandchildren.

At 3:30 p.m. they gathered together on a bench and Olivia opened her picnic basket. She had peanut butter and jelly sandwiches for the children and tuna fish or bologna for Karen and herself. Instead of canned pop, she had small cans of fruit juice for the kids.

As Olivia handed out the juice to the children, Karen smiled and said, "I hope none of those is prune juice."

Olivia laughed and said, "I like your sense of humor! No. I have apple and grape today. I left the prune juice home for my husband."

"I think we are going to be good friends, Olivia."

As they talked, Olivia volunteered some information about Hathaway to Karen.

"Robert spent his first ten years in South Dakota in a foster home. He doesn't know who his parents are. He was abandoned at a hospital when he was two years old. From age twelve to seventeen, he lived in a boy's village community in Texas. Robert said it was similar to Boy's Town. After high school, he earned money doing various jobs in construction. When he was twenty-five, he went to college and then law school. He applied for a job at Abbott and Finnegan two years ago. He has been doing so well with the firm, they would

hate to lose him. Everyone says he is top notch."

"Wow. How did you find all this out, Olivia?"

"Mostly from Robert at parties and some from my husband. I think he considers me a mother figure. He didn't tell me all this at once. I found out about his background over the last couple of years. Robert is such a nice guy and he is very clever."

"And he's very handsome, too," added Karen.

"Yes. You and Robert would make a great couple."

"That seems to be what everyone is telling me. I know he likes my children."

"If he asks you out, you'd better go. I don't think you could go wrong with Robert. I wonder if he is a virgin?"

"Olivia! You come up with some surprising things."

"That's what my husband says. Sometimes my mouth gets me in trouble."

"Well, if he asks me out, I will have to buy something to wear. I can use some of the money from the ornaments."

"That won't be necessary, dear. I have several nice dresses that I have outgrown a little bit. Come to think of it, maybe a lot. I have hardly worn some of them. You can try them on and we can get them altered if you like."

"That would be wonderful, Olivia. But some day I want to be able to shop for something really nice and pay cash. In a few years, perhaps I will be far enough ahead financially to be able to splurge a little."

"Remember, dear, if you are Mrs. Hathaway, you won't have anything to worry about, at least financially."

"Olivia, you are so funny! You sure have created a rosy picture."

After eating, everyone wanted to go home. Sarah and John were fast asleep in the stroller and the four-year olds were having trouble holding their eyes open. They would probably fall asleep in the car on the way home. Sharon and Suzy were having an animated talk about the hands-on science exhibits and the animatronic dinosaurs.

While Olivia drove the Suburban to the Ekstrom's, Karen reviewed the pictures she had taken. She was developing a plan for painting the portraits. By the time they reached the apartment, she had decided how to paint the grandchildren. She had also developed an approach for painting her children.

John and Sarah were still fast asleep when the car stopped to let the Ekstrom's out. The women exchanged a parting thank you. Olivia told Karen she would bring the dresses over tomorrow morning. Karen scooped John up and was carrying him toward the building.

"Bye Karen!" Olivia yelled.

"Bye Olivia!" Karen yelled back.

CHAPTER 13

Alterations and Truths

There was knocking at the door of Ekstrom's apartment at 8:00 a.m. Wednesday.

The kids hadn't finished breakfast yet and Karen was in a bathrobe. The knocking wasn't unexpected; Olivia was supposed to come over with some dresses. Sure enough, when Karen opened the door, Olivia was standing there, smiling. She had a large plastic bag containing some dresses she had outgrown.

"Come in Olivia."

"Good morning Ekstroms! Grandma Olivia is here!"

Suzy and Larry said, "Good morning Mrs. Ostrum," but John's cheeks were puffed out, full of milk and cereal. He couldn't say anything but he waved his spoon.

"Here, let me take your coat."

Olivia slid her arms out of the coat and Karen hung it up in the closet. Olivia was opening the bag and pulling the dresses out. Karen saw dresses of four different colors, white, red, blue and green. Olivia held up each dress separately so Karen could see the style and type of material used.

"Are you ready?" Olivia asked.

"I guess so. The kids are dressed and fed. Suzy has some school work to do so I have time to try on the dresses."

"What is your color preference?"

"I like the blue one best and the green one is the runner up."

"Okay. Put on the blue one and I'll get out my pins and chalk."

Karen disappeared into the bathroom and reappeared wearing the blue dress. It was about two sizes too big but the length was about right. Olivia was kneeling on a pillow in the middle of the living room floor. Karen stood next to her and the work began. Olivia gathered the material at the waist, pinned it in place and made some chalk marks. It took her about ten minutes to make all the markings for the alterations.

When Karen first emerged from the bathroom in the dress, Suzy made a comment to Larry and John.

"John. Larry. Look at Mom! Doesn't she look pretty?"

Suzy was the only one of the three who had ever seen Karen in a dress before. That had been at their father's funeral. The two boys were too young to remember.

"I like the color," commented Larry.

"Pwetty," uttered John.

Nearly an hour later, all four dresses and been marked for alterations. The first, the blue one, had taken the longest. Olivia was a little out of practice. Almost twenty-five years had passed since she worked as a seamstress in a large clothing store. She hadn't forgotten the tricks she had learned. She just had to limber up her fingers. But, she only poked Karen and her own fingers a couple of times.

"Now. What about shoes, dear?" Olivia queried.

"There is a boutique close to the glass shop. It's called "Head to Toe". I think they'll have what I want."

"Well, I guess we're finished here. I'll take the dresses home and make the alterations. Shall we try things on again in the morning?"

"Sounds like a plan to me, Olivia. Thanks so much for doing this. I don't know what I would have done without you."

"You are welcome, Karen. You will look beautiful at the party."

"I sure hope so. Now, Robert has to ask me."

"Don't worry about that. If he doesn't, I'll sue him," laughed Olivia.

Olivia left for home at 9:30 and Karen got dressed. Since she

was going to see Bob, she decided to wear something better than a sweatshirt and jeans. She also put on a little more makeup than the small amount she usually applied for work at Finley's.

She worked with the children until noon. Karen didn't feel like eating any lunch. She was getting nervous about Bob asking her to the Christmas Party. The kids had peanut butter and jelly sandwiches and apple slices. She let the kids play until 1:15 and then readied them for the walk to Finley's. Karen made sure she had her camera so she could start sketching Olivia's grandchildren on canvas.

Finley was happy to see Karen and the children. Their absence of only one day made him realize more than ever how much he missed his wife. He regretted that he and Eveline had decided not to have a family. Forty-five years earlier, however, the assassinations of politicians and clergymen and general unrest in the country had convinced the couple to not have children.

Karen showed Finley the pictures she had taken at the museum and told him her ideas for the portraits. Finley remarked that he had seen Olivia prior to her visit to the store on Monday, but he couldn't recall where.

"Hathaway came in Monday after you had gone. We talked about the ornaments. He acted as if he didn't know anything about them. He was worried he had some competition."

"Really? That makes me wonder who did leave the ornaments."

"Well, he said he would be back today to talk to you."

"Thanks for the info, Evan."

Customers were entering the shop so Karen busied herself with the portraits after she got the kids working on some craft projects. Finley was busy selling ornaments and taking customer's orders.

It seemed like only a few minutes had elapsed since Ekstroms had arrived at Finley's. In reality, an hour had passed when Karen realized someone was behind her watching the work progressing on the portraits.

She heard Bob Hathaway say, "You are doing a good job on my sister's kids."

She turned around and said, "Oh! Hi Bob."

Karen thought for a second and said, "But you're really not related, are you?"

Hathaway was a little surprised and said, "Sure I am, they're my sister's kids."

"But Olivia told me you were an orphan."

"Oh! No! My Mom told you that?"

"You mean Olivia is your real mother? Wow! She really told me a whopper!"

"I'll bet she did! I know what happened. I have to apologize. Let me explain."

"Okay. I've got to hear this!"

"After my junior year in college, I brought a girl home to meet my parents. My dad had her investigated and he found out she was a gold digger. When she realized my father was the CEO of a big company, she had plans to marry me and get a big settlement from a divorce. After that incident I assumed a different name, Robert Hathaway. It wasn't as easy for people to trace who I really was, Bobby Ostrum. Mom assumed I wanted you to be unaware that my father was the owner and CEO of Abbott and Finnegan."

"She was so believable. Your mom is really good at telling a fib."

"It's my fault, I should have told her not to tell you that story. When I put her name at the top of the list I gave you, I didn't know she would want some artwork done for Christmas and my dad's birthday. I thought it would be later on next year."

"Who are Abbott and Finnegan?"

"They were bankers that financed the firm at the beginning. Dad thought if he used the names of the financiers in the name of the company, they would more readily put up the money. He was right, it worked."

"Bob, I just got an idea. What would Olivia do if I tell her we are going to be married?"

Bob laughed, "Boy, you have a sinister streak in you! I came by

today to ask you to go to a Christmas party next Sunday evening, but what a good idea! We could have some fun with my parents. Would you be my date at the party?"

"I'd like to go to the party; thanks for asking. Do you think saying we're getting married would upset your parents?"

"Oh yah! You and I have known each other for less than two weeks. My father would go nuts! He's very conservative, but Mom would want to help plan the wedding. I'm pleased that you'll go to the party. It's semi-formal and in a penthouse where the firm's most important clients stay when they're in town. All the firm's employees and their wives or significant others will be there. I imagine about fifty people will come. If you have any questions about what to wear, just ask my mom."

"She hasn't told you she is altering some of her dresses for me?"

"Is that right? Boy, she is getting sneaky. She must really like you, Karen. That's two of the Ostroms. I'm positive my sister will like you. As soon as Dad gets to know you, he'll be on board too."

Karen couldn't help but smile and said, "That'll make the wedding easier, won't it?"

Bob laughed again, "You have a great sense of humor."

Bob gave Karen a hug and said, "I'll pick you up for the party at 7:00 p.m. It should be fun! Do you think we should make an announcement?"

"You are just as nutty as I am, Robert."

Hathaway went over to the card table and said hi to the kids before he left the store. Karen couldn't hear what Suzy and Bob were saying but Hathaway leaned over the table and wrote something on a piece of paper.

As Bob went out the door, he turned around and stuck his head back in the shop, smiled, and said, "Bye dear."

Karen started laughing and said, "You'd better get out of here; I'm still working."

Karen must have smiled for several minutes. Her exchanges with Bob had been illuminating to say the least. Work on the portraits

continued for another fifteen minutes before curiosity got the best of her. Karen couldn't wait any longer. She had to ask Suzy what Bob had written. She put down her brush and walked over to the card table.

"Suzy, what did Mr. Hathaway write on your paper?"

"I asked him to print Merry Christmas and Happy New Year on one of my pictures."

Karen suddenly remembered she had forgotten to ask Bob if he had left the ornaments outside their door. But, now she had an example of his printing to compare to that on the messages from inside the ornaments. She was still going to do some detective work! Who, other than Bob, would have left the ornaments at her door?

CHAPTER 14

Inconclusive Evidence

When Ekstroms arrived at the apartment, Karen started preparing dinner. They watched the news, listened to the weather report and had their meal. As Karen did the dishes she asked Suzy to find the notes that were found in the Christmas ornaments. Karen put the notes and Suzy's picture with Bob's printing side by side on the kitchen counter so she could compare them.

"Hmm. These don't look at all alike."

Karen noted that the letters on the little notes slanted backward and those on Suzy's picture slanted forward. She remembered from a TV crime show that left handed writing sometimes slanted backward.

"So, who do we know that is left handed? Suzy, do you know any adults that are left handed?"

Suzy thought for a moment and answered, "No Mom. I can't think of anyone."

Karen returned Suzy's picture to her daughter and put the little notes in a kitchen drawer. As the evening progressed, Karen decided the ornaments might have come from someone that worked for the clothing company who wanted the children to have a Merry Christmas. A thousand dollars would certainly guarantee that outcome. She felt a little guilty about the amount of money they were given so she decided to donate some of it to a charity. Tomorrow, when Olivia arrived, she would ask Bob's mother what charity could best use the money.

Thursday started just as Wednesday had. Olivia knocked on the door a few minutes after 8:00 a.m.

As soon as she entered the apartment, Olivia asked, "Did Bobby ask you to go to the party?"

"He did, and I said yes, of course."

"Good! I only had time to do the alterations on two of the dresses. I'll do the others tonight or tomorrow."

"No hurry. I only need one for the party."

Olivia had the altered blue and green dresses for Karen to try on again. Karen slipped into the blue one and put on a pair of black heels. She hadn't had time to find some blue ones to go with the dress.

"Karen, you look fantastic! A little makeup, blue heels and you'll be good to go."

"Olivia, you did a great job on the dress. I don't know how to thank you! You are a real lifesaver! Now I have to wear heels around the house for a while to get used to them. I haven't dressed up in a long time."

"I noticed you were a little unsteady in the heels, but you'll be fine. Try on the green one and see how it fits."

"Okay. Just a minute."

Karen went to the bedroom and changed into the green dress. She looked at herself in the mirror and decided the blue one was much nicer. The blue material had a metallic luster; the green one was shiny but not metallic and the back was cut a little too low. When Olivia saw Karen in the green dress, she remarked, "I like the blue one better, Karen."

Karen smiled, "You have good taste, Olivia. That's my opinion also."

"I'll alter the white one next. Then you'll have three dresses to wear. I'll do the red one later. You can use it for Valentine's."

"The white one is really nice. I can use it for my wedding dress."

"Wedding dress?" Olivia quizzed.

"Oh! I meant to tell you when you first arrived; Robert and I are getting married on Christmas Eve."

Olivia was stunned. She didn't know what to say at first. She put her hand to her mouth and thought for a few moments. Karen watched Olivia and fought off laughter. Karen just smiled and said, "When Bob asked me to the Christmas party, he also asked me to marry him."

"I can't believe Robert would be that impulsive. It's just not like him! His father is going to have a heart attack!"

"You think your husband will be upset?"

"Oh yes! He hasn't even met you yet. I think you are a wonderful person, Karen, but this just isn't the way we do things. Bob should take time to get to know you, maybe a year to eighteen months, before there is a wedding."

"Well, we talked about that. But since the children and I like Bob so much and he likes all of us, we thought we would go ahead. Since I am just developing my art business, marrying Bob offers my family some needed security."

Karen thought she might be laying it on a bit too thick, but she would tell Bob everything she said to his mom. Besides, she and Bob would set things straight at the party.

"Don't get me wrong, Karen. I would love to have you as my daughter-in-law. I just think this marriage thing is too soon."

"I understand your concern, Olivia. But after Bob and I talked it out, I thought it would be all right. However, the kids don't know about it yet. I intend to tell them tonight. I think they'll be happy to have a new daddy."

"Uh huh. Well, I'd better go now. I have some errands to run and need to get some more Christmas cards sent. I'll have more to say in my cards now, that's for sure."

"Thank you for the dresses, Olivia. You did a professional job. I'll get some shoes today. I'll take a few minutes off from Finley's and pick up the shoes. Oh yes! I have a question for you. What is a good charity to give some money to? I want to give some of the thousand dollars from the ornaments to someone who needs the money more than I do."

"What a nice thing to do! How about the Salvation Army? They can always use money during the holidays to take care of people."

"That's a good idea, Olivia. Thank you. Bye now, see you later."

Olivia had on her coat, her hand on the doorknob. She had a concerned look on her face. She opened the door and looked back a Karen.

"Goodbye, Karen…dear."

The door closed. Karen walked over and locked it.

"Phew!" She took a deep breath, "That went fairly well."

Karen thought to herself. Olivia is really concerned. Maybe telling her that Bob and I were going to be married wasn't such a good idea.

"What did you say, Mommy?" Suzy asked as she walked toward her mother.

"Oh nothing. I was just talking to myself again."

"I need some help with some new words. What does designate mean?"

Karen helped Suzy with the new words and then changed into her work clothes.

When Karen and the kids arrived at the glass shop, Finley was already busy with customers. Nearly half an hour slipped by before Karen was able to talk to Finley. She told him about the joke she and Bob were playing on Hathaway's parents.

"I hope it doesn't backfire, Karen. A set of angry in-laws is not a desirable thing to have."

"We'll tell them about it at the party on Sunday. Hopefully, they'll laugh at the joke. I need to go to a store and buy some blue heels for the party. Could you please watch the kids for about fifteen minutes?"

"No problem. It looks like John is already napping."

"Thanks Evan, I'll be right back."

On his way back to his workbench, Finley stopped to see what Suzy and Larry were drawing. Suzy was making decorations and Larry was drawing Santa Claus and his helpers.

"Who is the fellow in blue, Larry?"

"Superman."

"Superman?" Finley quizzed.

"He is going to help Santa deliver the presents. He goes so fast; he can deliver things faster than Santa can. Santa will be able to take a break and rest a little bit."

"That is a clever idea, Larry."

Amused at Larry's logical thinking, Finley returned to his workbench.

Karen returned in about twenty minutes with a plastic bag containing a shoebox.

"Any problems, Mr. Finley?"

"Nope. Everyone behaved. I think they realize Christmas is coming soon and being naughty isn't good for Santa to know about."

Larry and Suzy looked up at Mr. Finley when they heard naughty and Santa in the same sentence.

"Mom, we've been good," contributed Suzy.

"Yes, no fighting," added Larry.

"Mr. Finley, may I use the phone to call my sister? I need her to baby-sit on Sunday evening. The quarter is over and school is out until the first week in January, so Jen should be free."

"Go right ahead, Karen. You have a big date Sunday!"

Karen arranged for Jen to come to dinner Sunday evening and take care of the kids while she was at the Christmas party with Bob. Karen also asked Jen to stay with her and the kids for Christmas. Jen was so busy with graduate studies very little time was left for dating. She didn't have a steady boyfriend, but had pizza and beer with several other graduate students about twice a month. Most of her evenings were spent in the lab working on her research, studying for exams or preparing for undergraduate tutorials and labs. After Jen

finished her master's degree she wanted to find a job. The thought of pursuing a doctorate was far from her mind.

CHAPTER 15

The Party

Friday and Saturday went by in a flash. Great strides were made with the portraits and Finley's thriving business was keeping the elderly gentleman extremely busy. The window paintings and the change in the store name seemed to be having a positive influence on his sales. Or, maybe it was having Karen and the kids in the front of the store. Karen's artwork was drawing the attention of many of the shoppers. Some people would visit the shop everyday to monitor the progress on her portraits. And, some returning visitors would buy additional Christmas decorations to give as gifts.

As Karen and her kids were getting ready to leave the shop Saturday, Finley talked to Karen.

"I looked over all the receipts since you painted the windows and sales are up 30% over last year. Karen, your paintings on the windows and the renaming of the store have really influenced my business. I owe you a lot for your good work."

"Thank you for the opportunity to earn some money and for the use of your store as a studio. The kids and I are having a lot of holiday fun. You have been good to all of us."

"I hope you enjoy your Christmas party on Sunday. On Monday, let me know how it turned out."

"I'll give you all the details, Evan. See you on Monday. Good night."

"Good night Ekstroms!"

"Good night Mr. Finley," answered the children.

Bob climbed into the driver's seat at 6:20 p.m. He let the car warm up for about five minutes before he drove from the below ground level parking onto the street. The car thermometer indicated the outside temperature was 19 degrees. It would take about twenty minutes to drive to Karen's so he would be a few minutes early. He turned on the seat heaters to warm up the cold leather. He was pretty sure Karen would appreciate a warm rear and legs. She probably wasn't a fan of goose bumps. It would take them another fifteen minutes to get to the party from Karen's apartment.

Bob knocked on Karen's door. He heard someone say "Just a minute!" so he leaned against the opposite wall. In about ten seconds, the door opened.

Suzy greeted him. "Hi Mr. Hathaway! Come in. Mom's almost ready."

"How have you kids been?" Bob asked with a smile.

"We've been great. Jen is staying with us while you and Mom go to the party. You can sit on the sofa with me while you wait. Can I smell you?"

"Sure you can. Do I pass the smell test?"

Suzy leaned over to Bob, inhaled and said, "You smell really good!"

"Thank you. Now it's my turn!"

Bob leaned over to Suzy, inhaled and said, "You smell like flowers!"

Suzy giggled and said, "I washed my face and hands after dinner."

Bob responded, "Didn't you wash your hands before dinner?"

"Sure I did, silly."

"Oh, I see. You ate with your fingers," Bob winked at Suzy.

Suzy laughed and sat down to watch TV.

John walked over to Bob and pulled on his trouser leg.

Bob smiled at John and said, "How are you John?"

John held out his flashlight and said, "Batman."

Bob answered with "That's a flashlight isn't it?"

John tilted back Batman's head and the light came on but it was very dim.

"I think you need some new batteries for Batman, John. We'll see if we can take care of that."

The bedroom door opened and Jen came out followed by Karen. Jen stepped aside so Bob could get a full view of her sister. Karen was almost unrecognizable. Bob almost gasped audibly. Karen was one of the most beautiful women he had ever seen. He stood and all he could say was "Wow!"

"You like?" asked Karen as she pirouetted.

"Yes! You are gorgeous! All the women at the party are going to be jealous. And the men are going to envy me. We are going to have a great night at the party. My dad is going to be happy I brought such a beautiful lady to the party."

"Thank you. I'd like you to meet my sister, Jennifer. She's a graduate student in chemistry. Jen, this is Bob Hathaway."

Jen and Bob shook hands.

Jen smiled at Bob and said, "Karen, I think you have a keeper."

Bob said, "Brains and beauty in the same family!" Bob suddenly said, "That didn't come out the way I wanted. You sisters are both smart and pretty."

Jen smiled, "I'm very happy to meet you, Bob."

"And I'm pleased to meet you. Thanks for taking care of the kids while we're at the party. We shouldn't be too late."

"Have her back by 11:00!" Jen said with a stern look, then laughed.

Bob smiled and said, "Is that p.m. or a.m.?"

Karen had gone back into the bedroom and returned with a long fur coat. She handed it to Bob and he helped her into it. Estelle, the elderly lady from down the hall, had loaned Karen the coat for this special occasion.

"Thank you sir."

"You are welcome, ma'am. Let me talk to Larry before we leave."

Larry was on the floor next to the Christmas tree building a garage out of Lego's for his transformer. Bob knelt down beside him and said, "You're the man of the house while we're gone Larry. Take care of your brother and sister. O.K.?"

"O.K., Mr. Hathaway."

Larry held up his transformer and said, "We'll take care of everyone."

"Good boy, Larry. We'll see you later."

About fifteen minutes later, Karen and Bob were entering the penthouse on the top floor of a thirty floor high rise. Bob's parents were welcoming the guests as they exited the elevator entering the large lavishly decorated living room.

"Dad, I'd like you to meet Karen Ekstrom. Karen, this is my father, Vernon Ostrum."

"I've heard so much about you, sir. It's nice to finally meet you. I see where Bob gets his good looks."

Karen extended her hand and Mr. Ostrum clasped her hand in both of his.

"I see one of the reasons Bob is interested in you. You are a very beautiful young woman. Olivia told me you are a very talented artist."

"Thank you. I'm still learning, sir. Each time I take on a project I learn new ways of doing things."

"That sounds like me with architecture, Karen. I hope you enjoy the party."

"Hi Olivia. The party decorations are beautiful."

"Thank you, dear. I think you are the prettiest woman here tonight. Let me take your coat."

Olivia handed Karen's coat to a hatcheck girl who gave Karen a ticket.

Karen stuck the ticket in Bob's suit coat pocket. Bob took Karen's hand and the couple started mingling with the other guests. After the guests had all arrived, the accordion-like room separator was removed and everyone was asked to take a seat.

The turkey and dressing meal was not sumptuous, but certainly adequate. Drinks were served, but no alcohol, which surprised Karen. She had expected to see the spectacle of at least one drunken act at the party. The ringing sound of a fork tapping on a glass drew the attention of everybody to Vernon Ostrum, who was standing.

He cleared his voice, "I have an announcement."

The room became silent except for a few caterers moving around pouring coffee and soft drinks.

"I would like everyone to know that my son Robert and his beautiful companion, Karen, are going to be married Christmas Eve."

Karen's mouth dropped open and she grabbed Bob's arm. They looked at each other in surprise.

"Oh, my gosh!" Karen said quietly, leaning toward Bob.

"I'll take care of this," Bob stated as he pushed back his chair and stood up.

When Bob stood, everyone applauded. "I just want to straighten things out.

Karen and I are not getting married this Christmas Eve."

Bob looked at Karen, smiled and continued, "We might plan that for next Christmas Eve. We have only known each other for about three weeks. We thought we would play a trick on my parents, but we didn't fool them at all. We should have known they were too smart to fall for such a ruse. They knew that both Karen and I are too mature to rush into a marriage without investing the time to develop a strong relationship."

Bob smiled, looked at his mother and father and said, "We're sorry we tried to fool you. We were curious to see how you would react. We should have known you wouldn't fall for our sudden marriage decision. If Karen and I try to trick you again, it will be after much more thought has gone into it."

Everyone laughed and applauded again. Bob sat down and Karen grabbed his hand and gave it a little squeeze. She smiled at Bob and said, "That was really good!"

"Thank you! Did I sound like a lawyer?" he asked with a grin.

"Nope. You told the truth; we were just having some fun."

Mr. Ostrum gave out some awards and each couple had their choice of several gifts. Karen and Bob chose a bottle of wine to share at a later date. After about an hour of sitting at the tables, the guests were free to move around the penthouse. It seemed like everyone at the party wanted to meet Karen. She hadn't shaken hands that often since her wedding. She was happy she wasn't a politician or a celebrity.

After another hour, Karen noticed people were beginning to leave. Bob looked at his watch and noted it was about half-past ten.

"Have you had enough, Karen?" he asked.

Karen smiled, giving a little sigh. "I think so. I believe I met everyone in the building except the janitors."

Bob laughed. "We could stay and you could meet the cleaning crew — just kidding. I'm glad you met my dad and my sister Lisa. They both think you're great. The people I work with enjoyed meeting you also. I'll get your coat."

When Bob was getting Karen's coat, Karen walked over to Olivia and thanked her for such a nice party.

Karen spoke more seriously, "I wanted to confess that it was my idea to say we were getting married. I didn't mean any harm. Bob and I both thought it would be a good joke."

Olivia said, "When Vernon and I discussed it, we figured you two were just pulling our legs, so we thought we would turn the tables on you. I was watching you when Vernon made the announcement. You looked shocked and I had a good laugh. You and Bob are a good fit. I hope it works out for you both. We would love to have you in the family and your kids would double the number of grandchildren."

"Olivia, you are so nice. Your whole family is wonderful. Thanks again for the wonderful evening."

Bob helped Karen into her coat and they moved toward the elevator.

Vernon and Bob shook hands and Karen said, "Thank you for the great party, Mr. Ostrum. You and Olivia were very clever with that announcement."

Karen stepped toward Vernon and gave him a hug.

Vernon hugged her back, smiled and said, "We certainly enjoyed having you here tonight. I hope we see you often."

CHAPTER 16

Returning Home

Bob and Karen were about ten blocks from Karen's apartment. Bob took his foot off the gas and coasted slowly to a red light. They had been talking about some of the guests at the party and there was a lull in the conversation.

Bob commented, "Boy, this red light is taking forever."

In a few seconds, the light turned green and Bob stepped on the gas. When they were about half way through the intersection, Karen noticed movement from the right and yelled at Bob.

"Watch out!"

Bob stepped hard on the gas pedal and the car surged forward. There was a loud crunching noise and the car was spun around in the intersection. The air bags inflated and forced Karen and Bob back into their seats. The car stopped along the curb to the left of the direction they had been traveling. The car had spun 270 degrees. Karen couldn't see anything and at first she thought she was blind. The air bags deflated and she saw Bob looking at her from the driver's seat.

"Karen, are you all right?"

"I...I think so. My wrist hurts. I think the air bags pushed my arm against my forehead. What about you?"

"My right arm and shoulder hurt. I can't feel anything in my right hand. I hope nothing is broken. I'm going to call 911. Did you see who hit us?"

Karen answered, "I think it was a small white truck."

Bob had his cell phone in his left hand and dialed 911.

"We've been in an accident. Someone hit us at Jefferson and 9th. I think it was a white truck. No. We're okay except for some sore arms from the airbags hitting us. No. We aren't bleeding. Okay. Thank you."

"They're sending a police car and an ambulance, just in case."

Someone tapped on Bob's door and motioned for him to lower the window. It was a policeman holding a flashlight in his right hand. Bob lowered the window and the officer asked, "Anybody injured in there?"

"My date and I both have sore right arms."

"An ambulance is on the way. Would you mind stepping out of the car and taking a sobriety test?"

"No, I don't mind. We just left a party but haven't had any alcohol."

Bob opened the door and got out of the car. He looked around and could see another officer directing traffic in the intersection. The back end of the truck that hit them was jutting out into the intersection. It had come to rest against a street light pole. The driver was sitting on the curb with his head in his hands, his elbows on his knees.

Bob passed the field sobriety test and the officer walked over to the truck driver and had him stand. It only took a few seconds for the officer to determine the truck driver was intoxicated. He put handcuffs on the driver and placed him in the back seat of his police car.

Bob didn't bother to look at the damage to his car. He went to Karen's door, opened it and helped her out. When Karen stood up, she was a little dizzy and Bob held onto her elbow to keep her from falling. He had to hold her up with his left hand, his right arm was sore and his fingers were numb. Bob moved his arm around and decided he must have hit his funny bone. Sensation was returning to his fingers and he felt a tingling in his forearm. An ambulance

appeared at the intersection and pulled over beside Bob's car.

An EMT from the ambulance approached them and asked, "May I check you for injuries?"

"Yes. Please check Karen first. She seems to be a little dizzy."

Karen related her suspicions about her arm hitting her in the forehead. The EMT checked her pulse and eye movements and then her arm and forehead.

The EMT remarked, "You might have had a slight concussion. You should be checked by a doctor at a hospital to make sure its nothing serious."

Karen was glancing at the temperature on a building sign and it read "22 F". No wonder she was feeling cold. Bob was noticing the breath of the EMT and said to Karen,

"I think you'd better get back in the car."

Bob assisted her and closed the car door. As soon as Karen sat down she began moving the deflated airbags out of the way. Bob was talking to the officer that had administered the sobriety test. Bob gave the officer his license, registration and insurance. The policeman motioned for him to get back in the car.

Bob opened the door and got in. "It will be a few minutes and we'll drive to the hospital and be examined by a doctor. I have to sign a report for the officer before we can leave. Do you feel all right now?" Bob displayed a concerned look.

"I'm feeling better now," Karen smiled a little apprehensively.

Bob moved the air bags out of his way and tried the ignition. To his surprise, the car started and he turned on the seat warmers. He got out of the car to see the damage to the right rear of the vehicle. The truck had made contact with the back of the car behind the back wheel and the tire was not damaged. The fender was bent toward the tire but not enough to keep it from rotating. The taillights were mangled and the trunk lid was bent but hadn't sprung open.

The officer approached the car as Bob was getting back into the driver's seat. He lowered the window and the officer returned his papers, then handed him a report.

"Mr. Hathaway, please sign where I have marked the form with an X."

Bob took the form, read it and signed it with his left hand; his right hand was still a little numb.

Karen watched as Bob signed the form. She suddenly realized Bob was writing with his left hand. Now she had him! Bob must have put the money in the ornaments! She was not going to let him know that she had discovered what he had done. That would come later. She smiled and felt great satisfaction figuring out who their benefactor was. What a great guy Bob was! He had been clever, but not quite clever enough. She thought how patience is sometime rewarded.

Bob handed the form to the officer and was told they could go. Bob knew where the nearest hospital was; he drove past it on his way home nearly every night. Bob drove to the emergency room and a doctor examined Karen's arm and forehead. He checked her eyes and coordination and said she probably suffered a small concussion. She should rest for a couple of days. Another doctor had Bob go though some arm movements and shoulder rotations. He told Bob not to overdue any exercise with his right arm. The numbness should go away by morning. With that, they left the hospital and Bob took Karen home.

Bob escorted Karen to her apartment. She was no longer dizzy but Bob put his arm around her anyway. It was after midnight. Karen knocked and they waited for Jen to open the door. When the door opened, Jen said, "Well, it's about time!" Jen smiled at Bob and continued, "I thought I told you to have Karen home by eleven."

Bob replied, "We were delayed. We were involved in an accident."

Jen got serious and with a concerned look said, "Really?"

Karen and Bob entered the apartment, took off their coats and tossed them on the sofa. After they were all seated, Karen related the night's activities to Jen. Jen yawned, said she would talk about it in the morning, excused herself and went to bed.

Bob said, "I'd better go. You need some rest. I'm going to leave my cell phone with you in case you need to make an emergency call.

I've got another one at home. I'll call you in the morning to make sure you're all right."

He handed Karen the phone and put on his coat. Karen followed him to the door and said, "Thank you for an exciting evening. I really enjoyed the party."

"Thank you for going with me. You were really great with everyone, especially my dad and sister."

Bob opened the door, turned, took Karen in his arms and kissed her.

Karen smiled and started laughing.

Bob was surprised and said, "Is there something funny the way I kiss?"

"No!" Karen could hardly speak due to her laughing. "I never thought I'd kiss a lawyer! And I liked it!" Her laughter stopped but she couldn't stop smiling.

Karen kissed Bob again. Bob said. "I think it's getting warm in here! I'd better go. Good night Karen."

"Good night Bob. Talk to you tomorrow."

Karen closed the door, sighed and leaned against it smiling.

"Wow, what a night!"

She looked at her watch, "Ugh, it's 12:30; time for bed."

Someone was tapping on Karen's car window. She was stopped at a red light but the car was backwards. How was she going to turn the car around? There was too much traffic. There was another tap on her door and a policeman was saying, "Karen, are you all right?"

"Karen?"

Karen woke up and realized she had been dreaming. She looked at the nightstand clock. It was 9:03 a.m. She sat up and rubbed her eyes.

"Who is it?" she asked.

Jen opened the bedroom door and leaned into the room. "Hey sleepyhead, are you feeling okay?"

"Uh. I guess so. I was dreaming. For a second, I didn't know where I was."

Karen sat up in bed and stretched her arms over her head. She looked at her right forearm and could see a bruised spot about the size of a quarter. "That's what hit me in the head when that idiot hit Bob's car," she explained to Jen.

Jen sat down on the bed and said, "I'm glad you're okay. I was afraid your little concussion might be a problem so I thought I'd better wake you up. So what do you think of Bob?"

Karen smiled and said, "He is really a good man, Jen---and a good kisser. I never thought I'd ever kiss a lawyer. Oh! He's supposed to call me this morning. I'd better get up. What are the kids doing? I don't hear them."

"I've got them making Christmas decorations on the kitchen table. I told them to be quiet so you could sleep after coming home late. I've got to tell you something really funny. After you left last night, we were watching TV. During some commercials, I went into the kitchen to make some popcorn. In about a minute, Suzy came in the kitchen and asked me what decapitated coffee was."

"Really! I'm sorry I missed that," Karen smiled but disappointment showed too.

"I told her it was decaffeinated coffee and explained what caffeine is. Do you think Suzy will become a chemist?"

"Anything but an artist, or a writer! Did you tell her what decapitated means?"

"Nope. She didn't ask and I didn't volunteer the information. I thought it was better that way."

"Good thinking, Jen."

Bob's cell phone rang. Both women were startled. Karen leaned over to the nightstand and picked up the phone.

"Hello Bob. Oh, I'm fine except for a bruise on my arm. How are you?"

"I got up this morning and couldn't move my right arm so I went to the hospital."

A look of concern appeared on Karen's face.

Jen got off the bed and went back to the kitchen so Karen could talk in private.

"You're in the hospital?"

"Yah. I called a taxi to take me to St. Luke's. It's closer to my condo than the hospital we went to last night. The doctor said I probably have some tendon and ligament damage. He said I might also have pinched a nerve. I've got my arm in a sling so I can't drive. Are you all right?"

"I'm fine. I just woke up from a confusing dream."

"Was I in the dream?"

"Nope." Karen smiled and laughed. "I'll tell you about it later. I have to get up and get a move on. I have to go to work at Finley's today. Are you staying home?"

"Yep. I've got to get used to doing things with my left hand. I'm supposed to rest my arm for at least a week."

"Well, take care of your arm. I'll talk to you later. Thanks for calling. Bye."

"Okay. See you later."

Karen dressed quickly and went to see what the kids were doing. They were having fun cutting out pictures of toys from a catalog and gluing them to colored paper to make wrapping paper of their own designs.

"Bob is in the hospital," Karen volunteered to Jen.

"What happened?"

"When he got up this morning, he couldn't move his right arm. Some tendons and ligaments were damaged so he has to wear a sling for the next week or so. He can't use his right arm at all for at least a week."

"Wow. That's a bummer. But he doesn't need his arm for kissing," Jen winked at Karen.

Karen smiled and said, "I think you are getting jealous!"

"Maybe, but right now the chemistry I'm doing is with molecules

in the lab."

"I guess he'll use a taxi until his arm heals and his car's repaired," Karen commented. "At the party, Bob told me this week was going to be busy winding up some end of the year contracts. But, he wanted to make sure we attend the Christmas party on Friday 'cause Santa would be there for the kids. It starts at 2:00 p.m."

"That should be nice since Friday is Christmas Eve," Jen added.

"Can you come too?" Karen asked her sister.

"Sure. Will there be cake and ice cream?"

Karen laughed. "I don't know. But just think, Jen, you can sit on Santa's lap and ask him to bring you a handsome man for Christmas."

"Hey! Maybe I can find someone to write my thesis. I just hope he's a good kisser like Bob is." Jen smiled and moved away from Karen as if her sister might throw something at her.

"You're coming over for Christmas aren't you?" Karen asked.

"Sure. I have some presents for the kids and you, dear sister."

"I hope you didn't waste any of your TA money on us."

"Nope! I spent a total of two dollars on you and the kids."

"Just don't go wild. They will have plenty for Christmas this year." Karen stated.

Jen was lying but she knew Karen didn't want her to spend more than a few dollars on each of them.

Karen checked the kids to see what they were doing. Suzy stopped using the scissors and looked up at her mother.

"Mom, your face is dirty."

"Really? I'd better look in a mirror."

Karen went in the bathroom and said, "Jen, why didn't you remind me that I didn't wash off my makeup last night?"

Jen smiled, laughed and replied, "Oh! I thought those were bruises as a result of the car wreck!"

"Jen, you are so bad! You joke around more than I do!"

"I would have told you before you went outside."

Karen came out of the bathroom and looked at Jen. "I have to get the kids ready to go to Finley's. What are you doing this afternoon?"

"Absolutely nothing. Why don't you go to Finley's and I'll stay with the kids?"

Jen smiled, "That will give you a chance to buy some things."

"That would be wonderful. What a great sister you are!"

"I am good, aren't I? You'd better remember this when you're shopping," Jen chuckled.

CHAPTER 17

Awesome Results

Karen called Bob from the glass shop. Home from the hospital, he was getting used to doing things with his left hand. Combing his hair was difficult and he found that if he didn't look in the mirror, he accomplished the task more quickly. Fortunately, he had an electric can opener and preparing things to eat wasn't too difficult. He wasn't a very good cook anyway and could always get things delivered if necessary. On Tuesday, he was going back to his office to wrap up end of the year final details.

Mr. Finley was curious about the party on Sunday and wanted to hear all about it from Karen. But first, he asked, "Where are the kids today?"

"Jen is staying with them this afternoon so I can do shopping for presents."

Karen told Evan about the people she had met and the results of their practical joke that had backfired. Finley smiled when he heard the results. Karen mentioned the traffic accident briefly.

Finley wasn't sure he had heard Karen correctly.

"And on the way home you had a wreck — with Bob driving?"

"Oh! It wasn't Bob's fault. A drunk hit the back of the car with a delivery truck.

Bob hurt his right arm and has it in a sling. I just got a little bruise."

"I'm sure glad neither of you was badly hurt. That would have messed up your Christmas."

"Speaking of Christmas, I have to call Olivia and tell her she can pick up the painting of her grand kids. I think she'll want to wrap it as a gift for her husband."

Karen extracted the cell phone from her pocket and called Olivia.

"Hi Olivia. This is Karen. I've finished the portrait. When do you want to pick it up?"

"Hi Karen. How about tomorrow at 3:00 o'clock?"

"That would be fine. I'm going to do some shopping this afternoon."

"Bob told me about the wreck. Are you sure you're all right?"

"I'm fine. Thanks for asking. I'll see you tomorrow. Bye."

"I'm glad you are okay. Bye."

"Mr. Finley, I'm going to do some shopping. I should be back in about an hour."

"Okay, Karen. I'll be here making cherubs and angels," Finley smiled and waved to her as she exited the store.

Karen couldn't remember the last time she felt reasonably secure financially. She could afford to get Jen a really nice sweater, but what to get for Bob and Finley? The kids and Jen came first. She would still have some time left before Christmas to buy things for Bob and Evan if she couldn't think of anything today. Boy, having some money sure complicates life. She normally would get presents for the kids and that would be it. Oh, she had almost forgotten Olivia and she couldn't forget Estelle. She told herself to not go overboard, the money had to last until she could depend on a steady income from her artwork, if there were such a thing.

Almost an hour later, Karen was back at Finley's with several packages. Finding things for the kids and Jen was easy. But what would she get for Bob? He seemed to have everything. Karen decided to ask Olivia tomorrow when she came to pick up the painting.

Karen had gone into a men's store on the way back to Finley's

and bought some cologne and aftershave for Evan. It was a new musk scent but wasn't too strong. Evan wouldn't use it if he thought it was too strong for his clientele.

"Karen, I sold your "New Friends" painting. Here is $125 cash. Mrs. Dixon bought it."

Karen tilted her head a little to the right; a questioning look formed on her face.

"Do I know a Mrs. Dixon?" Karen inquired.

"She's the detective that was working for the clothing manufacturer."

"Oh, that's right."

Evan held out the money to Karen.

"Thank you Evan. I'll have to bring in some more of my work. Maybe I'll have another sale before Christmas."

Karen smiled, accepted the money, folded it and pushed it into her jean's pocket.

She stashed her packages under the front window display area out of sight of prying eyes and started a new painting. This one was going to be analogous to illustrations by Rockwell. It was going to be a policeman giving a ticket to a man driving an SUV full of kids with a Christmas tree tied to the roof of the vehicle. Karen smiled as she thought of the title for it to be "Merry Christmas."

A steady flow of customers for Finley's creations made it a little difficult for Karen to make very much progress on her painting. People were milling around the shop and interrupting her sketching to ask questions. She finished a few pencil sketches, decided on proportions and it was time to go home. After telling Mr. Finley goodbye until tomorrow, Karen went to Clausen's Antiques and found a teacup and saucer as a gift for Estelle.

Tuesday arrived with steady snowfall and the temperature had dropped into the twenties. Jen had to visit her lab to check some reactions she had started on the previous Saturday. When Jen could leave her lab, she would come to Finley's. She and Karen would take

the kids shopping after Olivia came to pick up the painting of the grandchildren.

Suzy was on vacation from home schooling for the rest of the year so Karen no longer had to plan lessons. But she had to arrange for Suzy to go to public school. Karen was thinking she would have to spend more time with the boys, since Suzy wouldn't be available until after 2:30 starting next year. She didn't expect Suzy to be a babysitter, but her daughter knew everyone's schedule and helped keep the boys busy and prevented fighting. Suzy deserved something special for Christmas. Karen would have to look at her bank account and decide how much they could afford to buy new school clothes for Suzy; she certainly needed some new things to wear.

Karen and the kids left the apartment at 1:30 and walked to Finley's. The snow slowed them down a little bit because Karen had to carry John part of the way. John couldn't move his short legs fast enough to allow him to keep up. The wind had started blowing around noon and the wind chill made the temperature feel like it was about 15 degrees. They each wore a scarf around their chin and mouth so only their nose stuck out. Running wasn't an option; many of the streets and sidewalks hadn't been plowed or shoveled yet. They all had red cheeks and noses by the time they arrived at the glass shop.

Karen was relieved that the kids had warm winter coats. She would never know who had generously supplied the clothing. She was certain Mrs. Dixon wouldn't divulge the name of the benefactor.

When they arrived at Finley's, Evan was standing just inside the door. He opened the door and ushered them into the shop.

"Good day everyone!" he exclaimed.

"Hi Mr. Finley," they all answered.

Karen helped John out of his coat and gave him a tissue to wipe his runny nose.

Evan held the Kleenex box in front of the other Ekstroms and they each pulled out a tissue. John wasn't very effective with the tissue so Karen cleaned up the aftermath.

Larry observed, "Coming inside on a cold day is like eating soup;

everyone's nose starts running."

"Good observation, Larry," commented Mr. Finley.

Karen smiled and said, "It's so nice and warm in here after that cold walk."

"The wind-chill is terrible, but it's sure good to see you all today."

"Guess what Mr. Finley," Suzy smiled and looked a Finley.

"You bought a car!" Finley quipped.

"No, silly. We get to see Santa Claus on Friday. That's Christmas Eve."

"Oh yes! Bob invited me to come to the party at the Architect's Building Friday afternoon. Is that where Santa is going to be?"

"I don't know." Suzy looked at her mom for help.

"That's right. We'll all go together; Jen's going too."

A customer entered the shop and Evan went to the counter. Karen got the kids busy at the card table and continued working on her new painting. She looked at her watch and noted that Olivia would be showing up in about fifteen minutes to get the painting for her husband.

The next time Karen heard the tinkling of the doorbells, she looked up to see Olivia.

"Hi everybody," was Olivia's cheerful greeting.

"Hi Olivia. Kids, look who's here!"

The kids all said "Hi" but didn't budge from the table. They were all coloring in Christmas coloring books, except John, he was scribbling with crayons on a sheet of white paper. Their minds were on Santa and what he might bring them.

"You have something for me?" inquired a smiling Olivia.

"It's in back. I'll get it, I hope you like it." Karen replied.

Karen returned in a few seconds holding the painting wrapped in brown paper to keep it clean. She put the portrait ensemble on top of the counter and pulled off the paper, revealing the finished artwork.

Olivia's face lit up. "Oh, Karen, this is beautiful! You have

captured the personality of each child."

"I'm so pleased you like it," Karen stated with a big smile.

"Like it? I love it! This is beyond all expectations. What can I pay you?"

"You decide, Olivia."

Olivia got out her checkbook and picked up one of Finley's counter pens. She started writing a check as Karen rewrapped the painting. Karen tied some string around the wrapping so it wouldn't come off and then wrapped some plastic around the brown paper to keep the snow from getting it wet.

"There we go. All ready to travel," announced Karen. She placed the package on the floor by the front door. "I need to ask you about a present for Bob. What can I get him for Christmas?"

Olivia thought for a moment and said, "Don't get him any aftershave or cologne. He gets his from a friend in Texas. It's not a national brand and the scent he likes isn't available here. You could get him some handkerchiefs; he always needs them. Or, a pair of gloves would be nice. He buys large and he likes the light colored leather ones with a liner. Oh, yes, he could use a new thermos."

"Thanks Olivia, that gives me several options."

Olivia handed Karen the check and said, "Thank you Karen. You did a marvelous job!"

"You're welcome, Olivia."

Karen looked at the check in disbelief. The amount was $2,750.00. She immediately thought Olivia had made a mistake. She must have meant the check to be $275.00. Karen looked at the written amount and read it twice, two thousand seven hundred fifty dollars.

"Oh, Olivia! That's too much!"

"No it isn't, dear. I checked with some galleries and the Internet. I'm getting a bargain for the amount I'm paying you. Big name artists charge up to $5,000, and I'm not sure they could do any better than you did. I'm very happy with your work."

"Well, since you put it that way. Thank you so much."

"You are very welcome. Now I have to find a nice frame."

"Mrs. Ostrum, there is a furniture store four blocks from here that has some nice frames. I'll give you the address," volunteered Finley. Evan wrote the address of Colton's Furniture and Appliance on a small piece of paper and handed it to Olivia.

"Thank you, Mr. Finley. That's not far from here. I can walk there from where my car is parked. And before I go, I want to invite everyone to my house Christmas day for dinner. We'll be ready for guests after 3:00 p.m. and we'll eat about 6:00 o'clock. You don't need to bring a thing."

"Thank you, Olivia. I'm having my sister and a neighbor over for Christmas breakfast and to watch the kids open their presents. But we should be finished with that by noon."

"Well, everyone is invited. In fact, I'll drive the suburban over and pick you up at your apartment. I'll call you. You still have Bob's phone?"

"Yes, I do. That would be awesome," Karen smiled and almost laughed when she used the word awesome. She explained to Olivia that kids use the expression "awesome, dude" for something excellent or impressive. Olivia hadn't heard the expression before.

"Okay. I'll see you on Friday. I'm going to be helping Santa with the children. I'll be over to pick you up on Christmas day at 3:00 p.m."

"That sounds awesome, Olivia," Karen smiled.

Olivia answered, "Later, Dude." They both laughed as Olivia left the shop.

CHAPTER 18

Where is Bob?

Karen ran over to the bank and deposited Olivia's check. She withdrew several hundred dollars from her account. The primary use for the money was for Christmas presents, but she also wanted to pay Finley a commission. When she got back to Finley's, Karen presented Evan with three hundred dollars.

"Whoa, Karen. What's this for?" exclaimed Finley.

"That is ten percent of my December sales. Remember our deal?"

"Well, all right. Olivia must have paid you well. She sure liked your painting."

"It looks like the poor days are over, Evan. Since you allowed me to use the store as my studio, I have made over three thousand dollars. I will probably have to pay taxes for this year. What a bummer!" her smile turned to an expression of disgust.

"Yep. There is always something to tarnish the silver lining, isn't there?" Evan smiled.

"There is a good side though. Having to pay taxes makes me feel like I'm a real member of society. Living off food stamps and such doesn't do much for one's self esteem."

"I probably don't need to tell you this, but make sure you keep some for a rainy day," advised Finley.

"Yes. I've set up a savings account as a nest egg."

It was nearly 4:00 p.m. when Jen arrived. While she warmed up, the two women had tea with Finley. After the tea and some oatmeal

raisin cookies for all, they bundled up the children and set off for Karen's apartment. The two women talked like schoolgirls all the way home. Even though the temperature was still in the twenties, they didn't even notice the cold. Karen told Jen of her plans to have Evan, Bob and Estelle over on Christmas morning. Then, in the afternoon they would all go to Ostrum's for Christmas dinner.

"Karen, this Christmas is turning out to be awesome!" Jen laughed.

Laughing, Karen replied, "Awesome, Dude!"

Wednesday morning, Bob called to see how everyone was. He said he was still adapting to using his left arm and hand. Doing things with his left hand certainly slowed him down. Though he still wore the sling, feeling had been slowly returning to his right hand, however, he thought the doctor had been a little optimistic about the recovery time. He deduced it was going to take at least two weeks, maybe longer. He told Karen he would see everyone on Friday afternoon when the kids visit with Santa. Karen said she would take her camera to the party. She wanted to get pictures of the kids talking to Santa.

Jen was going to watch the kids while Karen went to Finley's but Karen needed help carrying more of her paintings to the store. Karen asked Estelle if she could watch the kids for about an hour. Estelle agreed and the two younger women carried six paintings to Finley's. After arriving at Finley's, Jen warmed up a bit before returning to the apartment to relieve Estelle. Jen was to ask Estelle to come over Christmas morning for breakfast and watch the kids open their presents. Karen didn't want Estelle to get the kids any gifts. If Estelle wanted, she could bring something to eat, perhaps some cinnamon rolls.

Karen priced her artwork and put it on display. Hopefully, someone looking for Finley's sculptures would buy a painting before Christmas. As she was putting price tags on the paintings, Karen came up with an idea for a gift for Olivia.

"Evan, could you make a Santa kissing Mrs. Claus for me to give to Olivia? I was thinking of something that could be a table

centerpiece or would decorate the mantel above a fireplace. I'll pay you for it."

"No you won't! Sure, I can do that. I'll get started on it tonight after I close the shop. It should be ready by Friday. You can give it to Mrs. Ostrum when we go over for Christmas dinner."

"Thank you! That would be great! You are really a good man. I'll tell Santa you have been a very good boy." Karen smiled, happy that she would be able to give Olivia something unique.

Now she only had to get something for Bob and Mr. Ostrum. She made up her mind to get gloves for Bob and handkerchiefs for his father.

"I'm going to the men's store for a few minutes, Evan. I'll be back shortly."

Karen slipped into her coat and nearly ran the half block to the specialty store. She was back in twenty minutes. She was relieved that she had all the bases covered and had plenty of money left over.

Finley's was extremely busy so Karen decided to skip trying to paint. She greeted customers and helped Mr. Finley with sales until about four o'clock. Customer traffic had greatly diminished and Karen asked Mr. Finley if it would be all right for her to go home.

"Sure Karen. Thank you for the assistance. I needed an extra set of hands today. This was one of the busiest days I can remember. I'll see you tomorrow."

Karen grabbed her coat, slid it on and was out the door.

"Bye Evan!"

"Bye Karen!"

Two days before Christmas and Karen had to find some time alone to wrap the presents for the kids and Jen. She decided that she would have Jen come to Finley's with the kids. While Jen took the kids for some treats and last minute shopping, Karen would wrap their presents.

Jen and the kids were gone for an hour and Karen got everything wrapped. She packed the gifts into a large shopping bag and taped

the bag shut. Jen helped Karen wrap the other gifts she had for Evan, Estelle, Bob and Mr. Ostrum. The two women helped Evan with some customers for half an hour. Karen, Jen and the kids left the store at 4:30. The temperature outside had risen to above freezing so the walk home was pleasant compared to the treks two days earlier. Jen and Suzy helped carry the shopping bags full of gifts ready for Christmas. Karen carried John on her right hip and a bag on her left arm. Larry was assigned the task of watching for slick spots and puddles.

Friday morning started a day of excitement for the kids. It seemed like every few minutes they were asking Jen and Karen if it was time to get ready to see Santa. Karen went down the hall to Estelle's and asked her to join them for the party. Estelle declined, stating the walk would be too much for her, but she would go with them tomorrow for Christmas dinner at Ostrum's. While the kids were seeing Santa, Estelle was going to prepare some things for Christmas morning at Karen's. Instead of buying presents, Estelle was making cookies and candy for the kids.

Karen gave the kids cheese, crackers and fruit juice for lunch. She knew they would be eating at the party and didn't want any throwing up later in the day. Jen suggested to Karen they should skip lunch so they could pig out at the party. Karen thought her sister was a little crazy at first but decided to go along with it. She didn't want any winter flab to start accumulating on her body.

Karen announced, "It's 1:15. Time to get ready."

She had let the kids stay in their pajamas. But she didn't have to tell them to get dressed. They scurried for their clothes and left their pajamas where they fell. Jen helped the boys with their shoes and Karen got the kid's coats from the closet.

"Is everyone ready?" Jen asked.

Karen inspected the kids and said, "Let's go!"

The architecture building was about as far as Finley's but at right angles to the route to the glass shop. They arrived with time to spare and joined the throng waiting to see Santa.

"Where did all these kids come from?" Jen asked.

"Most of them are from foster homes," Karen replied. "Each Christmas the firm invites children from foster homes to come see Santa and get presents. Bob told me what they were going to do today. Each child gets a toy they selected from a list at the foster home."

Jen rose up on her tiptoes and looked around. "I don't see Bob."

A loud siren sounded on the street as a fire truck rolled up to the building's entrance. Everyone watched as Santa and five male helpers carrying large bags filed into the building. A lady with a large jar of candy canes followed the helpers. Even though the lady wore a wig and was dressed in a red velvet dress, Karen recognized her instantly. She wore bright red makeup on her cheeks and exhibited an enormous smile.

"Jen! That's Olivia Ostrum. She's fitted with a mic and earphone."

Santa and the helpers climbed two steps onto a raised platform and stashed the bags of toys behind a large armchair which Santa occupied. Two young women, dressed as elves, were Santa's helpers stationed with the bags of toys behind Santa. They also were equipped with mics and earphones, as was Santa.

Olivia, the lady with the candy canes, spoke, "All the children four and under are first. Please gather over here beside me."

The young children gathered near Olivia, some with older siblings and some with parents or guardians. Olivia took out a list and called the name of the first child to talk to Santa. As each child approached Santa, one of the helpers assisted the youngster onto Santa's lap. Karen watched and noticed Santa was using both arms to help lift and hold the children. She dismissed the thought of Bob being Santa. But where was Bob? Besides, whoever Santa was, he had a full face and was heavily built. Of course, Santa suits probably come with padding.

"John Ekstrom," announced Olivia.

"Oh! John, that's you! Let's talk with Santa."

Karen picked John up and carried him to the platform and encouraged him to walk over to Santa. John hesitated and looked up at Karen.

"It's okay John. I'm right here."

John ran over to Santa and was lifted onto Santa's lap.

"Hi John. I have a special present for you."

Santa took a small package from one of the elves and gave it to John.

"Merry Christmas, John."

"Merry Kissmas, Santa."

John wiggled to get down and Santa stood up and steadied John on the platform so he could walk back to Karen.

Karen waved to Santa and said, "Thank you!"

"Let's go see Jen and Suzy and open your package, John."

Larry waited with the other children until his name was called and returned with his present from Santa.

As the older children assembled near the platform, John unwrapped his package and found a lighted magnifier and a package of twenty batteries.

"What is it?" asked John.

"It makes little things bigger so you can see them better and it has a light like Batman." Karen noticed the batteries would also fit John's Batman flashlight. Larry's gift was a large set of Lego building blocks. Larry was going to be able to construct numerous objects and Karen imagined she was going to be stepping on Lego blocks for years to come.

The procedure was repeated until everyone had a gift. Suzy came skipping back from the platform after talking with Santa. She had a package about the size of a shoebox.

Karen had been watching Suzy while she talked with Santa and was curious about the conversation. Suzy started unwrapping her present.

"What did you talk to Santa about, Suzy?"

"I asked him to bring me a new daddy," she answered nonchalantly.

"Look Mom! It's a Barbie!" Suzy held up the box containing

the doll.

"When you asked for a new daddy, what did Santa say?"

"He asked if I had anyone in mind."

"What did you say?"

"I told him somebody like Mr. Hathaway. Oh, look! There's a makeup set, a comb and curlers for her hair."

Suzy looked away from her doll and right at her mom and said, "Santa smells just like Mr. Hathaway."

That did it! That's where Bob is! Karen asked Jen to watch the kids for a minute. She walked over and climbed the stairs to the platform and as Santa finished giving a present to the last child, Karen sat down on Santa's lap.

"Okay, Bob. The jig's up! Did you put the money in the ornaments?"

Santa started laughing almost uncontrollably.

"You…you must have me confused with someone else ma'am. I'm just your everyday Santa Claus handing out gifts to children."

"So you want me to do a lap dance?" Karen threatened.

"Okay. I give up. How'd you know I was Santa? I thought my disguise was pretty good."

"Suzy said you smelled like Mr. Hathaway. You said you would be here, but I didn't see you. You had to be Santa. But I was a little confused since you were using your right arm. Is it all right?"

"Yes. This morning the body shop returned my car. When I opened the door, I moved my shoulder and there was a little pop in my upper arm. Suddenly the feeling came back and the soreness was almost completely gone. It must have been a pinched nerve."

"That's great. Now, please answer my question or I'll start gyrating."

"No! Don't do that. I confess. I put the money in the ornaments."

Karen uttered, "You little devil." Then she leaned over and kissed him.

Suzy was watching her mom sitting on Santa's lap. "Look, Larry! Look, Jen! Santa is kissing Mom!"

Jen smiled and said, "No Suzy, I think your mom is kissing Santa Claus."

Suzy looked at Jen and frowned.

Bob looked around the lobby and said, "Karen, we'd better be careful. People are beginning to stare."

With some resignation, Karen said, "Oh, all right." Karen stood up and said to Bob, "Thank you, Santa, for all you have done for us. Will you come over in the morning to watch the kids open their presents? Estelle, Evan, Jen and I are going to have breakfast. Will you please join us?"

"Well I'll be pretty tired after delivering billions of gifts around the world, but I think I can make it. How about 8:00 a.m.?"

"That sounds great. You can watch the kids while I sleep in," Karen smiled ear to ear and then laughed.

"I've got to get out of this costume. It's starting to itch. I'll be back in about ten minutes and we can all have something to eat."

Santa waddled off to an elevator and returned just like he said he would but five minutes late. He was dressed in a sweatshirt and jeans. Karen had never seen him before in casual clothes. She was impressed with his informal look.

"I'm sorry the change took so long. I had to remove the rubber pieces from my face. It took longer than I expected."

"That's okay, you're here now. Let's get some hotdogs and hot chocolate. We had a light lunch and our stomachs are starting to growl."

They all walked over to the portable hotdog stand and found Evan eating a hotdog smothered in chili.

"Hi everybody!" Evan greeted Ekstroms, Jen and Bob. His mouth was stuffed with a big bite of bun partially sticking out. He poked the bun into his mouth with his finger.

He lifted his plastic fork and pointed at the food as they came

closer and said, "This is so good! I'm going to have a giant case of heartburn. But I don't care. I've got some antacid tablets back at the shop."

He put down his fork so he could shake hands with Bob. "Congratulations, you did a wonderful job with the kids." He was careful to not say Santa in front of the children. He didn't want to spoil any beliefs they may have. He was confident the kids didn't know Bob had been Santa.

The kids from the foster homes were climbing into buses and the staff members were thanking Mrs. Ostrum for the visit with Santa, the food and toys. Karen, Bob and Jen helped the Ekstrom kids get hotdogs and hot chocolate. After the adults filled their plates, they all sat on the edge of the platform to eat.

Evan joined them with a second helping of chili on a hotdog bun. Bob smiled and said, "Mr. Finley, if you are going to work with a flame tonight, you'd better be very careful. All that gas in your shop might cause an explosion."

Bob was sitting between Karen and Jen and they both slugged him playfully.

Evan smiled and answered back, "Since tonight is Christmas Eve, I think I'll stay at home. I'll light a candle so my cat doesn't get too much gas and try to run away."

Evan finished the last bite, stood up and disposed of his plate and fork. He came over to Karen and said, "I'll bring that sculpture to you tomorrow, when I come over for breakfast. I'll get it out of the annealing oven early in the morning."

Karen said, "Thank you Evan. We'll see you tomorrow. Merry Christmas!"

Everyone told Finley "Merry Christmas" and he started toward the door. When he had his coat zipped up and opened the door, he leaned back in the building and said loudly, "Merry Christmas everyone!"

CHAPTER 19

Christmas Day

It was 1:00 a.m. when Karen and Jen finished putting gifts around the Christmas tree. They sat in the kitchen talking for only a few minutes before Karen started dozing off.

"Karen. Go to bed. I'll clean up the table and wipe off the kitchen counters. See you in the morning."

Karen sighed, "Okay. Thanks Jen."

As soon as Jen finished cleaning up, she prepared the sofa bed. Following a quick trip to the bathroom, she slid between the inviting sheets and pulled the thick comforter up to her neck. She thought for a moment, threw back the covers, got up and turned on the lights on the little Christmas tree. There was something soothing about the multicolored lights reflecting off the walls and ceiling. Jen swung her legs under the heavy blanket and closed her eyes.

Jen felt someone sit on the sofa bed. She stirred; opened the eye not buried in her pillow and saw Karen.

"Sorry Jen, but I've kept the kids quiet as long as I could."

Jen yawned and said, "What time is it?"

"It's ten to seven."

Jen smiled and said, "Is that a.m. or p.m.?"

"I'm going to let the kids each unwrap one present now and then they have to wait till everyone gets here."

"That will never happen, Karen. How will they react to torture?"

"Well, I'll think about letting them open another one in an hour. I'm going to need your help getting things ready for breakfast. We need to go to Estelle's and help her carry the goodies she has made. So please, get up!" Karen slapped Jen on the butt and went in the kitchen.

"Boy, you are the bad witch and it isn't even Halloween!" Jen laughed as she tossed the covers back. She dressed quickly, concealed the pullout mattress in the sofa and replaced the cushions. Karen had started the coffee and the kids were asking if they could open anther present…just one more.

"Oh, all right, but just one. Then you have to wait until our guests arrive."

Jen said, "Hah! I knew you couldn't do it!"

Karen went to the door and asked Jen to watch the kids while she went to Estelle's. In about ten minutes, Karen returned with Estelle and three dinner plates full of cookies and frosting coated cinnamon rolls. The plates were set on the kitchen table and Jen lifted the wax paper to take a look. There were three layers of cinnamon rolls, each layer different from the others. Jen couldn't help but poke her index finger into the frosting on one of the rolls and lick the glistening icing from her finger. She scolded herself and poured a cup of coffee.

Estelle had been watching Jen and she said, "I did that too, dear."

Jen replied, "Estelle, that is so good!" and licked her lips. "I can hardly wait to eat a whole cinnamon roll!"

Karen was telling the kids to remember who gave them each gift so proper thanks could be given. The doorbell rang. Suzy ran to the door and opened it. Both Evan and Bob were standing in the hallway with packages.

In unison, Bob and Evan said, "Merry Christmas!"

Suzy opened the door as far as she could and said, "Merry Christmas! Please come in. What's in the packages?"

Evan said, "Oh, all kinds of things. We might even have something for you!"

Suzy turned toward the kitchen and yelled, "Mom, Mr. Finley

and Mr. Hathaway are here! Can we open some more presents?"

"Let's eat first and then we can open the gifts, okay?"

Suzy answered disappointedly, "Oh, all right,"

The kids had some eggs, a cinnamon roll and a small glass of juice. They finished quickly and were back under the tree handling all the packages. Karen had to wash John's face; the icing had been randomly spread from his chin to his eyebrows.

Before the adults sat down to eat, Estelle was introduced to Evan and Bob. Estelle didn't eat much, but she took over the kitchen and kept the mugs full of steaming hot coffee. She cooked some sausages and bacon on the gas stove and warmed the cinnamon rolls in the microwave.

In the middle of breakfast, Karen said, "Estelle, sit down with us and eat something. You don't need to be our chef and waitress."

Estelle replied, "As I cooked during the last couple of days, I ate enough to last me for a week." Her eyes sparkled, she smiled and said, "I don't want to lose my girlish figure and I'm pretending you young people are my children."

Evan retorted, "Young people? I beg your pardon."

Estelle said, "Young man, I'm old enough to be your mother!"

"Well, many amazing things have been accomplished with today's technology, but back in 1943, I don't think that could have been possible."

Everyone laughed, including Estelle. The dirty dishes were removed from the table and the adults joined the children in the living room.

Karen, Jen and Estelle sat on the sofa, Evan occupied the rocking chair and Bob grabbed one of the chairs from the kitchen table.

Karen said, "Let the spectacle begin! Suzy, please bring me the small red cubical package." Karen handed it to Estelle and said, "Merry Christmas."

Estelle removed the card, read it and put it in her lap. "Thank you Karen." She appeared to be a little flustered.

Jen said, "Open the box Estelle, we want to see what's in it."

Estelle carefully removed the tape and unwrapped the small box. She folded the paper as if to save it and opened the box.

"Oh, my. What a beautiful teacup and saucer! Thank you so much!" She got up, went to Karen and gave her a big hug.

"You are welcome, Estelle."

The kids tore the paper off their presents in record speed. Pieces of wrapping paper became airborne, apparent random motion of arms and legs and excited voices resembled the disruption of a small tornado. The flurry was over in about five minutes. The sudden calm was a relief for the adults.

Karen broke the silence. "Suzy, would you please deliver the presents to the adults. You can have Larry help you. Just tell him who they belong to."

As the adults received their gifts, the kids played with the toys they had received. When a gift was opened, appropriate thanks and comments were exchanged. Bob noticed that John had his lighted magnifier but wasn't using the foldout lenses, just the light.

"John, where is Batman?" Bob inquired.

John got up and went in the bedroom. He returned with the Batman flashlight and handed it to Bob. Bob flipped the head back but there was no light; the batteries hadn't been changed. "John, can you get the batteries you got from Santa yesterday?"

John just stood and looked at Bob. He didn't understand batteries.

Karen was observing Bob and John interacting and she said, "John, Santa gave you a heavy package when he gave you the one with the light. Can you bring the heavy package to Mr. Hathaway?"

John disappeared into the bedroom and returned with the battery pack, which he gave to Bob.

"Now we're cooking, John. Good boy. Let me show you how to fix Batman so his light will work again. Then I will show you how to use the magnifier."

Karen smiled, enjoying the sight of Bob and John installing the new batteries. She looked over at Estelle. Suzy and Estelle were playing with the Barbie that Suzy had gotten from Santa the day before. Evan was talking to Larry, who was asking for help with the directions for building a bridge out of Legos.

Karen turned toward Jen and said, "It looks as if I have found three more babysitters."

"I know one you'll be having over, but I doubt it will be for babysitting." she winked at Karen. Karen just smiled.

After all the presents from under the tree were distributed and opened, Karen said, "Well, kids, let's clean up the mess."

Bob and Evan both stood and Bob said, "Wait a minute, we're not done yet. Evan, show Karen what you made for my mom."

Evan opened a medium sized box near the front door and took it over to Karen. Karen carefully opened the box. The object was wrapped in tissue paper which Karen removed very slowly to expose a glass sculpture of Santa sitting in a chair looking at a list and Mrs. Claus leaning over kissing him on the cheek.

Karen could hardly believe what she saw and said, "Oh, my God, this is beautiful! Evan, this is truly a work of art! Look everyone! Evan, I can't thank you enough."

Evan smiled and answered with, "I guess I did what you wanted. And I have something else for you, Karen." Evan handed Karen an unsealed green envelope.

Karen accepted the envelope with a quizzical look on her face. She opened it and took out the contents. She counted out one hundred fifty dollars in twenties and tens.

"Thank you Evan, but you can't afford to give away money like this."

"Oh! It's not my money. I sold one of your paintings yesterday afternoon. After the party, I had to go back to the shop and a customer came in and wanted to buy the painting of the wildflowers in the mountain meadow. Prices weren't marked on the paintings so I just told the gentleman it was $150. He took out his wallet and paid me."

Karen smiled and said, "I was going to mark that one $85. I'd better let you put the prices on my artwork, Evan!"

Bob gave Jen a nice pen and pencil set saying she might use it when writing her thesis. Evan was given some new business software for his computer and Estelle received a pastry cookbook. Bob told Karen he would give a present to her at his parent's house later.

"I think we need a toast…not a piece of toast, a drink. What will it be, coffee, tea or orange juice?" Jen laughed as she stepped into the kitchen.

When everyone had their drinks, Jen raised her glass of orange juice and said, "I'm so happy to be in the presence of such nice people at Christmas time. Merry Christmas. Now let's have some more to eat."

Evan's eyes twinkled when he said, "Nicely done, Jen. I think I need another cinnamon roll. They are outstanding, Estelle."

They all enjoyed the rest of the morning and early afternoon. They talked, played with the kids and had a great time together. The television was never turned on.

There was a knock at the door and Karen went to see who was there. She opened the door to "Merry Christmas!" It was Olivia; she had arrived to give them a ride to her house for Christmas dinner. Karen introduced Jen, Evan and Estelle to Olivia.

Everyone put on their coat and went down to Olivia's suburban. Bob and Evan said they would see everybody at Olivia's house and climbed into Bob's car. As soon as the women and the kids were all buckled up, Olivia drove home.

As they were getting out of the suburban, Olivia noticed the box Karen was carrying.

"What's in the box, Karen?" quizzed Olivia.

"Oh…it's just a little surprise. I'll show you later," Karen smiled.

Inside the house, which was warm and highly decorated, were the rest of the Ostrum family and Evan. Bob and Evan had arrived a few minutes ahead of the suburban. After all the introductions, wine and cheese were served to the adults and the six children had

sodas or juice, and cookies decorated with green and red icing. The kids gravitated to the Christmas tree, which was over eight feet tall. John had his lighted magnifier and was observing the pine needles. He leaned into the branches and smelled the tree and then looked at his mom and smiled. Karen's children joined the Ostrum grandchildren and began playing with the new toys delivered by the real Santa Claus.

About 4:00 o'clock, it started snowing and by 5:00 the sky was nearly dark. Olivia was standing at the picture window watching the snow falling on the window ledge and began closing the window drapes. Karen approached her with the box she had brought in earlier.

"This is the Ekstrom's present for you Olivia. I hope you like it."

Olivia accepted the box, placed it on the dining room table and began unwrapping the white tissue paper from the sculpture. As she folded back the last piece of paper covering the glass figures, her eyes widened and her mouth opened.

"Oh my gosh! What beautiful figures! This is so cute!"

"I asked Evan to make it for me so I could give you something unique."

"Oh, thank you Karen. It is wonderful. I know just the place for it so it won't get damaged and everyone can see it. Bob, could you please help me?"

"Sure, Mom. What can I do for you?"

"Take down that ugly starburst clock above the mantel. Then put this work of art in the niche the clock was hiding. Do that for me and you'll be my favorite son."

"Gee...thanks Mom." Bob interchanged the clock and the sculpture and everyone applauded.

Lisa looked at Olivia and said, "Mom...what can I do for you to become your favorite daughter?"

Everyone laughed. They knew that Bob and Lisa were Olivia's only children. Olivia thought she would give Bob a hint so she said, "You already are; you've given me three grandchildren."

Bob reacted with "Ouch" and everyone laughed again.

Olivia noticed that Estelle was very quiet. Olivia went over to Estelle and placed her hand on the older woman's shoulder and said, "Estelle, would you like to help me in the kitchen?"

"Oh…I thought you'd never ask."

When Olivia and Estelle went into the kitchen, Karen, Jen and Lisa checked to see what the kids were doing and then joined the older women in the kitchen. As they began putting food in serving vessels, they heard the sounds of the piano from the living room.

Olivia asked, "Who's playing the piano? Robert and Vernon don't know where the keys are. I never could get them to learn to play."

Before the other women could answer, they heard girl's voices singing with the piano music. Karen looked into the living room and saw Evan playing the piano. Suzy and Sharon were standing on each side of him singing the Christmas carol. Karen ran for her purse and took a picture of the trio.

It was nearly six o'clock and the women began putting the serving dishes, nearly overflowing with food, on the dining room table.

Olivia announced, "Okay, everyone, dinner is ready. Kids, remember to wash your hands. Evan followed the kids to the bathroom and Sharon said, "You're not a kid!"

Evan answered with, "Oh yes I am. I'm much younger than Estelle and I'm just a little older than you are."

Suzy commented, "Lots older," and smiled at Finley.

As soon as everyone was seated, Vernon said grace, followed by "Let's eat!" The food was going fast and Olivia seemed to be jumping up and getting things while everyone else ate. Karen decided to take her place the next time a request came for more food. She went into the kitchen looking for more dinner rolls. She heard someone behind her and spoke, "Olivia, where are the dinner rolls?"

"It's not Olivia. They're in the microwave waiting to be warmed up. Thirty seconds should do it," instructed Bob.

"Thank you, Chef Bob," Karen turned and smiled.

"I followed you in here to give you something."

Karen half expected him to kiss her but he was holding a small silver box in his right hand. He extended his hand and Karen took the box. Her mind was racing with several thoughts. Is he giving me a ring? No, it's too soon for that, but it's got to be some jewelry. Well, I'd better open the box and see what it is.

Karen opened the little hinged box and found a pair of earrings, swirls of silver metal with sapphires in the center.

"Oh my God! They're beautiful. Is that silver?"

"Nope. Silver will tarnish. This metal won't tarnish."

"Oh Bob…thank you! But they are too expensive!"

Bob stepped toward Karen and placed his hands on her hips. "Karen, you deserve some nice things."

The microwave was beeping and Jen came into the kitchen just as Karen kissed Bob.

"Oops…sorry to interrupt. I need to get some dinner rolls."

Karen was still kissing Bob. She pointed toward the microwave.

Jen popped open the microwave door, retrieved the rolls and went back to the dinning room. Her big grin was from a mixture of embarrassment and amusement.

Vernon said, "Hey you two! Get back in here. Estelle has something she wants to say."

Karen and Bob came back to the table grinning from ear to ear.

After they were seated, Estelle stood up and holding onto the chair, moved behind it, turned and faced her new friends. "When I was growing up, it was the time of the Great Depression. My family, like most others, had very little. My family consisted of my mom and dad and sister. My sister was a year younger than I and we played together all the time. You know, my sister lives in San Francisco. I'll have to call her later tonight. The West Coast time is three hours earlier than East Coast time. Oh, yes…my mother was a seamstress and my father was a plumber but one year the only work he could find was digging ditches. I think I was seven years old.

"About the time of Thanksgiving, my father broke his leg and couldn't work. My mother didn't make enough to keep us going for long. We had to sell some of our furniture to have enough money to buy food. My father had a gold coin he had kept in reserve for emergencies, but he had to use it for medical bills. Mom had saved some money in a savings account and we used a little each week so we could eat. As I recall, we had about thirty dollars until my father could work again.

"That year, Christmas was very bleak. We had no money for presents or even a Christmas tree. But we had each other and our imagination. For presents, we cut out pictures of things from newspapers and magazines. We gave each other the pictures. I remember I gave my sister a picture of a bicycle. She gave me a picture of a dog. We went to bed early Christmas Eve after singing some Christmas carols. When I got into bed, I began to think of people and things I liked during the past year. In my imagination, I created a Christmas tree. The tree had stars for lights. I pretended to place the stars so they looked like the constellations. I decorated each branch of the tree with angels, cherubs, kings and queens, shepherds, their wives and children. Those were my ornaments representing the people I knew. And, I had a few animals too. There were dogs and cats and the milkman's horse.

"Well, I have kept up that idea for all these years and the tree has gotten very large. Of course, I have never run out of stars. When I close my eyes, I can see the constellations in the tree. This year, I have added several branches to my tree. All of you are on my tree. You have become angels, shepherds and wives, kings and queens. The children are the little cherubs. All of you are my ornaments of value. Thank you for such a wonderful Christmas. Merry Christmas everyone."